Letters
to the
Lost

Letters
to the
Lost

BRIGID KEMMERER

BLOOMSBURY
LONDON OXFORD NEW YORK NEW DELHI SYDNEY

Bloomsbury Publishing, London, Oxford, New York, New Delhi and Sydney

First published in Great Britain in April 2017 by Bloomsbury Publishing Plc
50 Bedford Square, London WC1B 3DP

First published in the USA in April 2017 by Bloomsbury Children's Books
1385 Broadway, New York, New York 10018

www.bloomsbury.com

A CIP catalogue record for this book is available from the British Library

ISBN 978 1 4088 8352 5

MIX
Paper from
responsible sources
FSC® C020471

Typeset by Newgen Knowledge Works (P) Ltd., Chennai, India
Printed and bound in Great Britain by CPI Group (UK) Ltd, Croydon CR0 4YY

3 5 7 9 10 8 6 4 2

For Michael
I'm so lucky to be on this crazy ride with you.
(Mostly because we keep each other from jumping off.)

CHAPTER ONE

There's this photograph I can't get out of my mind. A little girl in a flowered dress is screaming in the dark. Blood is everywhere: on her cheeks, on her dress, in spattered droplets on the ground. A gun is pointed at the dirt road beside her, and you can't see the man, but you can see his boots. You showed it to me years ago, telling me about the photographer who got the shot, but all I remember is the scream and the flowers and the blood and the gun.

Her parents took a wrong turn or something. In a war zone, maybe. Was it Iraq? I think it was Iraq. It's been awhile and I'm fuzzy on the history of it. They took a wrong turn, and some spooked soldiers started firing at the car. Her parents were killed instantly.

The little girl was lucky.

Unlucky?

I don't know.

At first you see the horror because it's so perfectly etched in the girl's expression.

Then you see the details. The blood. The flowers. The gun. The boots.

Some of your photographs are equally gripping. I should probably be thinking of your work. It seems wrong to be leaning against your headstone and thinking about someone else's talent.

I can't help it.

You can see it on her face. Her reality is being ripped away, and she knows it.

Her mother is gone, and she knows it.

There is agony in that picture.

Every time I look at it, I think, "I know exactly how she feels."

I need to stop staring at this letter.

I only picked up the envelope because we're supposed to clean up any personal stuff in front of the gravestones before we mow. I usually take my time because eight hours is eight hours, and it's not like I'm getting paid for this.

My grease-stained fingers have left marks along the edges of the paper. I should throw it away before anyone knows I touched it.

But my eyes keep tracing the pen strokes. The handwriting is neat and even, but not perfect. At first I can't figure out what's holding my focus, but then it becomes clear: a shaky hand wrote these words. A girl's hand, I can tell. The letters are rounded just enough.

I glance at the headstone. It's newish. Crisp letters are carved into shiny granite. *Zoe Rebecca Thorne. Beloved wife and mother.*

The date of death hits me hard. May twenty-fifth of this year. The same day I swallowed an entire bottle of whiskey and drove my father's pickup truck into an empty office building.

Funny how the date is etched into my brain, but it's etched into someone else's for something entirely different.

Thorne. The name sounds familiar, but I can't place it. She's only been dead a few months, and she was forty-five, so maybe it was in the news.

I bet I got more press.

"Hey, Murph! What gives, man?"

I jump and drop the letter. Melonhead, my "supervisor," is standing at the crest of the hill, wiping a sweat-soaked handkerchief across his brow.

His last name isn't really Melonhead, any more than mine is Murph. But if he's going to take liberties with *Murphy*, I'm going to do the same with *Melendez*.

Only difference is that I don't say it to his face.

"Sorry," I call. I stoop to pick up the letter.

"I thought you were going to finish mowing this section."

"I will."

"If you don't, then I've gotta. I want to get home, kid."

He always wants to get home. He has a little girl. She's three and completely obsessed with Disney princesses. She knows all her letters and numbers already. She had a birthday party last weekend with fifteen kids from her preschool class, and Melonhead's wife made a cake.

I don't give a crap about any of this, of course. I just can't get the guy to keep his mouth shut. There's a reason I said I'd handle this section alone.

"I know," I say. "I'll do it."

"You don't do it, I'm not signing your sheet for today."

I bristle and remind myself that being a dick would probably be reported to the judge. She already hates me. "I said I'd do it."

He waves a hand dismissively and turns his back, heading down the opposite side of the hill. He thinks I'm going to screw him over. Maybe the last guy did. I don't know.

After a moment, I hear his mower kick on.

I should probably finish clearing the mementos so I can get on my own mower, but I don't. The September sun dumps heat on the cemetery, and I have to shove damp hair off my forehead. You'd think we were in the Deep South instead of Annapolis, Maryland. Melonhead's bandana almost seemed like a cliché, but now I'm envying him.

I hate this.

I should be grateful for the community service, I know. I'm seventeen, and for a while it looked like they were going to charge me as an adult—but it's not like I killed anyone. Only property damage. And lawn maintenance in a cemetery isn't exactly a death sentence, even if I'm surrounded by it.

I still hate this. I say I don't care what people think of me, but that's a lie. You'd care, too, if everyone thought you were nothing more than a ticking time bomb. We're only a few weeks into the school year, but half my teachers are probably counting the minutes until I start shooting up the place. I can already imagine my senior portrait in the yearbook. *Declan Murphy: Most likely to commit a felony.*

It would be hilarious if it weren't so depressing.

I read the letter again. Pain flares in every word. The kind of pain that makes you write letters to someone who will never read them. The kind of pain that *isolates*. The kind of pain you're certain no one else has felt, *ever*.

My eyes linger on the last lines.

> You can see it on her face. Her reality is being ripped away, and she knows it.
>
> Her mother is gone, and she knows it.
>
> There is agony in that picture.
>
> Every time I look at it, I think, "I know exactly how she feels."

Without thinking about it, I fish a nubby pencil out of my pocket, and I press it to the paper.

Just below the girl's shaky script, I add two words of my own.

CHAPTER TWO

Me too.

The words are shaking, and I realize it's not the paper; it's my hand. The foreign handwriting is almost burning my eyes.

Someone read my letter.

Someone read my letter.

I look around as if it just happened, but the cemetery is empty. I haven't been here since Tuesday. It's Thursday morning now, so it's a miracle the letter is still intact. More often than not, the envelope is gone, taken by weather or animals or possibly the cemetery staff.

But not only is the letter *here*, someone felt the need to add commentary.

The paper is still shaking in my fist.

I can't—

This is—

What—who would—how—

I want to scream. I can't even think in complete sentences. Rage is burning up my insides.

This was private. *Private.* Between me and my mother.

It has to be a guy. Greasy fingerprints line the edges, and the handwriting is blocky. It smacks of arrogance, to insert himself into someone else's grief and claim a part of it. Mom used to say that words always carried a bit of the writer's soul, and I can almost feel it pouring off the page.

Me too.

No, *not* him too. He has *no idea.*

I'm going to complain. This is unacceptable. This is a cemetery. People come here to grieve privately. This is my space. MINE. Not his.

I stomp across the grass, refusing to allow the cool morning air to steal any of my fire. My chest hurts and I'm dangerously close to crying.

This was ours. Mine and hers. My mother can't write back anymore, and his words on my letter seem to drive that point home. It's like he stabbed me with the pencil.

By the time I crest the hill, tears hang on my lashes and my breathing is shuddering. The wind has turned my hair into a mess of tangles. I'm going to be a wreck in a minute. I'll show up late for school with reddened eyes and running makeup. Again.

The guidance counselor used to have some sympathy. Ms. Vickers would pull me into her office and offer a box of tissues. At the end of my junior year, I was getting pats on the shoulder and whispers of encouragement to take all the time I needed.

Now that we're in the middle of September, Mom's been dead for months. Since school started, everyone has been wondering when I'm going to get my act together. Ms. Vickers stopped me on Tuesday, and instead of giving a kind look, she pursed her lips and asked if I was still going to the cemetery every morning, and maybe we should talk about more constructive uses of my time.

Like it's any of her business.

It's not *every* morning anyway. Only the mornings when Dad leaves for work early—though half the time I'm convinced he wouldn't know the difference either way. When he's home, he makes himself two eggs and eats them with a bowl of grapes I've washed and pulled from the vines. He sits at the table and stares at the wall and doesn't speak.

I could light the place on fire and it'd be even odds that he'd get out in time.

Today was an early-work morning. The sunlight, the breeze, the peaceful tranquility of the cemetery all seemed like a gift.

The two words scrawled on my letter feel like a curse.

A middle-aged Hispanic man is blowing leaves and lawn clippings from the paved road, and he stops when I approach. He's wearing some type of maintenance uniform, and the name across his breast reads *Melendez*.

"May I help you?" he says with a hint of an accent. His eyes aren't unkind, but he looks tired.

There's wariness in his voice. I must look fierce. He expects a complaint. I can tell.

Well, I'm about to give him one. There should be some kind of regulation against this. My fist clenches around the letter, crumpling it, and I inhale to speak—

Then I stop.

I can't do this. She wouldn't want me to do this.

Temper, Juliet.

Mom was always the calm one. Level-headed, cool in a crisis. She had to be, what with jetting from war zone to war zone.

Besides, I'm about to sound like a jacked-up freak of nature. I already look like one. What am I going to say? *Someone wrote two words on my letter?* A letter I wrote to someone who *isn't even alive?* It could have been anyone. Hundreds of graves line the field around my mother's. Dozens of people must visit every day—if not more.

And what's the lawn-care guy going to do? Babysit my mother's headstone? Install a security camera?

To catch someone with a hidden pencil?

"I'm fine," I say. "I'm sorry."

I walk back to her grave and sit down in the grass. I'm going to be late for school, but I don't care. Somewhere in the distance, Mr. Melendez's leaf blower kicks up again, but here I'm alone.

I've written her twenty-nine letters since she died. Two letters every week.

When she was alive, I wrote her hundreds. Her career kept her on the cutting edge of technology, but she craved the permanence and precision of the old-fashioned. Handwritten letters. Cameras with film. Her professional shots were always digital, stuff she could edit anywhere, but film was her favorite. She'd be in some African desert, shooting starvation or violence or political unrest, and she'd always find time to write me a letter.

We did the normal thing, too, of course: emails and video chatting when she had a chance. But the letters—those really meant something. Every emotion came through the paper, as if the ink and dust and smudges from her sweat lent weight to the words, and I could sense her fear, her hope, and her courage.

I'd always write her back. Sometimes she wouldn't get them for weeks, after they'd filtered their way through her editor to wherever she was on assignment. Sometimes she was home, and I could hand her the letter on my way out the door. It didn't matter. We just thought on paper to each other.

When she died, I couldn't stop. Usually, the instant I get to her grave, I can't breathe until I'm pressing a pen against the paper, feeding her my thoughts.

Now, after seeing this response, I can't write another word to her. I feel too vulnerable. Too exposed. Anything I say could be read. Twisted. Judged.

So I don't write a letter to her.

I write a letter to him.

CHAPTER THREE

Privacy is an illusion.

Obviously you know this, since you read my letter.
It wasn't addressed to you. It wasn't for you. It had
nothing to do with you. It was between me and my
mother.

I know she's dead.

I know she can't read the letters.

I know there's very little I can do to feel close to
her anymore.

Now I don't even have this.

Do you understand what you've taken from me?
Do you have any idea?

What you wrote implies that you understand
agony.

I don't think you do.

*If you did, you wouldn't have interfered
with mine.*

My first thought is that this chick is crazy. Who writes to a random stranger in a cemetery?

My second thought is that clearly I'm not one to throw stones here.

Either way, she doesn't know me. She doesn't know what I understand.

I shouldn't even be standing here. It's Thursday night, meaning I'm supposed to be mowing on the other side of the cemetery. It's not like I have tons of spare time to stand around reading a letter from a stranger. Melonhead gave a glare at his watch when I walked into the equipment shed five minutes late. If he catches me slacking off, there'll be hell to pay.

If he keeps threatening to call the judge, I'm going to lose it.

After a moment, my initial irritation seeps out, leaving guilt behind. I'm standing here because I felt a connection with the last letter. I wanted to see if another had been left.

I didn't expect anyone to *read* what I'd written.

It's a slap in the face to realize she must have felt the same way.

I dig in my pockets for a pencil, but all I find are my keys and my lighter.

Oh wait. Rev needed a pencil in seventh period. It's unlike him not to return something he borrowed, even something as stupid as an old pencil.

Maybe this is fate's way of telling me to stop and think before I speak. Before I write. Whatever.

I fold up her rant and shove it in my pocket. Then I pull on my gloves and go to find my mower. I hate being here, but after weeks of doing this, I've found that hard labor is good for thinking.

I'll work, and I'll think.

And, later, I'll be back to write.

CHAPTER FOUR

I don't think you understand agony yourself. If you did, you wouldn't have interfered with mine.

Did you ever think that my words weren't meant for you to read, either?

"Jules?"

I look up. The cafeteria is nearly empty, and Rowan is standing there, looking at me expectantly.

"Are you okay?" she asks. "The bell rang five minutes ago. I thought you were going to meet me at my locker."

I refold the tattered letter I found this morning and shove it into my backpack, jerking at the zipper. I don't know when he wrote it, but it must have been last week, because the paper is crinkly like it's been wet and dried again, and we haven't had rain since Saturday.

It was the first weekend I didn't go to the cemetery in a while. A little part of me is irritated that this letter sat for days. His self-righteousness has probably faded, while mine feels fresh and new and hot in my chest.

I'm glad I went this morning. They mow on Tuesday nights, and it probably would have gotten thrown away by the staff.

"What were you looking at?" says Rowan.

"A letter."

She doesn't push past that. She thinks it's a letter to my mother. I let her think that.

I don't need anyone to think I'm any crazier than they do already.

The late bell rings. I need to move. If I get another tardy, I'll end up in detention. Again. The thought is enough to add extra speed to my step.

I can't get another detention. I can't sit in that room for another hour. The silence hurts my ears and leaves me with too much time to think.

Rowan is right beside me. She'll probably escort me to class and sweet-talk the teacher out of writing me a late slip. She doesn't need to worry about tardies or detention—teachers love her. She sits in the front row of every class and hangs on their every word, as if she wakes up every morning thirsting for knowledge. Rowan is one of those girls you love to hate: delicately pretty, with a kind word for everyone, and a seemingly effortless straight-A average. She'd be more popular if she weren't so perfect. I tell her that all the time.

If we're calling a spade a spade, she'd be more popular if she weren't best friends with the senior-class train wreck.

When I found the letter this morning, I expected to read it and start crying. Instead, I want to find this loser and punch him in the face. Every time I read it, I get a bit more furious.

Did you ever think that my words weren't meant for you to read, either?

The fury helps cover up the little part of me that wonders if he's right.

The hallways are empty, which seems impossible. Where are the rest of the slackers? Why am I always the only late one?

Besides, it's not like I wasn't *here*. I'm physically in the building. It's not like I'm going to turn into a model student once a teacher starts doing the Charlie Brown at the blackboard.

By the time we reach the language arts wing, we're half running, skidding through turns. I grab hold of the corner to help propel me down the last hall.

I feel the burn before I feel the collision. Hot liquid sears my skin, and I cry out. A cup of coffee has exploded across my chest. I slam into something solid, and I'm skidding, slipping, falling.

Some*one* solid.

I'm on the ground, eyes level with scuffed black work boots.

In a rom-com, this would be the "meet-cute." The boy would be movie-star hot, first-string quarterback, and class valedictorian. He'd offer me his hand, and he'd coincidentally have an extra T-shirt in his backpack. I'd change into it in the restroom, and somehow my boobs would be bigger, my hips would be smaller, and he'd walk me to class and ask me to prom.

In reality, the guy is Declan Murphy, and he's practically snarling. His shirt and jacket are soaked with coffee, too, and he's pulling material away from his chest.

If the rom-com guy was the star quarterback, Declan is the senior-class reject. He's got a criminal record and a frequent seat in detention. He's big and mean, and while reddish-brown hair and a sharp jaw might turn some girls on, the dark look in his eyes is enough to keep them away. A scar bisects one eyebrow, and it's probably not his only one. Most people are afraid of him, and they have reason to be. Rowan is simultaneously trying to help me up and pull me away from him.

He looks at me with absolute derision. His voice is rough and low. "What is *wrong* with you?"

I jerk away from Rowan. My shirt is plastered to my chest, and I can guarantee he's getting a great view of my purple bra through my pastel-green shirt. For as hot as the coffee was, now I'm wet and freezing. This is humiliating and horrible, and I can't decide if I want to cry or if I want to yell at him.

My breath actually hitches, but I suck it up. I'm not afraid of him. "You ran into *me*."

His eyes are fierce. "I wasn't the one running."

Then he moves forward sharply. I shrink away before I can help it.

Okay, maybe I am afraid of him.

I don't know what I thought he was going to do. He's just so *intense.* He stops short and scowls at my reaction, then finishes his motion to lean down and grab his backpack where it fell.

Oh.

There probably is something wrong with me. I want to yell at him all over again, even though all this was my fault. My jaw tightens.

Temper, Juliet.

The memory of my mother hits me so hard and fast and sudden that it's a miracle I don't burst into tears right here. There's nothing holding me together, and one wrong word is going to send me straight off an edge.

Declan is straightening, and that scowl is still on his face, and I know he's going to say something truly despicable. This, after the chastising letter, might be enough to turn me into a sopping mess.

But then his eyes find mine, and something he sees there steals the dark expression from his face.

A tinny voice speaks from beside us. "Declan Murphy. Late again, I see."

Mr. Bellicaro, my freshman year biology teacher, is standing beside Rowan. Her cheeks are flushed and she looks almost panicked. She must have sensed trouble and gone running for a teacher. It's something she would do. I'm not sure whether I'm annoyed or relieved. A classroom door hangs open behind him, and kids are peering into the hallway.

Declan swipes at drops of coffee clinging to his jacket. "I wasn't late. She ran into *me*."

Mr. Bellicaro purses his lips. He's short and has a round gut that's accentuated by a pink sweater-vest. He's not what you'd consider well-liked. "No food is allowed outside the cafeteria—"

"Coffee isn't food," says Declan.

"Mr. Murphy, I believe you know the way to the principal's office."

"Yeah, I could draw you a map." His voice sharpens, and he leans in, glowering. *"This isn't my fault."*

Rowan flinches back from his tone. Her hands are almost wringing. I don't blame her. For an instant, I wonder if this guy is going to hit a teacher.

Mr. Bellicaro draws himself up. "Am I going to have to call security?"

"No." Declan puts his hands up, his voice bitter. His eyes are dark and furious. "No. I'm walking." And he is, cursing under his breath. He crumples his paper cup and flings it at a trash can.

So many emotions ricochet around my skull that I can barely settle on one. Shame, because it really *was* my fault, and I'm standing here, letting him take the blame. Indignation, for the way he spoke. Fear, for the way he acted.

Intrigue, for the way the darkness fell off his face when his eyes met mine.

I wish I had a photograph of his face at precisely that moment. Or now, capturing his walk down the shadowed hallway. Light flashes on his hair and turns it gold when he passes each window, but shadows cling to his broad shoulders and dark jeans. I haven't wanted to touch my camera since Mom died, but all of a sudden I wish I had it in my hands. My fingers itch for it.

"For you, Miss Young."

I turn, and Mr. Bellicaro is holding out a white slip of paper. Detention. Again.

CHAPTER FIVE

You're right:

I shouldn't have interfered with your grief.

I'm sorry.

That doesn't mean you were right to read my
letter. I still kind of hate you for that. I've been
trapped here for fifteen minutes, staring at a blank
piece of paper, trying to remember how it felt to write
to her, to know my thoughts were more permanent
than a conversation.

Instead, all I can think about is you and your
"Me too" and what it meant and whether your pain
is anything like mine.

Not that it's any of my business.

I don't know if you'll even read my apology, but I need

to say the words to someone. Guilt has been riding my shoulders awhile now.

Not guilt because of you. Because of someone else.

I owe this "someone" an apology, but I don't know him any better than I know you. I'm certainly not going to start writing notes to two strangers. For now, this is the best I can do, and I'll just have to hope that the guilt catches up.

Have you ever heard of Kevin Carter? He won a Pulitzer for a photograph of a dying girl. It's a pretty famous photo, so maybe you've seen it. A little girl was starving in the Sudan, trying to reach a feeding station. She needed to stop to rest because she was barely more than a skeleton held together by a stretch of skin. She needed to rest because she wasn't strong enough to get to the food in one trip.

So she rested in the dirt, this tiny little girl, while a vulture sat nearby, waiting.

Do you get it? Waiting. For her to die.

I think of that picture sometimes. Of that moment.

Sometimes I feel like the girl.

Sometimes I feel like the bird.

Sometimes I feel like the photographer, unable to do anything but watch.

Kevin Carter killed himself after he won the Pulitzer.

Sometimes I think I understand why.

I need a cigarette.

Moths flutter around the porch light, pinging against the glass bulb. It's almost midnight on Thursday, and the neighborhood is nearly silent.

The house behind me is not. Alan, my stepfather, is still awake, and my mother's out with friends, so I'm not ready to go inside yet.

Alan doesn't like me much.

Trust me. It's mutual.

The letter had been sitting in my back pocket all night. I have no idea when she wrote it, but it had to have been within the last forty-eight hours. It wasn't there on Tuesday night, because I looked. Melonhead was riding me then because I was late, and no one ever wants to hear my excuses.

"I had detention," I said when I finally showed up.

He was pouring fuel into one of the mowers in the equipment shed. It was hot as hell in there, and his shirt was sticking. The space isn't all that big, and it always smells like a mixture of cut grass and gasoline. I like it.

I didn't like the way Melonhead looked at me, a disgusted glance, as if I were just another slacker.

"You can make up your lost hour on Saturday," he said.

"I can make it up on Thursday."

"No, you'll make it up on Saturday."

I held up my slip. "I'm only assigned to work Tuesdays and Thursdays."

He shrugged and turned toward the door to the shed. "You're assigned to work from four till eight. It's ten past five. You can make up your hour on Saturday."

"Look, man, I can stay until nine—"

"You think I want to stay late for you?"

Of course not. He wanted to get home to his wife and kid so he'd have more stories to bore me with next time. I punched the wall beside my mower and swore. "You think I want to be here at all?"

He stopped in the doorway, and for a second, I wondered if he was going to take a swing at me. But he looked at me, and his voice didn't change. "You should be grateful to be here. If you want me to sign your slip for eight hours, you'll show up on Saturday." Melonhead began to turn but paused. "And watch your language. I don't want that talk here."

I opened my mouth to fire back at him, but he just stood there, sunlight at his back, and I knew he'd be on the phone with the judge in a heartbeat if I pushed it.

I hate that he can hold this over my head. I remember the sentencing, thinking that mowing a cemetery would be *easy*, that no one would hassle me. I didn't realize this program would involve a guy who'd get a power trip from ordering me around.

I half crumpled the slip in my fist. "You can't make me work on Saturday."

"If you don't like it, show up on time."

Tonight I showed up early, hoping I'd earn a gold star and a free pass. No dice. But I did find a letter from the cemetery girl.

Part of me wonders if I'd be better off without it here in my hands. It's depressing and intriguing and frightening all at once.

I don't know the photograph she's talking about. I didn't know the first one, either, with the *scream and the flowers and the blood and the gun.* I almost don't need to see them, because her words zoom in on the details with a painful focus.

But now, reading her lines about the vulture and the little girl, I want to go look it up.

The side gate rattles, and I fold the letter up to slide it under my thigh. I'm expecting my mother, but then I hear the sniff, and I know it's Rev. He's allergic to everything, including most people.

"You're out late," I say. Rev is more likely to drag me out of bed at six in the morning than to come calling near midnight.

"They took in a baby this afternoon. She won't go to sleep. Mom says it's separation anxiety. Dad says she'll settle soon. I said I needed to take a walk." He's not irritated. He's used to it.

Geoff and Kristin are foster parents. They live on the other side of the block, but their backyard is diagonal from ours, so we've always gotten a firsthand look at the kids who roll through their house.

Rev was the first. He showed up ten years ago, when he was seven and scrawny, with Coke-bottle glasses and allergies so bad he could barely breathe. His clothes were too small, and his arm was in a cast, and he wouldn't speak. Geoff and Kristin are the nicest people on the planet—they're nice to *me*, and that's saying something—but Rev ran away from them anyway.

I found him in my closet, curled up in the back corner, peeking at me through shaggy hair while clutching a ratty, old Bible.

I had a box of Legos in there, so I thought he was there to play. Like kids routinely showed up in my closet or something. I don't know what I was thinking. I folded myself in there with him and started building.

Turned out he was scared of Geoff and Kristin because they're black. His dad had told him that black people were evil and sent by the devil.

The irony here is that Rev's dad used to beat the crap out of him.

He usually quoted the Bible while he did it.

Geoff and Kristin adopted Rev five years ago. He says it was no big deal, that they'd been the only parents he'd known for years anyway, and it was just a piece of paper.

But it was a big deal. It settled something inside him.

He wears contacts during the day now, but his hair is still on the longish side. My sister, Kerry, used to say he hides behind it. When Rev was eight, he told Geoff he didn't want anyone to ever be able to hurt him again. Kristin signed him up for martial arts the next day. He's kept up with it, almost to the extreme. If the glasses and the allergies and the shyness had you thinking *loser*, you wouldn't say it to his face. He's built like an MMA fighter. Add a best friend with a record—*me*—and most kids at school give him a wide berth.

Also ironic, because Rev is about as aggressive as an old golden retriever.

I move over to give him room to sit down, and he drops onto the step beside me.

"What were you reading?" he says.

He must have seen me from across the yard. I hesitate before answering.

And that's ridiculous. He knows every secret I have. He watched my family fall apart, including my mother's misguided attempts to glue the pieces back together. He even knows the truth about Kerry, and I thought I was going to take that to the grave with me last May.

I still hesitate. I feel like maybe I'm breaking a confidence if I tell anyone about the cemetery girl.

Not like I even know who *she* is.

I deliberate for another moment. Rev doesn't say anything.

Finally, I pull the slip of paper out from beneath my leg and hand it to him.

He reads silently for a minute, then hands it back. "Who is she?"

"I have no idea." I pause. "The daughter of Zoe Rebecca Thorne."

"What?"

I turn the letter over in my hands, sliding the paper between my fingers. "I found a letter sitting against a gravestone last week. I read it. It was talking about . . ." I hesitate again. No matter what Rev knows, it was easier to talk about life and death with an anonymous reader. I have to clear my throat. "It was about losing someone suddenly."

"And you thought of Kerry."

I nod.

We sit there in silence for a while, listening to the moths dance against the lightbulb. Somewhere down the road, a siren flares to life. Just as suddenly, it's gone.

Rev says, "But this is a different letter?"

"Yeah. I wrote back to the first one."

"You wrote back?"

"I didn't think she'd read it!"

"What makes you so sure it's a girl?"

It's a good question. I'm not entirely sure. Then again, his first question was *Who is she?* "What makes *you* so sure it's a girl?"

"The fact that you wouldn't be sitting here mooning over a letter from a guy. Let me see it again."

I do. While he reads, I play his words back in my head. *Mooning*? Am I mooning? I don't even know her.

"'Sometimes I feel like the girl,'" he quotes.

"Exactly."

"This is notebook paper," he says.

"I know." The cemetery is local. It has occurred to me that she might be another student at Hamilton High School.

"Dude. She could be, like, *eleven*."

Okay, that hasn't occurred to me.

I snatch the letter back from him. "Shut up. It doesn't matter."

He sobers. "I'm just yanking your chain. She doesn't sound eleven." He pauses. "Maybe that letter was left for you."

"No, she was pretty pissed that I wrote back."

Now he hesitates. "I don't mean that *she* left the letter for you."

It takes me a second to figure out his tone. "Rev, if you start preaching at me, I'm going in the house."

"I'm not preaching."

No, he's not. Yet.

He still has that old Bible I found him clutching in my closet. It was his mother's. He's read it about twenty times. He'll debate theology with anyone who's interested—and I'm not on that list. Geoff and Kristin used to take him to church, but he said he didn't like that he couldn't live by his own interpretation.

What he didn't say was that looking up at a man in a pulpit reminded him too much of his father.

Rev doesn't walk around quoting Bible verses or anything—usually—but his faith is rock solid. I once asked him how he can believe in a providential god when he barely survived living with his father.

He looked at me and said, "Because I did survive."

And there's no arguing that.

I'm wishing I hadn't told him about the letters now. I don't want a religious analysis.

"Don't call it God, then," he says. "Call it fate. Don't you find it interesting that of all the people who could have found that letter, *you* did?"

This is one of the things I love best about Rev. He'll never force anything on anyone. I nod.

"Do you want to write back?"

"I don't know."

"Liar."

He's right. I do want to write back.

In fact, I'm already planning what to say.

CHAPTER SIX

I'd say you're kind of dark, but I'm writing to a girl who leaves letters in a cemetery, so I guess that's a given.

You said you were wondering if my pain was anything like yours.

I don't know. I don't know how to answer that.

You lost your mother. I haven't lost mine.

Don't you think it's funny how people say "lost" as if they were just misplaced? But maybe it's a different meaning of "lost," in that you don't know where they went. My best friend believes in God and heaven and eternal life, but I'm not sure how I feel about all that. We die and our bodies are absorbed back into the earth in some kind of biological cycle, right? And our soul (or whatever) is supposed to go on forever? Where was it before?

My friend would die if he knew I was talking to you about this, because this is the kind of thing I won't discuss with him.

If I'm being strictly honest, I'm about ready to crumple up this letter and start over.

But no. Like you said, there's some safety in writing to a complete stranger. I could fire up the computer and Google your mom's name and probably find out something about you, but for right now, I like it better this way.

My sister died four years ago. She was ten.

When people hear about her dying so young, they always assume we spent her last days surrounded by oncologists and nurses. We didn't. We didn't even know they were her last days. She was the picture of health.

Cancer didn't kill her. My father did.

I could have stopped it, but I didn't.

So when you say you feel like the photographer, unable to do anything but watch, I think I know exactly what you mean.

It's Sunday afternoon, and I've been sitting in the sunlight for two hours. It's a popular day at the cemetery, and I've watched mourners come and go all afternoon.

I've read his letter seventeen times.

I read it again.

He lost his sister. I think back to the first letter, when he said, *Me too.*

He's thought of looking me up. Well, my mother. Considering I'm practically staking out her grave to see if he shows up, I can't exactly hold that against him.

He can use any search engine he wants; he won't find much about me. She had already built her name as a photojournalist before she got married, so she sure wasn't changing it. Googling "Zoe Thorne" isn't going to lead anyone to Juliet Young. My last name isn't even mentioned in the obituary.

Zoe is survived by her husband, Charles, and her daughter, Juliet.

Survived. This guy is right. The words we use to surround death are bizarre. Like we're hiding something.

I guess the obituary wouldn't read right if it said something like, *Zoe died on the way home from the airport, after nine months on assignment in a war zone, leaving her husband, Charles, and her daughter, Juliet, with a Welcome Home cake that would sit in the refrigerator for a month before either of them could bear to throw it away.*

So maybe we are hiding something.

Now I understand his inability to compare our pain. I'm an only child, so I can't relate to losing a sibling. Since my mother died, my father and I seem to orbit separate planets of grief, barely interacting unless strictly necessary. That said, I'm pretty sure Dad's not homicidal. He barely rates as conscious these days.

Cancer didn't kill her. My father did.

Four years ago. I rack my brain, trying to remember anything that might have been in the news about a father killing his daughter. Four years ago, I was thirteen. Not exactly the type of story my dad would have shared at the dinner table, and Mom was a better source for world news—if she was even home. Mom could talk geopolitical warfare with heads of state, but local crime? Forget about it. Below her pay scale, she'd say.

Wait.

Four years ago, his sister was ten. That means she'd be fourteen now.

Is Letter Guy an older brother—or a younger one? Could I be exchanging letters with a twelve-year-old? Or someone in his early twenties?

Our conversations are too mature to be written by a twelve-year-old. His letter is written on notebook paper, just like mine. That says high school or college.

He writes in pencil, which makes me think high school. But I don't know for sure.

Twenty feet away, an older man is laying roses at the base of a gravestone. Sunlight reflects off the plastic.

It's a waste of money, because they mow this section on Tuesdays, and I'm pretty sure they chuck all the crap that people leave lying around. That's why I've never left anything but letters.

They chuck all the crap.

The letters. The maintenance guy. What's his name, Mr. Melendez?

Suddenly I feel exposed, even though it's a Sunday afternoon and they never mow on Sundays.

And ick. He's, like, forty.

It can't be him. Right? It doesn't feel like someone that much older. Besides, that age gap between a brother and sister would be unusual. Not impossible, but pretty rare.

The man with the roses is leaving. He may have noticed me here, but no one ever really *looks* at me. I never look at them, either. We're all united by grief, and somehow divided by the same thing.

My sister died four years ago.

I'm such an idiot. Letter Guy is probably a visitor—and he all but told me how to find his sister's grave. She has to be buried near here. How else would he have found my letters?

I start walking the rows of graves, spiraling outward, looking for headstones that are slightly weathered. A few times, the year of death is correct, but not the age or gender. The grass crunches beneath my feet as I walk, and I eventually reach the iron fence at the edge of the property. It's late in the afternoon now, and everyone has gone home to dinner or families. I'm alone, and I've walked a radius of at least one hundred feet from my mother's grave.

Well out of the range where a casual visitor could see a letter left under a rock at the base of a gravestone.

Hmm.

My cell phone vibrates against my thigh, and I fish it out of my pocket, expecting a message from Rowan.

No, my dad. He's sent me a picture.

I frown. I can't remember the last time he texted me. And a picture? I swipe my fingers across the screen to unlock the phone.

It's the kitchen table. For a moment, I can't make out what's spread across it. Then it snaps into focus, and my heart stops beating.

Her photography gear. All of it.

He might as well have dug up her body and laid the skeleton on the kitchen table, then sent me a photo of *that*.

I can name every piece of equipment. If you show me one of her photos, I could probably tell you which camera she used. Her bags are hung from one of the chair backs, and I can smell the scent of the leather mixed with literal blood, sweat, and tears from her assignments. Every time she came home, I'd help her unpack, and the weight of those cameras and the smell of her bags are wrapped up tightly in those memories.

Every time except that last time.

I haven't touched her bags since she died. I haven't *touched* them.

Those are her things.

Those are *her things*.

She and I always unpacked them together. She would tell me secret stories from her travels, and we'd stay up late and watch a chick flick together after Dad went to bed. There's still an untouched pint of Ben & Jerry's Cherry Garcia in the freezer, almost unrecognizable under the ice crystals now. I picked it up to split with her. I'll never eat that flavor again.

He never cared for her stories. He *never cared*.

And now he's TOUCHING HER THINGS.

My fingers are shaking. Sweaty. I almost can't hold on to the phone.

A line of text appears beneath the photo.

CY: Ian offered to take these off our hands. He's coming
over to make me an offer. Is there anything you want
before I let him take it?

WHAT.

I think I'm having a panic attack. Wheezing sounds choke out
of my mouth.

Somehow, the phone finds my cheek and my dad's voice is in
my ear.

"What are you doing?" I say. I want to be yelling, but my
voice is thin and reedy and thickening with tears. "Stop it! Put
it back!"

"Juliet? Are you—"

"How could you?" Now I am crying. "You can't. You can't.
You can't. How could you?"

"Juliet." He sounds stricken. It's the first emotion I've
heard out of him since she died. "Juliet. Please. Calm down. I
didn't—"

"Those are hers!" My knees hit the ground. I press my forehead against the wrought-iron bars of the fence. "You never—
those are *hers*—"

"Juliet." His voice is hushed. "I won't. I had no idea—"

He is killing me. Pain is ripping me apart. I can barely hold
the phone.

I hate him. I hate him for this.

I hate him.

IhatehimIhatehimIhatehimIhatehimIhatehim.

Temper, Juliet.

My eyes blur and the world spins, and it feels like a long time before I realize I'm lying in the grass and his voice is a tinny echo shouting out of the phone.

I press it to my ear. Spots flash in front of my eyes.

"Juliet!" He's yelling. "Juliet, I'm about to call nine-one-one. Answer me!"

"I'm here," I choke. I sob. "You can't. Please."

"I won't," he whispers. "Okay? I won't."

The sun keeps beating down on me, turning my tears to itchy lines on my face. "Okay."

I should apologize, but the words won't form. It feels like apologizing for getting mad that someone drove an iron spike through your chest. My breath won't stop hitching.

"Do you need me to come get you?" he says.

"No."

"Juliet . . ."

"No."

I can't leave yet. I can't go home and see all her things on the table.

"Put it back," I say.

He hesitates. "Maybe we should talk . . ."

I'm going to be sick. "Put it back!"

"I will. I will." He hesitates again. "When are you going to be home?"

He hasn't asked me this since she died. It's the first indication I've had that he even knew I still existed.

I should probably be thanking my lucky stars that he bothered to ask if I wanted any of her things.

He's probably regretting the hell out of sending that text message.

"When I'm ready."

Then I end the call.

CHAPTER SEVEN

You can look up my mother if you want. If you search for "Zoe Thorne Syria Photo," you'll find one of her most famous photographs. A little boy and a little girl are on a pair of swings, laughing. Behind them is a bombed-out building and two men with assault rifles. Everyone's clothes are filthy, caked with sweat and dust. The men are sweating and exhausted and terrified. There's nothing left but that swing set.

I've never been able to decide whether the photograph is depressing or hopeful.

Maybe both.

My mother's equipment has been stashed in a back corner of the basement since she died. No one has touched any of it—until today. This

afternoon, my father was ready to sell it all to my
mother's former editor.

I didn't take it well.

It's a lot of gear, and it cost a ton of money.
Thousands of dollars. Probably tens of thousands
of dollars. We're not rich, but we're not hard up
for cash. Dad said he didn't care about the money,
and for that, I wanted to punch him. If he didn't
care about the money, then why do it? Why get
rid of her most precious things? It's so like him,
though. I asked if he'd be so cavalier about selling
her wedding ring. He said she'd been buried with it.
Then he started crying.

I felt ~~like shit~~ terrible. I still do.

It's ridiculous for me to cross that out. Force
of habit, I guess. Mom never tolerated profanity.
She said she spent too much money learning to use
words and pictures effectively, and it seemed a waste
to drop an f-bomb.

The only reason I knew my dad was getting
rid of her stuff was because he asked me if I
wanted any of it. I haven't touched a camera
since she died. I was supposed to be in honors
photography this year, but I dropped the class.
The teacher has told me at least six times that he'd
welcome me back if I change my mind, but there's
as much chance of that as there is of her coming
back from the dead. I can't press a camera to

my face without thinking of her. I haven't even
wanted to take a picture.

No. That's not true.

Last week, I saw someone with so much
emotion trapped in his eyes that I wanted a camera
in my hands, right that instant. I barely know
him, and I only saw him for a minute, but it's like
a shutter clicked in my brain. Mom used to say
that a picture wasn't worth anything if it didn't
produce a reaction, that it takes talent to capture
feeling with an image. I don't think I ever really
understood what that meant until that moment.

But I didn't have a camera, and it's not like you
can snap a picture of a random stranger without
generating a few questions.

Look up her Syria picture if you get a chance.
I'm curious to hear what you think.

My mom was there when the bomb went off. She
was lucky to get out alive.

I know she was lucky because my father used
to tell her that all the time. He was usually a little
irritated when he said it. "You're lucky you're
here, Zo. You're going to use up all your luck
one of these days. Can't you take meaningful
pictures in Washington, DC, or downtown
Baltimore?"

She'd laugh and say she was lucky to get the
photograph.

42

He was right, though. She did use up all her luck. She was killed in a hit-and-run crash on her way home from the airport.

She was only in a cab because I'd begged her to hurry home, and she'd caught an earlier flight as a surprise.

Sometimes I think fate conspires against us. Or maybe fate conspires with us.

I know you know what I mean. Don't you feel the same about your sister?

Melonhead isn't here. I've been sitting against the door to the equipment shed for half an hour, and I'm starting to wonder if he's going to show up. I know the routine now, and I could start mowing without him, but I don't have a key.

I pull out my phone and search for the photograph that Cemetery Girl described. She's right: the kids show a glimmer of hope. Their smiles are bright, and you can sense the motion of the swings. The guys with guns look like they don't have any hope left. One has blood trickling from a wound on his temple. I wonder why the hell anyone would let kids swing after the town had been blown to bits, but then I realize that there's probably nowhere left to hide them.

"Hi!"

I look up. A little girl in a purple sundress is running across the grass. Her hair is so black it gleams in the sun. Curly pigtails bounce with every step, and she looks thrilled to be alive. "Hi!"

Who is she so excited to see? There's no one else here.

Then I see Melonhead. He's following her at a more sedate pace. This must be his kid.

I shove my phone in my pocket and stand up. I never know how to read this guy, but I'm tempted to lay into him about showing up late after he hassled me last week.

Then the little girl tackles my legs. I'm startled and stumble back a step. She giggles at my reaction but doesn't let go.

"Hi!" she says again, digging in with her fingers in a way that guarantees she's not letting go. She grins up at me, her mouth full of baby teeth.

"Marisol!" Melonhead jogs the last ten feet and scoops her up, flipping her over his arm to catch her against his shoulder.

She laughs, full out. "Stop it, *Papi*!"

"Sorry, Murph." Melonhead fishes a key ring from his pocket. His voice is tired. "She hugs everyone."

Something about it reminds me of the carefree innocence in the picture of the bombed village. This little girl doesn't know me. She doesn't see what everyone else sees.

It makes me want to warn her away.

Then again, Melonhead was pretty quick to snatch her up, like I would have done something.

I'm standing there, scowling, when he calls out to me from inside the equipment shed. He rolls up the garage door so we can get the mowers out. "You ready to work or what, kid?"

"I was ready to work half an hour ago."

I expect him to snap at me, but he doesn't. He tosses me a pair of work gloves. "I know. I'm sorry. Carmen had to work late, so one of us had to pick up Marisol. I thought I could make it back in time."

I wasn't expecting an apology, and it pokes a hole in my irritation. I pull the gloves on and grab a trash bag to collect tonight's assortment of mementos.

Melonhead climbs on a mower and calls to his daughter. "Want to drive, *Cotorra*?"

"Yes!" She abandons the wall of dust where she'd begun drawing flowers or monsters or whatever those nonhuman stick figures are supposed to be. She climbs onto the mower with a little help and settles in front of him, her tiny hands wrapping around the steering wheel.

For a second, I'm a child again, watching Kerry scramble into the truck to "help" our dad steer. We'd fight over whose turn it was to sit next to him.

I have to jerk my eyes away. I climb onto my own mower. Maybe this letter writing is a bad idea. I've said too much already, and each time I put pencil to paper, it's like taking a backhoe to memories I want to leave buried.

Melonhead's engine cranks hard, then catches. A second later, it dies. He mutters something in Spanish and tries again. This time it cranks and sounds like it won't catch at all, but it finally does.

And then it dies immediately.

He tries a third time. And a fourth.

There's a definition for insanity that talks about doing the same thing over and over again, expecting a different result.

"Hey," I call. He ignores me and tries again. Now it won't catch at all.

I kill my own mower and climb down. "Hey!"

He lets the key go and looks up, his expression impatient. "What?"

"It sounds like your fuel line."

"What do you know about it?"

I hate that. I hate when people treat me like some kind of idiot who can barely tell time. "I know it sounds like your fuel line. When's the last time you checked the filter?"

"I don't maintain the machines, Murph. They have a service plan."

"Then your service plan is crap."

"Your soovis plan is *crap*," Marisol says. She bounces in the seat. "Come on, *Papi*. Go, tractor. Go."

"Thanks a lot, kid." Melonhead looks aggrieved. He lifts her off the front of the mower and sets her on the ground. "I thought I was late before. Now *I'm* going to have to work on Saturday."

"Do you have tools? I might be able to fix it."

"I don't think you should be messing with it."

"Fine. Whatever." The hell with it. I offered. I climb back on my own mower and fire it up.

I'm driving it out of the shed when he calls out behind me. "All right! Come see what you can do."

The tractor is a mess. It takes me an extra minute to get at the engine because the hinge is rusty. I don't know who's been taking their money, but this thing hasn't been maintained at all.

While I'm in here, I check the oil pan. The oil is black and thick as soup. I tell him so.

"What makes you an expert on tractors?" he says. His daughter is crouching between us, like she's a key player in the repair effort. Her eyes dart back and forth. She repeats almost every word I say.

"I didn't say I was an expert on tractors. This is basic stuff." I wipe my arm across my forehead before sweat can get into my eyes. "An engine is an engine."

"You know cars?"

I shrug and keep my eyes on the engine as I slide the oil pan back into place. I'm used to Melonhead running on at the mouth, but he usually doesn't talk *to* me. "More about the insides than the outsides."

"Can you fix it so it'll run tonight?"

"Maybe. The fuel filter needs replacing, but I can probably clean it enough." I pull it free and blow on it.

Marisol leans forward and tries to do the same thing. I hold it out for her to give it a shot.

Melonhead watches this, and I pull it back, remembering how he grabbed her away from me.

"It's nice of you to let her help," he says.

I feel myself blushing and glance back at the engine. Rev is really better with kids. I don't get much practice. "It's not like she can hurt it."

"I not hurt it!" she says indignantly.

I smile. "Besides, she sounds like she's taking notes to make up a manual later."

He hugs her. "She's my little parrot."

She squirms free. "I helping!"

"You are," he says.

I wipe at the outside of the filter, then blow on it again. "I can't guarantee it'll hold all night, but this should get you through a section or two."

"Did your father teach you this?"

"Yeah."

"Is he a mechanic?"

"Not anymore."

He must hear the note in my voice, because I can hear his hesitation. He wants to ask. I'm surprised he doesn't know my whole history from the judge, but maybe he only gets the details of my crimes and not my father's.

He must think better of it. "Thanks, Murph."

I push the filter back into place, then look at him. I try to keep the irritation out of my voice, but a little slides in. "My name is Declan."

Melonhead doesn't miss a beat. He holds out a hand. "Nice to meet you. My name is Frank."

I blink. "Frank?"

He shrugs. "You'd feel better if I told you to call me Francisco?"

Now I look away, almost ashamed. It's not like I called him Pedro or something.

Though maybe that would have been better than *Melonhead*.

He claps me on the shoulder. "Your dad didn't teach you to shake hands?"

I pull the work glove off my hand and reach out to shake his.

48

"You're not a bad kid to have around, Declan," he says.

I snort. "You just haven't known me long enough."

My stepfather is sitting in the living room when I walk through the door. I usually check before walking in, but all I want is a soda and a shower and a chance to hole up in my room and not be accountable to anyone. A football game is on, the volume roaring. Alan and Mom bought the big-screen for each other as a wedding present. Mom can't stand loud noise, so I'm not surprised when she's not sitting next to him. Her car is in the driveway, though, so I know she's home.

I want to tell Alan to turn the damn volume down so she can enjoy the television, too.

I don't. I don't even look at him.

He watches me, though, like he's waiting for me to rage out. You could grab hold of the tension in the room.

"Where have you been?" he says.

What a dick. He knows where I've been. I stride past the couch toward the kitchen.

"I'm talking to you." He's half shouting over the television. "Don't you ignore me."

I ignore him.

I expect him to follow me into the kitchen, but he doesn't.

Alan sells insurance. I've seen him in full-on sales mode, and the bull practically oozes from his pores. The rest of the time, he's pretending to be a tough-guy sports nut. It's some kind of miracle that he's not sitting in front of the television with a foam finger and a felt pennant.

I have no idea what Mom sees in him.

No, that's not true. I know exactly what she sees in him: a sweet-talker who figured out how to get in her pants.

You know what I see in him? Another prick who's going to let her down so hard that a fall from a cliff would hurt less.

Not that anyone's sitting around asking for my opinion.

The refrigerator yields cold lasagna. I scoop some onto a plate but don't bother to heat it up. I grab a Coke and a fork and prepare to run the Alan gauntlet one more time.

He's glaring at the kitchen doorway when I emerge. The television blares behind him.

"I asked you where you were," he says.

I keep right on walking.

He stands up. Blocks my path.

Alan isn't a big guy, but he's not small, either. I have no idea what would happen if he took a swing at me. The only thing that keeps me from hitting *him* is that I know how much it would upset my mom.

I wonder if the same is true in his case.

I meet his eyes. We're dead even for height. Most people back down from me, but Alan doesn't. He knows what I did and he knows what I have to do, but it's still humiliating to have to admit it out loud. "I had community service."

"That ends at eight o'clock. It's after nine."

"My boss was late. We had a problem with one of the mowers." The plate in my hand is starting to feel heavy.

"You're supposed to report there and come home immediately after."

"I did."

"Don't lie to me."

It takes everything I have to keep the food in my hands instead of flinging it down. "I'm not lying to you."

"If I had my way, you wouldn't be driving at all."

My jaw is tight. I push past him before he can goad me into an argument. "I guess it's a good thing you don't get your way, then, huh?"

Actually, it's a good thing I had an expensive attorney, or I really wouldn't be driving at all.

Alan doesn't stop me, and he doesn't say anything as I ascend the stairs. I'm closing the door to my room when I hear his voice, bitter and resigned. "You're going to end up just like your father."

The television should be too loud for me to hear him clearly, but he wasn't quiet about it.

I slam my soda on the dresser and fling my door open so hard it bounces against the wall. My breathing is loud in my chest, and I have to force myself to stop at the top of the stairs.

"What did you just say to me?" I yell.

Now it's his turn to ignore me.

I hit the wall so hard the pictures rattle. "What the hell did you just say to me, Alan?"

"You heard me."

I hate him.

I hate him.

I hate that he's here. I hate that he's not my father. I hate that he makes my mother happy. I hate that he doesn't make her happy enough.

I hate everything about him.

The door at the other end of the hallway opens, and my mother stands in the doorway. Her dark hair is in a loose ponytail, and she clings to the molding like she might duck back inside if it's too scary out here.

That sucks some of the rage right out of me. My one hand is so tight I'm digging nails through my palm, and the other hand clutches a shaking plate of lasagna. My shoulders are hunched, and I'm sure my eyes are fierce.

I should apologize, but I can't. There's too much weight behind it. I owe her apologies for much bigger things. The letter from the cemetery was right: fate does seem to conspire against us. The guilt sits on my shoulders and presses me into the floor until I'm unable to move.

My mother doesn't move, either.

I wonder if she heard what Alan said. I wonder if she agrees with him.

I turn my back on her and enter my room. I don't slam the door, but the sudden silence is loud, despite the football game roaring downstairs.

She won't come in. She hasn't come in for years.

Maybe—

No, nothing will change.

I drop onto the corner of my bed. I don't want the lasagna anymore. I keep hearing Alan's voice in my head.

You're going to end up just like your father.

He's right. I probably will.

CHAPTER EIGHT

My father is in prison.

I've never visited him. I don't think my mother has, either, but it's not like we talk about it. It's a family secret that's not really a secret at all.

The real secret is that sometimes I want to see him. It's weird admitting that, even to you. I've never told anyone, not even my best friend. It would be easy to hate my father, but I don't.

I miss him. Not the same way I miss my sister. Never like that. She and I could fight like it was the end of the world—she was a little sister after all—but when it counted, we were close. People sometimes say that losing a family member is like losing a limb. Her death was like losing half of myself. I miss her, but I know I'll never get her back. There's no undoing it.

But I miss him, too, in a different way.

And prison isn't forever. Well, not for him.

That's wrong, isn't it? How messed up am I that I miss the guy who killed her?

I almost used a different expression than "messed up," but I remembered what you said about your mom. My best friend is the same way. He hates when I swear, so I make an effort. Usually.

I disagree with your mom, though. Words are words. Dropping an f-bomb wouldn't make me an idiot any more than saying "sesquipedalian" makes someone intelligent.

Both those words can easily make someone sound like a real douchebag, though.

Now I feel like I should cross out "douchebag." Your mom probably wouldn't like me much.

I looked up your mother's photograph. I don't think it's depressing. I don't think it's hopeful, either. It's life. When everything goes to hell around you, the only way to go is forward. Those kids on the swing set know it. The guys with the guns do, too.

How old are you? You mentioned honors photography, so I'm guessing you're in high school. Do you go to Hamilton?

Or maybe it's better if we don't know anything about each other.

Your call.

"I need your opinion on something."

Rowan lifts a hand and blows on her nails. She's painting them a pink so light it's almost white, and the opaque nails combined with her light hair and skin makes her look even more ethereal than usual. Her bedroom furniture is all white, trimmed with gold, and her carpeting is lavender. All she needs is a pair of wings.

"You're hiding," she says.

I straighten. That's out of the blue and has nothing to do with what I was about to ask.

Then again, maybe it's exactly on target. "I'm hiding?"

"From your father."

Oh. I scowl. "I don't want to talk about him."

She starts a second coat of polish. "He wasn't trying to hurt you, Jules."

I don't say anything.

She glances up. "You said yourself that her editor offered to take them. It's not like your dad dug them out and listed them on Craigslist."

She's right. I know she's right. I study my own nails, short and round and unpolished. "It feels like he's punishing her," I say softly.

"Maybe." She hesitates. "Anger is one of the stages of grief."

This conversation is making me jittery. I didn't want to talk about Dad at all. Or Mom. "Is that your psych class talking?"

She puts down the nail polish and turns the desk chair to fully face me. "Last night Mom asked me if she should call your dad."

"What?" My voice drops two levels. I glance at the door, ready to bolt. "Why?"

"Because you've been here until almost midnight for the last four days."

"Fine. I'll leave."

"No! Jules—stop!" She blocks me before I can make it out the door. Her hands fall on my shoulders, gingerly so she doesn't smudge the polish. "Wait. Okay? Wait. Mom also said you're always welcome here. Always." She pauses. "We're worried about you."

Rowan and her mother could be sisters. Seriously, people say so all the time. Mary Ann was twenty-two when Rowan was born, and she takes care of herself. You'd think Rowan would rebel by dyeing her hair black and eating Snickers bars for dinner, but she doesn't. They tell each other everything.

I shouldn't be surprised that they've been talking about me.

I *am* surprised at how envious I am. It hits me all at once.

"I know he wasn't trying to hurt me." I glare at her because this is the first time I realize she doesn't get it. "That's the problem. He didn't even know it would."

She hesitates.

"Say it." I harden my voice. "Whatever it is. Say it, Ro."

"Maybe you should let my mom call him."

"What? Why?"

"Maybe he needs a little . . . support. So he can help you."

"Sure." I can't even keep the disdain out of my voice. I turn for the door again.

"Come on," she says, following me down the hallway. "You're my best friend, Jules. I want to help you."

"I know. I just—I don't want it right now."

"Please stop."

I do stop, in the foyer. The overhead lights are bright, turning her hair to spun gold, making her blue eyes pop. My hair hangs dark and straight, and I'm wearing a touch of blush and lip gloss only because I'm sick of people telling me I need to get some rest.

"You seem so angry all the time," she says quietly, carefully.

"I am angry."

The words are out before I can consider their impact. Maybe she's right; maybe this is a stage of grief. I feel like I've been stuck on anger for a while now, though, and the rut has been dug so deep there's no escaping it.

In fact, if we stand here much longer, I'm afraid this anger is going to rattle me apart.

"I need to go," I say quickly, and grab the doorknob.

"Jules—" She stops short and sighs. "I didn't mean to chase you off."

"You didn't."

"What were you going to ask me about?"

I was going to ask her about the letters, but I can't now. She wouldn't understand. She would read our conversations about death and suicide and hopelessness, and she'd get it all wrong.

My father would *definitely* be getting a call in that case.

I look at her. "It's nothing. It's silly. I'll see you in the morning, okay?"

She starts to follow me out the door, but I put my hands up. "Enough, Ro. Enough. I just want to drive around for a bit. I'll be okay."

"Are you going to the cemetery?"

It's late, well after dark, and if I tell her yes, she'll flip out. "No. Not tonight." I jog down the steps. Rowan didn't throw me out, but her house doesn't feel like a refuge anymore. Not with her mother sitting around, waiting to analyze my grief.

"Good night, then," she calls.

"Good night," I call back.

I feel like a bad friend, but I can't help it. I can't force what I'm feeling to fit between chapters two and six in some handbook dealing with the death of a loved one.

My car is way at the end of the block because someone was having a birthday party after school. Now the street is deserted, and my car sits alone in the shadow of an elm tree. I half expect Rowan to come after me, but she doesn't. The sidewalk is pitch-dark, and my sneakers whisper against the pavement with every step. Nighttime has stolen the heat from the air, and now a breeze lifts my hair and cools my neck.

I inhale, breathing in cut grass and tree bark and humidity.

A man coughs nearby. I jump a little, startled. I glance around, but I don't see him.

The hairs on the back of my neck stand up. My hands fumble with the keys.

The lock gives, and I drop into the driver's seat. The air inside the car clings to my skin, smelling of slightly stale coffee and too-warm upholstery. Anger wars with unease as I press the key into the ignition and turn it.

Nothing happens.

I try again.

Nothing. The accessory lights flicker and die.

I hit the dashboard. "*Damn* it."

My voice is loud in the confines of the car, and I wince. *Sorry, Mom.*

For what it's worth, I think I agree with Letter Guy. Words are just words.

A flicker of guilt pokes at me, like I'm somehow betraying her memory.

A hand knocks on the window, and I nearly jump out of my skin. A guy is standing there, his face in shadow under a dark hoodie. I can see the edge of a jaw and a slice of longish hair, but that's it.

"Back off!" My hand finds my phone without my even thinking about it.

I have my finger over the nine, but his hands are up, and he takes a step back. I can't see him much more clearly, but the frame of a pair of glasses catches the light. He's tall with broad shoulders. The phrase "built like a brick outhouse" comes to mind. He could probably bench-press my Honda Civic.

He coughs again. "Sorry," he says, speaking a little more loudly than necessary so I can hear him through the window. "I wanted to see if you needed any help."

"I'm fine!" Didn't one of those stupid girl-safety chain emails talk about a gang initiation where they disable your car to trap you? I turn the key again. *Flicker-flicker-die.*

"Aren't you Juliet Young?"

I stop and look at him again. Is it a good thing or a bad thing that he knows my name?

He pushes back the hood of his sweatshirt. "I think we had English together last year."

For a moment, I can't place him at all. Then my brain decides to work. He's that freak loner who sits in the back of every class and never talks to anyone. His name is Red or Razz or something. He always wears hoodies or long-sleeved shirts, even when it's the dead heat of summer.

He looks like a serial killer.

"Do you need a jump?" he says.

I stare at him for a moment too long. "Do I need a *what*?"

"For your car," he says. "Battery dead?"

"I don't know. I'm fine." I could go back to Rowan's, but I'm not sure I want to get out of the car yet. He hasn't done anything wrong, but it's just me and him on this darkened street. This is the part of the movie where you'd scream at the girl to stay in the car.

Then I have an epiphany. "I'll call my dad to come get me."

"My friend's got a set of cables. He lives right over there." He points down the opposite street, then pulls a phone out of his pocket and starts texting. After a second, he glances back at me. "Pop your hood."

I'm stuck in this in-between place where I'm not sure whether he's being real or I'm being stupid. I glance at my own phone. I don't *really* want to call my dad. That would invite conversation, and since the camera incident, I'm *so* not ready for conversation.

Instead, I jot off a quick text to Rowan.

> JY: My car won't start and some guy from school is offering to jump-start it. Can you come out here?

Then I shove the phone in my pocket and pull the lever to pop the hood.

He doesn't wait for me to get out of the car. He steps to the front of the vehicle and lifts the hood, looking for the steel arm to hold it up. I hear him snap it into place.

The air inside the car is stifling, and I wish I had enough power to roll down a window. The sun set long ago, but the warmth in here is enough to make sweat bloom on my forehead.

Metal clicks on metal under the hood and I wonder what the guy is doing. I think of all the times my father offered to teach me basic car maintenance—and the equal number of times I told him "Later."

Then again, it's not like changing the oil and checking the tire pressure is going to fire up the engine.

Through the passenger-side window I see Rowan heading down the sidewalk toward us, her hair shining in the moonlight. Good. I won't be alone.

I hit the unlock button and fling my door wide. It hits something. Hard.

"Whoa!" a guy's voice exclaims.

I look up. Standing there outside my car door, a length of

jumper cables in his hands, is the only classmate I'd find scarier than the wannabe Goth guy poking around under my hood: Declan Murphy.

He looks super excited to see me, in the way the school janitor is super excited to discover a clogged toilet. Declan's hand has caught the frame, and he's blocking my path out of the car.

I need to apologize, but it's going to come out spiteful. I can feel the words on the back of my tongue. A smart-aleck sorry that's more about protecting myself and nothing about him getting pummeled by my door.

My eyes fall on the jumper cables in his hand.

I should apologize *and* thank him.

As he's staring down at me, his face loses some of the irritation, like in the school hallway last week. Light from somewhere crosses his face, forming a stripe over his eyes, leaving his remaining features in shadow. Like a superhero mask, but in reverse.

"Battery dead?" he says.

He looks huge standing over me. I swallow and think of the moment he made a quick move in the hallway—when I thought he was going to do something aggressive, but he was only picking up his backpack. "I don't know."

"What's it doing?"

"Um." I have to clear my throat. I glance at the dash. "Nothing. It won't start."

"I don't think it's the starter," calls the guy from under the hood.

"Thanks, Rev." Declan rolls his eyes skyward, then leans into the car. He's muttering under his breath, something like, "I teach him three things and now he's the expert."

I barely catch the words because he's leaning in front of me, reaching into the car. I suck back into the seat, but when he turns the key, I see he's not making a move toward me. I expect him to smell disgusting, like cigarettes and sweat and unwashed jeans.

He doesn't. He smells like cut grass and fresh laundry and some kind of sporty guy bodywash. The dash lights barely flicker when he turns the key, and then he's out of my space.

"Everything okay here?"

Rowan is on the sidewalk behind him, her blond hair shining from the nearby streetlamp. Declan turns. He doesn't seem surprised to see her. "She needs a jump. You have a car you can pull over here?"

Her eyes go from him, to the guy under the hood—*Rev?*—to me. "Yeah." She drags the word out. "Want to walk back with me, Jules?"

It's only the other end of the block, but it feels weird to leave them with my car, especially when Declan says, "Leave the keys."

Then again, the alternative is staying here with the two of them.

I grab my purse and fall into step with Rowan.

"They seem legit," she says quietly. "I thought Declan Murphy was trying something when I walked up."

I feel flushed and chilled at the same time. "He didn't even touch me."

"Good." Her voice is firm. "I'm glad you texted me."

I am, too. Sort of. There's this little part of me that wishes she hadn't walked up right then.

I glance back over my shoulder. Rev is still bent over the front end of my car. Declan is a few feet behind him. He's patting something against his opposite palm, then lifts his hand to his face. A red glow suddenly lights his features.

A cigarette. I hate smokers.

"Do you know that other guy?" I say.

"Rev Fletcher," she says. "He lives on the corner. Mom calls him the vampire. We hardly ever see him out during the day."

"He scared the crap out of me."

"I bet. Only you would have the two most socially awkward guys in the world show up to jump-start your car." Now she glances over her shoulder. "Maybe I should have Mom come back with us."

I think about what she said earlier about her mother wanting to call my father for "support," and I bristle. "We're not six years old, Ro."

We're back in her driveway now, and she pulls her keys out of her pocket and clicks the button to unlock her doors. "I don't want to end up on the evening news."

I don't, either. It's probably a lucky thing that my car battery is dead, or Declan Murphy could be five miles away by now, adding grand theft auto to his rap sheet. I'm glad I grabbed my purse before getting out of the car.

Rowan has to turn around in a driveway to make her car face mine. Her headlights illuminate Declan and Rev. It would make a great photograph, all overexposed and full of harsh contrast.

She kills the engine and the lights, and we start to get out of the car.

Declan waves a hand and takes a drag on his cigarette. "Leave the car on," he calls. "Headlights, too."

She does, and ten seconds later, we're on the sidewalk, looking at cables connecting our vehicles. He slides into my car's driver's seat and starts the engine. It fires right up.

"Is that it?" I say.

"That's it." I expect him to get out of the car, but he takes a drag on his cigarette and starts flicking dials.

"What are you doing?"

He doesn't glance at me, and he doesn't answer my question. "Where do you live?"

"I don't think that's any of your business."

That gets his attention. He shoves himself out of the car and looms over me. Everything about his posture screams, *Don't mess with me.* I take a quick step back before I can stop myself.

"Declan!"

I jump. The male voice is loud and to my left. A middle-aged man with a receding hairline is striding across the road, fury in his voice. "What are you doing? Leave those girls alone."

His tone implies that I might have been right to be cautious.

Declan hasn't moved away from me. "Her car wouldn't start." His voice grates with irritation. "I was helping."

"Yeah, it looks like you're helping."

Declan whirls and unclips the jumper cables from my car battery. They click together and sparks fly. "What the hell do you think these are, Alan?"

Rev moves close to him. His voice is low. "Easy, Dec."

Alan is braver than I am. He doesn't back away. "You're not allowed to walk out of the house whenever you want. You have a curfew. Do you understand what that means?"

A curfew? Declan Murphy has a curfew?

He jerks the cables free from Rowan's car and slams her hood. "I'm not breaking curfew. I was *helping*—"

"Get back in the house. I can't believe you keep putting your mother through this."

Declan's entire expression darkens. He drops the cables on the asphalt and starts forward.

Rev is quick. He's in front of Declan, a hand on his shoulder. "Hey. *Hey*. Think it through."

Declan stops. He's glaring at Alan, and his jaw is set. Both hands form fists.

Alan is glaring right back at him. His expression says, *Bring it, punk.*

Rowan is by my side now, and her breathing is loud in the night air. Her sudden anxiety wants to pull me into its grasp. She doesn't like conflict, and this is worse than the confrontation in the hallway. There's no teacher to come play referee.

Part of me wants to hide. Part of me wishes we *had* called Rowan's mom.

One of them is going to move, and it's going to spark a fight. The promise of violence weighs heavy in the air. Neither looks ready to back down. The tension is coiled so tightly that I don't think either of them will be able to unravel it.

My mother once wrote to me about a close call in West Africa. She'd been shooting the effects of an extremist group that had been leveling small towns. According to her letter, she'd been following her guides through the jungle, and they literally stumbled right into an extremist camp. She'd thought they'd be killed. I could feel her fear between the words. They grabbed her equipment and began destroying her cameras—until she told them that she was documenting their military victories. Not only did they let her live, but they also allowed her to travel with them for a day. Her photos had made their way into the *New York Times*, but her letter, the words meant for me, had been more powerful. She had painted a picture of sweat and guns and terror, but then she'd made me laugh.

Men can be like toddlers, Juliet. Sometimes all they need is something shiny to distract them.

I stoop to snatch the jumper cables from the pavement. I hold them out to Declan and do my best to lace my voice with sugar. "Thanks so much for coming out. I didn't mean to get you in trouble." I give an apologetic glance at Alan, though inside I'm shaking like a leaf. "I'm really sorry. I didn't know he had a curfew. My car wouldn't start, and I was so worried about getting home . . ."

Alan blinks, almost as if he forgot I was there. He glances at Declan, then at the cars, and finally back to me. "No harm done, I suppose." His eyes flick back to Declan. "Next time you want to help someone, you say something before leaving the house. Sneak out again, and I'm calling the cops. Then you can try sneaking out of Cheltenham. You hear me?"

A muscle twitches in Declan's jaw, and I can tell he's going to fire back. I thrust the jumper cables at him. "Do you think I need a new battery? Or should I be okay?"

It takes him a second, but he breaks the lethal eye contact and takes the cables from my hand. "It looks pretty old." His voice is rough, but under the aggression, there are notes of something else I can't identify. "You never answered my question about how far you have to go."

His question? I don't remember him asking a question.

Is that why he asked where I live?

Shame heats my face. "Oh. Just a few miles."

He nods. "Let it run for a bit before you turn it off. I'd get a new battery when you can."

I nod.

Declan turns and heads down the street.

Alan doesn't move. He's looking at Rev, who's shifted to lean against Rowan's car. "You need to let him fight his own battles, Rev."

Rev's expression is even. He coughs, then pulls his hood up. It throws his whole face in shadow. "Maybe I think his stepfather shouldn't be starting battles with him."

Alan draws himself up, but he must figure it's not worth it. He gives a humorless laugh and shakes his head, then turns away. "You kids always think you know everything."

The street is dead silent once he's gone.

"Wow," whispers Rowan. Her eyes are like saucers.

Rev looks at her. "That's nothing."

"Thanks for stopping Declan from—" She breaks off. "From . . . whatever he was going to do."

"I didn't stop him. He stopped himself."

That's not quite what it looked like, but I don't say anything. I like Rev's quiet voice, and the way he stood up to Declan's stepfather. It makes me feel bad for thinking he looked like a serial killer.

Especially when he glances at me and says, "Thanks for what you did, too. Do you think you'll be okay to get home?"

My heart is still thudding in my chest, but I nod. I have to clear my throat. "What's Cheltenham?"

Rev frowns. "What?"

"That Alan guy. He said Declan could try sneaking out of Cheltenham."

Rev's expression darkens, closing off. He coughs again, and his shoulders hunch a little. "It's a juvenile detention facility." He pushes away from Rowan's car. "Make sure you get a new battery. If he says you need it, you need it."

Then he slides into the darkness, leaving us alone.

CHAPTER NINE

I've started 35 notes to you, and they all start with, "I'm 17," but then I can't write any more. I don't want to ruin this. I don't want to lose it.

I sound like an idiot. I might as well be sitting here writing letters to the dark, waiting for a response.

I don't even know you, but I feel like I understand you.

I feel like you understand me.

And that's what I like so much about it.

She's my age.

I had suspected she was close, but this is confirmation. I don't know why it matters, but it does.

She likes this.

She likes this.

I've read the note at least sixty-seven times, and it still gives me a secret thrill. I glance around the classroom, checking to see if it's contagious, as if the rest of the class should be able to feel the jolt this one little note gives me.

I don't need to worry. We're studying poetry in English, and an espresso bar couldn't wake this room up. A girl in the front row is reading a Dylan Thomas poem out loud, but she doesn't give a crap about raging against the dying of the light, because she sounds like she's reading a shopping list. She twirls her hair around her finger and slumps back in her chair when she reads the final line.

I smooth my fingers along the lines of the note and read it again. I have it tucked under the edge of my textbook.

I feel like I understand you. I feel like you understand me.

A crazy, wild part of me wants to find her. To say, *yes, yes, I understand.*

Bored silence has overtaken the classroom. I swear you can hear three people texting. Our teacher, Mrs. Hillard, is hoping we're all absorbing the power of the poetry. She leans back against her desk, clutching the textbook to her chest. "Who can tell me what the poem is about?"

This will probably come as a shock, but no one answers.

Mrs. Hillard straightens and walks down the rows of desks, touching her fingers lightly to each one. Her long skirt swishes with each step, and she's wearing one of those patterned cardigans you only ever see on middle-aged high school teachers.

I slide the note farther under the book before she can get to me.

"What is Dylan Thomas raging against?" she says. "What is 'the dying of the light'?"

"Darkness," calls out Drew Kenney.

Mrs. Hillard nods but says, "On the surface, maybe." Her heels click down the aisle between the desks. "What else could he be talking about?"

"Nighttime?" calls another girl, her voice lilting at the end. It's a guess.

She sounds so dull, so uninspired. I think of my photography analysis with the cemetery girl and wonder if she'd be so bored with this class.

Wait. I wonder if she's *in* this class. I look around.

I have no idea. I don't *think* so, but I have no idea. It's not like you can look at a girl and know her mother is dead. There's no neon sign over my head flashing DEAD SISTER, either.

"Read it again to yourselves," says Mrs. Hillard. She taps on Elijah Walker's textbook and whispers, "Put your phone away."

He gives a heavy sigh and shoves his phone into his bag.

"Read it again." She stops beside my desk and barely gives me a glance, her fingers tapping the textbook absently before she moves on. Teachers never expect much from me. "Read it again and tell me what this poem is really about."

Someone coughs. Someone shifts.

Silence.

She turns at the back of the room, and for the first time her composure cracks. "Someone must have an idea. Someone. Anyone. There are no wrong answers here."

Says the woman who just told two people they were wrong.

"What is this poem about?" she demands.

My eyes skip to the page to see what the big deal is. *Do not go gentle into that good night.*

Before I know it, I've read the whole thing. It's not about nighttime or darkness at all.

Mrs. Hillard is still pacing the aisles. "He says, 'Rage, rage against the dying of the light.' What is Dylan Thomas *feeling*?"

"Desperation."

The word is out of my mouth before I can stop it. My voice is rough with misuse—I haven't talked to anyone since I split a bagel with Rev in the cafeteria three hours ago. I've drawn some focus, too. Half these people have probably never heard me speak.

Mrs. Hillard comes back up the aisle and stops beside my desk.

I don't look at her. I should have kept my mouth shut. I doodle on my notebook like someone else said it, but she's not an idiot.

"Desperation," she says quietly. "Why?"

"I guessed."

"You didn't guess. Why desperation?"

My hand goes still, and now I glare at her. You could hear a pin drop in the classroom. I don't like being the center of attention, and I want her to move on. "I *said* it's a guess."

"Okay, guess again," she says equably. "*Why* desperation?"

I slam my book closed, and two kids near me jump. "Maybe he's afraid of the damn dark."

She doesn't flinch. "Maybe he is. What kind of darkness?"

The wrong kind. Sudden emotion clocks me upside the head.

My shoulders tense, and I want to rip this book to shreds. My breathing is so loud I sound like a trapped wild horse.

"Give it a shot," she says. "What kind of darkness?"

Her voice is encouraging. I'm about to rattle apart, but she thinks she's somehow going to get through to me, to find shiny silver under a little bit of tarnish. I've seen this look before: in social workers, in school psychologists, in other teachers.

What they fail to understand is that there's no point in trying.

Keith Mason snorts under his breath a few rows over. "They probably don't read much poetry in juvie."

I push out of my chair so hard it scrapes the floor.

Mrs. Hillard is quicker than I'd give her credit for. Braver, too. I've got six inches on her, but she blocks my path.

"Prove him wrong," she says quickly. "Answer my question. What kind of darkness?"

It takes me a moment to filter intelligent thoughts. I tear my eyes away from Keith and look down at her. My head is spinning with emotion from the girl's note and the memories the poem evoked and the humiliation from another reminder of what I am. Of how these people see me.

"He's not wrong," I say, and my voice is rough again. I drop into my chair and keep my eyes on my book. I find my pencil and take up the same doodle.

She inhales to say something more, and my fingers threaten to snap my pencil. Without meaning to, I start digging a hole through the paper.

The bell rings, and the students around me explode into a flurry of activity. The teacher begins calling instructions about our homework assignment, some paragraph I'll probably write between classes.

I slip the girl's note into the textbook and shove it into my backpack. I have a clear path to the door. Everyone avoids me.

Except Mrs. Hillard. She steps in front of me again. "Do you have a minute?"

I'm tempted to ignore her. Students are streaming out of the room around us, and it would be simple to glance away and slip into the flow. If she looked like she was going to write me a detention or otherwise hassle me, I wouldn't hesitate.

She doesn't look like that, so I stop.

"Are you going to be late for your next class?" she says.

I shake my head. "I have lunch." Then I realize I could have lied and gotten out of here without too much trouble.

She nods at a desk in the front row. "Sit down for a minute."

I inhale and hesitate—but then I let it out in a sigh, and I slide into the seat. It's the first time I've sat in the front row of any classroom in this school.

"I want to talk to you about what you said," she begins solemnly.

Oh. *Oh.* I'm such an idiot. I begin to rise from the chair, and a familiar bitterness settles in my chest. "Whatever. Just write me a detention so I can get the hell out of here."

She blinks, startled. "I don't want to write you a detention."

I frown. "Then what do you want?"

"I want to know why you said *desperation*."

"It was a stupid guess! Maybe you should have asked—"

"Are you really so afraid to appear smart?" She leans back against her desk and folds her arms across her chest.

I scowl, but I don't say anything.

She doesn't say anything, either.

The weight of her words pins me in this chair. My pride picks them apart. *Afraid. Are you really so afraid? To appear smart?*

I'm not a bad student—that's a good way to get hassled, and I don't need to give these people any more reason to get in my face. There was a time when I was a *good* student, when my mother would pin my report cards on the refrigerator. Now I only bother with enough work to scrape by, making sure I don't fail anything.

Her words are a dare.

We sit there for the longest time.

"I'm missing lunch," I finally say.

Her shoulders fall. A little. Enough. "Okay," she sighs. She nods toward the door. "Go ahead."

I'm halfway down the hallway when her voice catches me. "Declan. Wait. Your assignment."

I turn, and she's coming down the hallway, a folded slip of paper between her fingers. "I heard it in class."

"No, I want you to write me something else." She holds out the paper. "Write me as little or as much of an answer as you want."

I take the paper, and her eyes light up.

Then I crumple it in my fist and turn away.

I skip the line in the cafeteria because Rev will have enough food to feed an army. Kristin always packs something extra for me.

I can't remember the last time my mother packed me a lunch. Not like I deserve it.

I drop the crumpled piece of paper on the table, then slide onto the bench across from Rev. We have the table to ourselves. Rain rattles the windows and the place is packed, but no one bothers us.

"You look like the grim reaper," I say, because he does. His hoodie has a skeleton silk-screened on the chest and arms, and as usual, the hood is up.

"I think that's the point." He uncrumples the paper and reads. "'Why is Dylan Thomas desperate?' What is this?"

"English homework. That's not the note I want to show you."

He pulls a sandwich bag out of his lunch sack and slides it across the table. "More from your girl?"

My girl. I shouldn't like that. But I do.

He knows we've kept up the communication, but I haven't shown him any of her notes since the night I told him about her. Our conversations have turned too personal, and I don't like the idea of her sharing my secrets with others. This note is short and vague, and I have to tell him.

He stares at the words while I unwrap two slices of banana bread. Each slice is spread with cream cheese and topped with raisins and walnuts. I'm instantly starving. I want to shove all of it in my face at once.

"She's our age," says Rev.

"Yeah."

He glances around, as if she could be watching us. Instead of the same glee I felt, his expression is serious. "Are you sure someone's not messing with you somehow?"

"Messing with me how?"

"She doesn't want to meet you. You don't *know* she's seventeen. She could be a fifty-year-old guy getting off on this whole thing."

I grab the letter out of his hands and jam it back into my backpack. "Shut up, Rev."

He watches me eat for a moment. "Let me see it again."

"No."

"Okay." He pulls a can of carbonated water out of his backpack and pops the lid.

Sometimes I want to punch him. I find the letter and slide it across the table.

He reads it again. It makes me feel all jittery inside.

His eyes flick up. "She likes you."

I shrug and steal his drink. It tastes like someone drowned an orange in a bottle of Perrier, and I cough.

Rev smiles. "You like her."

"How can you drink this crap?"

His smile widens. "Is it making you crazy that she won't reveal herself?"

"Seriously, Rev, do you have any regular water?"

He's no fool. "What do you want to do?"

I take a long breath and blow it out. I run a hand through my hair. "I don't know."

"You know."

"I want to stake out the grave. This waiting between letters is killing me."

"Suggest email."

"She doesn't want to tell me anything more than her age. She's not going to give me her email address."

"Maybe not her *real* email. But you could set up a private account and give her the address. See if she writes you."

It's so simple it's brilliant. I hate that I didn't think of it. "Rev, I could kiss you."

"Brush your teeth first." He reclaims his bizarre can of water.

"What if she doesn't write back?"

He puts down her note and taps the words *And that's what I like so much about it.* "She will, Dec. She will."

CHAPTER TEN

I don't want to lose this, either.
    But maybe we could take this digital, so
we're not at the mercy of the elements? I
set up an anonymous account.
    TheDark@freemail.com
    Your move, Cemetery Girl.

Wow.

The morning breeze is chilly, and it ruffles the paper. I read it again.

Wow. *Wow.*

Suddenly, I need to move.

I kiss my palm and slap it to the gravestone. "Sorry, Mom. I need to go."

CHAPTER ELEVEN

From: Cemetery Girl <cemeterygirl@freemail.com>
To: The Dark <TheDark@freemail.com>
Date: Wednesday, October 2   7:17:00 AM
Subject: Going digital

The Dark? Don't you think that's kind of ghoulish?

She actually sent me an email.

She sent me an *email*.

I'm sitting in the school library and grinning like an idiot. I haven't linked this account to my phone yet, because I really didn't think she'd respond. I almost didn't leave the note last night. Melonhead—Frank—kept asking why I was so jumpy.

I told him it was all the drugs, and he gave me a shove and told me I shouldn't joke about those things.

My eyes flick up to the time stamp. Wednesday. Today.

Not just today, but twenty minutes ago. My heart rate doubles. She could be here. She could be in the library right this instant. I cast a furtive glance around, trying to be inconspicuous about it. Most of the computers are occupied, but I have no way of knowing what anyone is doing. The monitors have those screen protectors that only allow someone to read the screen if they're looking straight at it. The students run the gamut from the freshman boy with leaking acne to an Asian girl with pink streaks in her hair who looks like she might be wearing pajamas.

Rev's voice echoes in my head. *She could be a fifty-year-old guy getting off on this whole thing.*

I shove the thought out of my mind and look around again. Everyone seems to be actively *doing* something, typing or clicking or reading. No one is sneaking glances the way I am.

I'm such an idiot. Why would *she* be sneaking glances? She could have sent the email from home anyway. It's not like the email came with a label like, *Sent from Hamilton High School Library.*

The librarian walks over to the computer bank. I have no idea what her name is, but she looks like she's pushing seventy. "Three minutes to the bell. Start saving your work if you haven't already."

I can't compose a reply in three minutes. Especially not a reply to something criticizing my email address.

I shut down the computer and sling my backpack over my shoulder. The hallways are packed with students on their way to class, but I let myself fall into the flow. I pull out my phone and start linking the email address so I'll get a notification when she writes again.

Then I stop. I don't like the idea of her emails being dumped into the same inbox with notices about court appearances and school detentions. It's too much of a reminder of who and what I really am.

I look to see if Freemail has its own app.

Bingo. Not only does the service have its own application, but there's also a chat feature and a customizable notification.

I should not be this excited about a chat feature. I don't even *know* this girl.

That doesn't stop me from looking to see if she's on. She's not. Maybe she doesn't have the app.

My homeroom teacher is trying to get everyone to take their seats when I walk into the classroom. It's louder than a pep rally in here.

They all ignore me. I don't care. I slouch into my seat at the back and start typing.

CHAPTER TWELVE

From: The Dark <TheDark@freemail.com>
To: Cemetery Girl <cemeterygirl@freemail.com>
Date: Wednesday, October 2   8:16:00 AM
Subject: Ghoulish

We met by exchanging letters in a cemetery. I don't think
either of us is in a position to call the other *ghoulish.*

I've been thinking a lot about what you said your
father did, about how he was going to get rid of your
mother's equipment. When my sister died, my mother
didn't want to get rid of anything. She refused to touch
anything Kerry had touched. Before she walked out of
the house, Kerry had eaten a grilled cheese sandwich,
and she'd left a plate by the sink with all the crusts
sitting there. She loved grilled cheese and made one just

about every day—which meant she left a stupid plate sitting there every day. My mom used to lay into her about it.

"The dishwasher is *right there*, Kerry! You're not going to have someone cleaning up after you for the rest of your life, you know!"

After she died, Mom couldn't touch the plate. It sat there for weeks, until mold grew on the crusts. It drew ants. It was disgusting. Once I tried to clean it up. I thought it would help, I guess—so she wouldn't have to do it.

She screamed at me and told me to never touch anything of Kerry's, ever again. She was so upset I almost couldn't understand her.

I ran. I hid.

It's embarrassing to type that out. I almost deleted it. But that's the point of all the cloak-and-dagger, isn't it?

I've never really been scared of my mother, but that day I was. I wasn't really afraid of her hurting me, though that was part of it. She's not a big woman, but that day she seemed huge.

I was scared of her grief. It seemed so much bigger than mine, and I worried it would overtake me. My father was in jail, my sister was dead, and my mother was trapped in her own private pain.

I was responsible for all of it.

I was scared she would do something irreparable.

I was scared I would lose her.

I didn't stay hidden for long. She came looking for me, and I didn't really have anywhere to go. I was thirteen. She found me in my closet. Her eyes were red, but she wasn't crying, and her voice was soft, so soft. When I came out of the closet, she put her hands on my cheeks and apologized. She kept stroking my hair, telling me that we only had each other now, and we had to help take care of each other. Then she said I could start by helping her with something in the kitchen.

The dish with the crusts was gone, and the counter smelled of bleach. Mom wanted me to box up all the dishes. She said she couldn't touch them anymore. I remember placing each dish in a box, so carefully, because I didn't want to do anything to set her off again.

I shouldn't have bothered. We took them all to the dump.

She made me throw them into the Dumpster while she stood there smoking a cigarette. I'd never seen my mother smoke, but there she was, staring down at the box of shattered dishes, a cigarette shaking between her fingers.

I'd never seen anyone do something like that. I thought she was losing her mind. A part of me wanted to run again, but a bigger part of me was scared to leave her alone.

After two drags, she stomped on the cigarette and said, "Let's go buy some dishes. You can pick them out."

I don't know what the point of this story is, except maybe to say that sometimes you get to a point where it

> hurts too much, and you'll do anything to get rid of the
> pain.
>
> Even if it means doing something that hurts
> someone else.

I feel like *I* need a cigarette.

No. That's not true. I hate smoking. It's disgusting.

But still. I need *something*.

I love the feel of his words. I'm supposed to be on my way to meet Rowan for lunch, but my steps are slow. The hallway is packed with people desperate for something other than class time, and they jostle me along. My thoughts aren't focused on any destination; they're trapped in time with a thirteen-year-old boy watching his mother lose her marbles.

"Juliet! What perfect timing."

Mr. Gerardi stands in front of me, leaning against the door to his classroom.

I don't know what I'm doing here. I haven't been down the arts hallway since she died. Tagboard-framed black-and-white photographs line the wall across the hall from him. One is magnificent, a shot of a man on a park bench, his skin weathered, a hat pulled low over his eyes. Despair pours out of the picture. Two are decent, but nothing special. The rest are crap.

A bowl of fruit, seriously?

I look back at Mr. Gerardi. "I was on my way to lunch. I didn't mean to come down this way."

He gives me a funny look. "Are you sure?"

The arts wing is an addition to the original school, so it's not really "on the way" to anywhere. The location made it easy to avoid anything related to photography after she died. It made it doubly easy to avoid Mr. Gerardi's attempts to get me to re-enroll in honors photography.

"You know, there's still time to change your schedule," he says. "But not much."

See?

I shake my head quickly. "No. I'm fine."

"Are you sure? Brandon doesn't have much competition anymore."

Brandon Cho. He's probably the one who took the photograph of the guy on the park bench. We used to have a friendly rivalry for who could get more space in the school paper and the year-book. Rowan always said that we would have made a cute couple, what with the cameras and all, but he's a little too pleased with himself to be right for me.

I almost roll my eyes. "I'm pretty sure Brandon is getting by just fine." Then I realize what he said when I walked up. "What's perfect timing?"

"I need a favor, and you're the perfect person to do it."

Mr. Gerardi is the school's only photography teacher, and when he needs a favor, it usually involves taking a picture of something.

"No," I say.

He frowns. "You didn't even let me say what I needed."

"Does it require a camera?"

He hesitates. "Yes."

"Then no." I turn and walk away. "I didn't mean to walk down here. I was distracted."

"It might be good for you to pick up a camera again," he said. "You'll never know if you don't try."

I keep walking.

He calls after me. "It'll only take an hour. And you'll get a volunteer credit."

I keep walking. I can barely hear him. Like I give a crap about volunteer credits right now.

He shouts, "You can use my Leica."

I can't help it. My feet stop, just for a second. It's an automatic reaction. Mr. Gerardi has an amazing Leica M digital camera. We all used to drool over it. He rarely lets a student use it, though he let me help shoot prom last year, so I'm familiar with it. It's as nice as Mom's field camera, which she never let me *touch*. She practically kept it on an altar when she wasn't working.

Right now it's sitting in a stained bag in the corner of my room.

My palms are suddenly sweating. I can't do this. I start walking again, turning the corner as quickly as I can.

I'm late for lunch, and the line is obscene. I have no appetite anyway. I see Rowan in our back corner, sitting at the end of the table.

I fling my bag under the table and all but collapse across from her.

She stops chewing her sandwich and raises an eyebrow. "You're not eating?"

"No." But I fish under the table for my water bottle.

"Why not?"

I don't meet her eyes. "It's not important."

"It kinda looks like it's important."

I heave a sigh, and it leaves my mouth with an edge. "Ro—"

But then I stop.

Sometimes you get to a point where it hurts too much, and you'll do anything to get rid of the pain. Even if it means doing something that hurts someone else.

He's talking about my father, but it makes me think of Rowan. Have I been doing that to her?

I fiddle with my water bottle and think about it. This is not a good feeling.

Rowan pulls open a bag of potato chips. "Does it have anything to do with Mr. Gerardi?"

My eyes flick to hers. "What?"

She nods toward the hallway. "Because he's heading over here."

I almost fall off the bench whipping around to see what she's talking about. He followed me?

For an instant, I cling to the naive hope that he's here to grab a soda or harass someone else. But no, Mr. Gerardi walks directly over and looks down at me. "At least let me ask you the favor."

My brain is already twisted up, thinking about how I've been treating Rowan. A sharp reply dies in my throat. I shrug and poke at a stained spot on the tabletop.

"I need yearbook photos for the Fall Festival," he says. "Spend an hour, take some pictures, and call it a day."

"That's tomorrow."

"I know."

It seems ridiculous to have a Fall Festival when it's still eighty degrees outside. We're barely into October. But it's a school tradition: Fall Festival and Homecoming game on Thursday, big dance on Friday.

"I wasn't going to go," I say. I wasn't going to go to any of it.

Rowan takes a sip of her soda and doesn't say anything.

Mr. Gerardi drops to straddle the bench beside me. "It's your senior year," he says quietly. "You won't get another chance to be a senior in high school."

I snort. "You think I'll somehow regret not taking pictures of football players getting whipped cream smashed in their faces?"

"Maybe." He pauses. "You can't tell me you haven't thought of picking up a camera again."

Declan Murphy comes to mind. The strip of light over his eyes as he surveyed my car, making him look like an inverse superhero. His expression in the hallway after I spilled the coffee, all aggression and fury—and something approaching vulnerability.

"You have," says Mr. Gerardi. "I know you have. You have too much talent to throw it away forever, Juliet."

I don't respond.

"Do you think your mom would have wanted that?"

"Don't *talk* about my mother." I slap my hand on the table, so hard that people nearby fall silent and tune in to our conversation.

He doesn't flinch. "Do you?"

No. She wouldn't want this. She'd probably be ashamed of me.

Oh, Juliet, she'd say, shaking her head. *Haven't I raised you to have some courage?*

The words don't inspire me. Instead, they make me want to shrink further into myself.

"You could probably find some freshman to do it," Rowan says.

"It's the yearbook," I snap without thinking. "Not Instagram."

She smiles and takes a drink of her soda. "Then *you* do it."

My hands are sweating again, and I roll my water bottle between them. I don't know what my problem is. It's a stupid camera. A stupid hour of time. A bunch of stupid pictures that won't matter after everyone has looked at them once or twice.

I think about dishes sitting smashed at the bottom of a Dumpster.

Mr. Gerardi is still waiting patiently. I look at him. "I can use your camera?" Because I sure can't use my mother's.

His expression doesn't change. I like that about him. "Yep."

"I only have to shoot for an hour?"

"Yes. All candid. Whatever you want."

I take a deep breath. I feel as though I'm standing at the edge of a cliff, and everyone is urging me to jump, including my mother. They're all telling me I'll be safe, but all I see is a gaping chasm.

"I'll think about it," I say.

I expect him to pressure me more, but he doesn't. He rises from the bench. "Sleep on it," he says. "Come see me before homeroom and let me know what you decide."

Sleep on it.

That, I can do.

My father brings home Kentucky Fried Chicken for dinner. I'm not really one for fast food, but I didn't eat lunch and my stomach is screaming at me to do something about the situation. The fried chicken smells so good that I have plates out of the cabinet before he's even set the bag on the table.

I start tearing into the plastic bag, shoving a biscuit into my mouth while I separate the sides. Mashed potatoes. Gravy. Macaroni and cheese. Everything is a varying shade of beige. Nothing colorful, not even green beans.

I can't make myself care. I break open the box of potato wedges and throw some on each plate.

Then I realize he's staring at me.

"What?" I say around the biscuit.

"One, you're home." He clears his throat. "And two, you're eating."

"I always eat."

"No, Juliet. You don't."

I look at him. He's so perfectly average it makes me wonder what my mother ever saw in him. She was vibrant in every way. She'd walk into a room and you couldn't help but be affected by her light.

He's completely unremarkable. Average skin, brown hair and eyes, stocky build. Like the food, there's a lot of beige. He's a nice-enough guy, I guess. We were close when I was little, but I think he was mystified by my first period and the resulting mood swings and decided to keep his distance after that.

"What changed?" he says.

"Nothing changed," I say evenly. "I didn't eat lunch. I'm hungry."

"Okay." He hesitates. "Want me to get drinks?"

"Sure."

He helps himself to a beer and places a glass of milk in front of me, which makes me roll my eyes. Milk. Like I'm six. I'm surprised there's not a straw.

I'm tempted to take a sip of the beer, just to see what he'd do. I've used up my courage for today, however.

We sit there and eat silently for a little while. I was excited by the smell of the chicken, but the skin feels slimy between my fingers, and I pull it all off. I slice into the meat.

"Did you finish all your homework?" he says.

He hasn't asked me about homework since the day school started. I glance at him. "I have a little left."

"Anything giving you trouble?"

I cut another piece of chicken. "School is fine."

He goes silent again, but I can feel his attention. I'm tempted to take my plate and go upstairs with it, but I'm thinking of the day he was going to get rid of her gear and the way I treated him. Maybe it hurts him to keep everything here.

Maybe it's hurting me and I don't realize it.

I have to clear my throat and keep my eyes fixed on my food. My voice comes out smaller than I'd like. "You can sell her stuff."

He draws a quick breath. "I don't need to do that, Juliet—"

"It's okay. I overreacted. It's stupid to keep it here."

He reaches across the table and puts his hand over mine. "It's not stupid."

I can't remember the last time he touched me. My eyes fill before I'm ready for it. I like the feel of his hand, the connection, the warmth. I didn't realize I'd been so far adrift until he grabbed hold of me.

I have to pull my hand away. He lets me go, but his hand stays there.

I press my fingertips against my eyes. "*I* was stupid. You probably thought I was being a hateful daughter."

"Never," he says quietly.

My shoulders are shaking. I can't look at him or I'm going to completely lose it. I'm curling into myself so hard that my elbows are jabbing into my stomach.

His arm comes around me, and it must be like holding on to a rock. I didn't even hear him come around the table.

Half-broken breaths are coming out of me in short bursts.

"You're not hateful," he says, stroking a hand over my hair.

"I miss her so much," I say, and my voice breaks on the last word. "I just wanted her to come home."

"I did, too."

I want to fall into him. I want to let someone else carry this weight, even if it's just for a little bit. But it's been too long. He's been too distant. I'd fall and he'd step back, leaving me to hit the dirt.

I sit there and shake. He sits there and strokes my hair.

Once I can speak without a hitching voice, I push a damp tendril of hair back from my face. "I meant it. You can sell her things back to Ian."

"Well." He sits back, but not too far. "Maybe we'll wait a bit before making that decision."

"They're just taking up room on my floor."

"They're not hurting anything."

I don't say anything, and after a moment, he says, "If you don't want them in your room, you can put them in the . . ." His voice falters, just a bit. "My room," he finishes. "Not the basement anymore. I'll watch out for them if you don't want to."

He doesn't want them there. I can hear it in his voice. He never liked her occupation while she was alive; there's no reason he should be head over heels for it now.

I straighten and pull away from him fully. "No. I'll keep them."

Suddenly, my appetite is gone. I can't reconcile the doting father with the absent one.

My plate slides across the table. Only half my chicken is gone, and I've barely touched the mashed potatoes. "I'm done."

"Are you sure—"

"I'm sure." I bolt for the stairs, sure he's going to try to follow me.

He doesn't. My door closes with a whisper, and I'm alone in my room.

Her things are there in the corner, a pile of bags and equipment and gear. I don't want to touch it, but a small part of me is glad that he doesn't want to get rid of it yet, either.

Like in the letter from The Dark, my father was ready to smash the plates, but now he's not.

I wonder what happened. What changed.

And what it has to do with me.

CHAPTER THIRTEEN

From: Cemetery Girl <cemeterygirl@freemail.com>
To: The Dark <TheDark@freemail.com>
Date: Thursday, October 3   3:28:00 AM
Subject: Can't sleep

I told my father he could sell my mother's things.

He's not going to do it, but I told him he could.

I didn't realize that the cameras and equipment might be his version of plates full of cheesy crusts and roaming ants.

Maybe they're mine. I'm not ready to throw them in the proverbial Dumpster.

Yet.

Do you believe in fate? Sometimes I want to. I want to believe that we all walk some path toward . . . *something*, and our paths intertwine for a reason. Like this, the way we've found each other. The way you told me the right story when I so desperately needed to hear it.

But that would mean my mother's path was predestined to end in that cab on the way home from the airport. Or your sister's path was predestined to end with your father. One simple change in direction might have led down a completely different path.

Or maybe one simple change of direction is what led them down the path they followed.

I begged my mother to come home early. She did. I know I didn't wreck that car, but she wouldn't have been in it if not for me.

I set her on that path. Me.

If I can't blame fate, who else is left?

I'm blinking sleep out of my eyes, and it takes me a minute to realize that's the end of her message. Like an idiot, I sit there swiping at the screen, hoping it will keep scrolling, but that's all she wrote.

If I can't blame fate, who else is left?

I know a lot about blaming myself.

I know what I did last May when I couldn't take it anymore.

I swing my legs out of bed like I have somewhere to go. I don't know her name. I can't call her. I don't even know where to find her for at least another ninety minutes—but even if I were reading this at school, there'd be over two thousand students to filter through. It's only ten after six anyway.

I know this kind of desperation. It's terrifying to sense it in her.

She's asking me about fate yanking people apart, and I can't help but wonder if this is fate's way of doing exactly that.

I tap at my phone until I get back to the main part of the app.

A little green circle sits beside her name. She's online. She's *alive*.

The air rushes out of my lungs, and I flop back onto my pillows.

Then I roll over and start typing.

CHAPTER FOURTEEN

From: The Dark <TheDark@freemail.com>
To: Cemetery Girl <cemeterygirl@freemail.com>
Date: Thursday, October 3   6:16:48 AM
Subject: Don't do that

If you're going to write to me at 3:30 a.m., you can't end
it like that.

   I'm not ready for fate to tear *this* apart, okay?
   Now write back and tell me you're all right.

My heart is beating fast, a light, unusual fluttering that's
almost painful in its strangeness. I didn't realize how heavy my
late-night email had gotten.

I can't look away from that last line.

Now write back and tell me you're all right.

He cares. About me.

My heart keeps fluttering, a butterfly trapped between cupped palms. Now that I think about it, I don't mind it one bit.

In fact, I quite enjoy the change.

CHAPTER FIFTEEN

From: Cemetery Girl <cemeterygirl@freemail.com>
To: The Dark <TheDark@freemail.com>
Date: Thursday, October 3   6:20:10 AM
Subject: I'm okay

I didn't mean to scare you. I wasn't in a good place last night.
I feel like everyone is waiting for me to get over her death.
My own best friend started quoting a book about the stages
of grief last week, like I should be on some kind of schedule.

In a way, I know she's right. I'm stuck in this rut of
anger and pain and loss, but the more people try to drag
me out of it, the more I feel determined to dig my heels
in and cling to the grooves in the dirt.

You never answered my question about fate. I
sometimes wonder if we're coming at this from different

sides. You could have stopped your sister's death, while I contributed to my mother's.

I keep wondering which is worse.

Her statement hits me right in the gut. I throw the phone at my pillow and storm into the bathroom. I shove the shower faucet with enough force that it creaks, and for half a second, I'm worried that I've broken something and water is about to start spraying everywhere.

I haven't, and it doesn't. Steam fills the bathroom almost immediately.

I squirt toothpaste with a vengeance and attack my teeth, but that hurts, so I dial back on the fury.

It takes effort. She keeps wondering which is *worse*? Like this is some kind of competition?

I slam the toothbrush onto the counter and spit into the sink, then wipe my face on a towel. My eyes are dark and angry in the mirror. I almost want to punch the glass.

Her words make me feel like a failure.

You could have stopped your sister's death.

I've told myself the same thing for the last four years. The words shouldn't have so much power. Not anymore. To hear them from *her*, though . . . All of a sudden, something that felt so safe feels like another opportunity for disappointment.

The water burns my skin when I step under the stream, but I let the pain run in rivulets down my back. The faucet runs hot for a good long while, and I force myself to take it. The heat on my skin takes some of the edge off my anger.

When I finally emerge from the bathroom, I smell bacon, but that's insane. Alan is usually gone by the time I go downstairs, and Mom always sleeps late. It must be a neighbor.

The scent wakes my stomach, and suddenly I'm starving. It doesn't help stave off my irritation. I stand at the foot of my bed and stare down at my phone.

Food first.

I leave my phone and move through the house like a ninja, well practiced in keeping silent in the morning so I don't disturb my mother. I slide into the kitchen to grab a granola bar.

Mom is sitting at the table with Alan. I stop short.

If they were talking, their voices were low. They stop and look up at me in surprise.

They're both in robes.

Any rage the shower bled off is back with full force.

Coffee mugs sit on the table in front of them. Used pans are on the stove, and food-caked plates are stacked in the sink. I smell eggs and see a few pieces of bacon soaking into a paper towel.

They had breakfast. Without me.

I don't say anything to them. Instead, I grab a travel mug from the cabinet over the coffeemaker and pour myself a cup.

My mother speaks first. Her voice is quiet. "Good morning, Declan."

I dump sugar into my mug. "Hi."

Alan watches me. I ignore him.

"Are you hungry?" my mother says after a moment. "I could make you a plate."

The way she says it makes me feel like an afterthought. Like until I appeared in the doorway, she'd completely forgotten I live here. "No."

My spoon clinks against my mug when I stir cream into my coffee, and the silence behind me presses against my back.

I am starving, and it takes every ounce of self-control to avoid grabbing the remaining pieces of bacon and shoving them into my mouth.

When I turn around, Alan is whispering something to my mother. I have no idea what he's saying, but it makes her giggle.

The rational side of my brain knows that they're not giggling about me, but the insecure side wants me to punch him. I settle for glaring at him over my mug. "What are you doing home?"

He looks right back at me. "I thought I'd surprise your mother and take the day off."

"We're going to take care of some things around the house," Mom says. "Then spend the afternoon together. Maybe see a movie."

I stand there and fidget with the lid of the mug. I should go upstairs and get ready for school, but this whole interaction is leaving me groundless, like if I walk out of this kitchen, they'll forget me altogether. "What kinds of things?"

"I'm going to power-wash the deck," says Alan.

I could do that. I *would* do that, if she'd told me she'd wanted it done. She never asks me to do anything anymore. Alan does everything around here, and hell if I'm going to offer to help him. Every time I try, he acts like I'm a delinquent who can't hold a screwdriver.

I set my jaw. "Sounds romantic."

"If you think that's romantic," Mom says, "you can imagine how I feel about him taking the car to get it serviced."

My grip on my mug tightens. "What's wrong with your car?"

"My car," says Alan. "Due for an oil change." An element of challenge hangs in his voice.

He *knows* I could do that. It's one of the things I've always done. In fact, I did it last May, right before their wedding.

Right before I totaled my father's truck and set myself down this rutted path of failure and disappointment. They don't need me. Alan is proving it right now.

I want to smack the smug look off his face.

I won't pick a fight in front of my mother.

I can do that much, especially if it's all I have left.

CHAPTER SIXTEEN

From: The Dark <TheDark@freemail.com>
To: Cemetery Girl <cemeterygirl@freemail.com>
Date: Thursday, October 3   6:48:57 AM
Subject: Fate

You want to know what I believe? I believe in fate, but I also believe in free will. Meaning, there's a path, but we're free to veer away from it. The only problem is that there's no way to know whose path we're following at any given moment. Our own? Or fate's? Other people are on their own paths, too. What happens when we intersect? What happens when someone else wipes our path clean, and we're left with no road to follow? Is that fate? Is that when free will kicks in? Is the path there, but invisible?

Who the hell knows?

I'm not in the right mood for this conversation.
Or maybe I'm tired. No one should have to discuss
existentialism before 7 a.m.

One thing, though: You didn't put your mother in that
car, Cemetery Girl. She made that choice. Or maybe fate
made the choice for her.

What's important is that *you* didn't.

I know that's not very reassuring. I know a lot about
anger and a lot about self-blame. We could reassure each
other until our fingers fall off.

It doesn't matter. We both know what we did.

Guilt is not a competition. Or at least it shouldn't be.

Mr. Gerardi teaches an elective, so he doesn't have a homeroom class, but I know from experience that I can usually find
him in his classroom before the first bell. Students crowd the
main hallways, making a racket of slamming lockers and shouting greetings, but down this hallway it's quieter.

I haven't been at school this early in forever. I'm usually sliding through the front doors right before the bell rings, but today
I have a mission, so I pinned my damp hair into a twist and
rushed.

Any other day I'd seek the quiet solitude the arts wing offers,
but today I wish for the wild cacophony of the other students. The
quiet lets my thoughts roam free, and they don't travel in happy
directions. The words from his email rattle around in my brain.

Was he mad at me? He seemed mad. I spent half an hour trying to puzzle out his tone. I didn't think it was possible to sound

encouraging, sympathetic, and pissed off all in one email, but somehow he managed it.

The classroom door is open, and I slide in without knocking. I need to rush, before I have a chance to trip over my anxiety.

Mr. Gerardi looks up in surprise. A student is standing beside him, showing him something in a notebook. She looks young. I don't know her.

I flush. I didn't consider that someone else might be here.

This is all wrong. I can't do this.

"Sorry." I edge toward the door. "I'll just—I'll come back."

Mr. Gerardi comes out of his seat. "Juliet. Wait."

"No—it was stupid. I'm going to be late for first period."

"I'll write you a note. Wait."

I don't wait. I walk out the door and stride toward the pandemonium.

My mother's voice shames me. *Have some courage, Juliet.*

That's the problem. I don't have her courage. I never have. If she was a firecracker, spreading light across the sky, I'm a lit match, going dark before doing much of anything at all.

The thought makes my feet slow. Am I following a predetermined path? Or am I choosing to hide behind my grief?

I don't like either of those options. I turn around.

Mr. Gerardi is in his doorway. I wonder if he was about to follow me—or if he was about to give up. I can't read his expression. It's some mix of disappointment and hopefulness.

It mirrors the way I'm feeling about myself. My fingers fiddle with the strap of my backpack. My voice is thready. "Just an hour?"

He nods like our conversation about photographs for the Fall Festival happened minutes ago instead of yesterday. He's not going to make me spell it out.

I have to clear my throat. "And I can use your Leica?"

"I have it charging right now."

I nod, then bite the inside of my cheek. The pain helps center me. "I'll be back after the final bell."

CHAPTER SEVENTEEN

From: Cemetery Girl <cemeterygirl@freemail.com>
To: The Dark <TheDark@freemail.com>
Date: Thursday, October 3   8:23:05 AM
Subject: Choosing new paths

I didn't mean to upset you this morning. You come across as having it all together, and I'm coming across like a complete freak who can barely tie her shoes in the morning.

But you're right. Guilt isn't a competition. I didn't mean to make it sound that way at all. I meant that I wonder if this guilt would feel cleaner if I'd been a more active participant—but then I'm not sure how that would play out. It's not like I would have pushed her in front of a car. It's not like that's what happened to your sister, either, right?

If I hurt you, I'm sorry.

I did want to tell you that your comments about fate inspired me. I did something unexpected. Not just unexpected to the people around me—I think showing up for school is unexpected at this point—but unexpected for myself. Everyone else is going to see this as some kind of turning point, I'm sure. *Oh look, she's back to herself.*

What they don't know is that I'm terrified.

That must mean I'm veering away from fate, right? Making my own way? Because the other path was a heck of a lot less frightening.

Mrs. Hillard is asking for volunteers to read their assignment from Tuesday. Each person has a paragraph interpreting the Dylan Thomas poem. It's about darkness. It's about nighttime. It's about Alzheimer's.

It's about time for these people to get a clue.

I doodle on my notebook and tune them out.

Your comments about fate inspired me.

The words light a little glow in my chest.

"Declan, would you like to share your thoughts?"

I ignore her and keep doodling. Mrs. Hillard is looking at me expectantly; I can see her in my peripheral vision.

"Declan?" she says again. There's no warning in her voice. She's giving me the benefit of the doubt, acting like there's some possible way I didn't hear her.

It makes me answer her. "I didn't do the assignment." My voice is low and rough. She's the first teacher to call on me all morning.

"Maybe you can answer my question from Tuesday on the fly, then. Why is Dylan Thomas desperate?"

Her tone is challenging, and it draws my eyes up. It reminds me of Alan because she's daring me. My pencil stops on the paper. Her expression is even, and her eyes hold mine.

I don't say anything. I can play this game all day.

The room falls silent as others pick up on the tension.

After a full minute, I realize she can play this game, too. Fine with me. We can all sit in silence. Like anyone is going to suffer because we won't get to hear Andy Sachs tell us that Dylan Thomas was lamenting over blind people who couldn't see lightning.

Over to my left, someone gives an aggravated sigh. It's a guy, but I can't tell who it is. Somewhere to my right, a girl shifts in her seat uncomfortably, then sighs, too.

People are beginning to glare. The tension in the room is dissolving into hostility.

Toward me.

Like that's anything new.

Mrs. Hillard turns to her desk and picks up a pad of Post-its. She writes a quick note, then walks to my desk and sticks it over my doodle.

It says, *Why don't you give them something new to think about you?*

I stare at it, and my pulse jumps. I think about the paths we choose. Cemetery Girl is right. This is terrifying.

I can't look at Mrs. Hillard anymore. I peel the note off my notebook and crumple it into a tiny ball in my fist. I can't make myself throw it away, however. I pick at the pointed edges. My chest feels like it's been tied in knots. My tongue refuses to work.

After a moment, Mrs. Hillard returns to the front of the room. She gives a small sigh and sets her planner on top of her desk. She's not looking at me anymore, and the room is still silent, waiting for one of us to break.

It's going to be her. I can feel it.

"He's afraid." My voice almost cracks. I keep my fist clenched around that tiny ball of paper and my eyes locked on my notebook. "He's afraid. That's why he's desperate."

She doesn't whip around. She simply turns, and her voice is as even as it was when she asked the question. "What is he afraid of?"

"He's afraid of losing his father." My hands are sweating, and I keep my eyes on that doodle. "He doesn't want his father to die. He wants—"

She gives me a breath of time, then quietly says, "What does he want?"

"He wants him to fight it."

"Does he feel his father's death is inevitable or preventable?"

I finally look at her. My hands are shaking, but her expression is so steady that it's like a lifeline. We could be the only people in the room.

"Inevitable." I hesitate.

She waits, but I'm not sure what I was going to say after that.

The bell rings, and I explode from my seat. I barely pause to shove my notebook into my backpack.

Mrs. Hillard calls my name before I make it through the door, but my nerves are shot. I let the flow of students carry me into the hall, pulling me back to a familiar path.

CHAPTER EIGHTEEN

From: The Dark <TheDark@freemail.com>
To: Cemetery Girl <cemeterygirl@freemail.com>
Date: Thursday, October 3   2:38:17PM
Subject: Unexpected

You don't have to apologize. I should be thanking you. I followed your lead and did something unexpected.

You're right. It was terrifying.

Let's do it again.

Mr. Gerardi's camera is smaller and lighter than my Nikon, and it feels unfamiliar in my hands. Mom wasn't a Leica girl—she was a Nikon devotee, which I inherited. That said, they're amazing cameras. Mom always said she'd buy me one if she ever won a Pulitzer.

I guess that's not happening.

Music pours across the courtyard, a booming bass that shakes the ground. Students are everywhere, dancing in small packs, drinking punch and soda from red plastic cups. Card tables are scattered across the quad, offering school-spirit games and activities. Face painting. Pie eating. Cookie decorating. You'd think we were all six, but everyone else seems to be enjoying it.

I cling to the shadows under the trees, my fingers sweating on the plastic camera casing.

I have yet to take a picture.

Rowan appears beside me, blue and white swirls on her cheeks. Someone has braided her hair into twin pigtails and tied blue pom-poms at the ends. Her eyes sparkle. She's thrilled that I'm doing this. Like I told my cemetery guy, she probably hopes someone flipped a switch and turned me back into the best friend she remembers. "Let me see what you've got so far."

"Nothing." My voice is rough, and I clear my throat. "I haven't taken any pictures yet."

"Nothing?" Her easy smile slides away. "The festival started twenty minutes ago."

I shift my feet. "I know."

"What's wrong?"

"I don't know."

She shifts closer to me. "Do you want me to find Mr. Gerardi? I can tell him you can't do it."

I swallow. "No. I want to do it."

"Do you need some inspiration?" She makes a ghastly face at me, rolling her eyes back in her head and sticking her tongue out sideways. "Want to take a picture of this?"

A laugh escapes before I can stop myself.

When I catch it, it turns into a sob. I press my fingers into my eyes.

"Jules," she whispers. Her fingers, featherlight, brush my forearms.

"I don't remember how to do this," I say.

"Yes, you do."

"No." I take a moment to breathe, because I don't want to cry. Not here. Not now. "Everything feels wrong. It's all so pointless."

She studies me for a moment, then takes the camera out of my hands. Her hands gently lift the strap from around my neck, and suddenly I can breathe more freely.

Then, to my surprise, she puts the strap around her own neck. "Say cheese."

"No! Ro—"

"Too late." She holds the camera out to check the display, then frowns when she sees a bunch of codes instead of the image a point-and-shoot would offer. "Where's the picture?"

"In the camera. Would you give that back to me?"

"No way." She sidles away, lifting the camera again to point it at a group of senior girls who are giggling uncontrollably while doing a Rockette-style line kick. I barely hear the shutter click.

"Ro."

She takes another picture, this time of a boy shoving his face into a pie plate filled with whipped cream. My fingers itch to grab the camera away from her, because the settings are all wrong for what she's doing. I know she's baiting me, but I'm sure she hopes some of these will end up in the yearbook. What she doesn't know is that she's just creating a big, blurred mess.

"Mr. Gerardi is going to flip out if he sees you using that," I tell her. "That's a ten-thousand-dollar camera."

"Shut up." She snaps a picture of some girls getting their faces painted.

"Seriously."

She lowers the camera and turns wide eyes my way. "He's letting you use a camera that costs more than my car?"

"Yeah." I put a hand out. "So quit screwing around."

She takes a step back. "I'm not giving it back to you until you agree to take a picture of something."

"I will."

She unwraps the strap from around her neck and gingerly holds out the camera. When I take it back in my hands, it feels heavier than before.

I begin to suck back into the shadows, but Rowan crosses her arms across her chest. "You promised."

"I know." My mouth is dry again, and I try to wet my lips. "I'm thinking." I wave a hand. "Go have fun. You don't have to do this."

She stares at me, then throws up her hands. "It's a stupid camera, Jules! Push the button!"

It's more than the camera. It's a statement that I can do this without my mother. My breath rushes in and out of my lungs, and for a terrifying moment, I'm worried I'm going to pass out. I lift the camera and put my eye to the viewfinder. Cheerleaders fill the frame, spreading extra blue icing on some cookies.

No, that can't be my first picture since her death. I keep my finger on the button and turn.

Some guys are playing basketball against the back wall. I hesitate on the scene. I like the colors, the grittiness of the game in an old area where the pavement is cracked and broken.

No, that's not the right shot, either.

This is what I spent the first twenty minutes doing.

My camera comes to a stop on two guys sitting at a bit of a distance from the festivities. One wears a dark blue hoodie, and he's leaning against one of the concrete barriers that prevent cars from driving onto the quad. His hood is up, and I can't make out much beyond the bare edge of his profile.

Then I see the guy with him, and my heart skips a beat. Declan Murphy.

I don't think about it. I twist the lens, bringing the shot into focus, then press the button.

The camera whispers a whir and a click, and it's done. I've taken a picture.

I feel like I've run a race. Sweat coats my fingers, and I might be shaking.

I press a few buttons on the camera, bringing the picture into view on the screen. I've framed the shot so it's wide, with Declan and his friend Rev isolated on the left, and the festivities going on to the right.

It looks like it should be in a pamphlet about the dangers of isolated teens or something. I can do better than that. I zoom closer, finding details. The line of jaw poking through the hood. Their backpacks in the dirt. Declan turning to ask Rev a question.

I like that last one. I hold the camera out to look at it on the screen. You can see the trust in Declan's expression. After watching his interaction with his stepfather, I get the sense he doesn't trust many people.

"Maybe you should be taking pictures of the actual festival," says Rowan.

"I know," I say quickly. I adjust a few settings and aim the camera at Declan and Rev again. "I will."

The sunlight is just to their left. I move out of the shadows of the tree until the light is more directly behind them. The technique is called *contre-jour*, "against daylight." Many people would seek a silhouette, but I still want some details.

I lift the camera. Sunlight beams behind them like an infinite halo, at odds with their defiant postures. The shutter clicks, and I look down and fiddle with the settings to see how it turned out.

"Um," says Rowan. "Jules."

"Hold on." I press a few buttons, widening the angle, then lift the camera. Declan's face fills the viewfinder.

I jump and swallow a scream. He's right in front of me, along with Rev, his shadow.

Declan frowns, studying me a little too intently. "Are you taking my picture?"

"Yeah. Sorry." Thank god the strap is around my neck, because I almost drop the camera. "I'm taking pictures of the Fall Festival."

"You're a photographer?"

His voice is dangerous, almost accusatory. I shake my head quickly and babble. "N-no. I'm just—the girl who was supposed to do it couldn't anymore. Mr. Gerardi asked me to fill in."

His features smooth over. "Oh."

"Can I see?" Rev says in his quiet voice.

I hesitate, then push a few buttons to bring the last picture up on the display. I turn until I'm beside Rev. "Here."

He looks down, and he's silent for a long moment. A very long moment. I'm not sure what to make of that.

Then he says, "That's cool. With the sun."

"Thanks." I'm out of practice, but I agree that it turned out well. Declan's hair is lit with gold from the sun, his profile clean and barely exposed. Rev's features are barely visible under the navy sweatshirt hood, which has turned black with all the light behind it. It looks like someone dropped a good angel and a dark one in the middle of our high school courtyard.

A dark one. I lower the camera and really look at Rev for a moment.

"Why do you always wear a hoodie?" says Rowan.

Rev looks at her, and his expression doesn't change. I can't tell if he's bothered by the question. "They're comfortable."

"It's eighty degrees outside."

He shrugs. His shoulder brushes against mine, and I can tell the sweatshirt hides some serious muscle.

Declan leans over and looks at the picture upside down. "Delete it."

I pull the camera closer to my chest. "No."

"Why?" says Rowan.

"Because I said so." Declan steps toward me and holds out a hand.

I take a step back. If I was hesitant to let Rowan handle it, there's no way in hell I'm letting Declan Murphy touch it.

"Delete it," he snaps.

Rowan pulls closer to me. "She's taking pictures for the yearbook. She doesn't have to delete it." Her voice is a little louder than necessary, and I'm sure she's hoping some teacher will hear her and intervene.

"I'm *in* the picture," Declan says viciously, "and if I'm telling her to delete it, she should delete it."

"What's going on here?"

It's not a teacher's voice. It's Brandon Cho, my former photography nemesis. Since dropping honors photography, I've barely seen him this year, but the summer break treated him well. He's grown a good four inches, and his shoulders have broadened. He used to be a bit lean and scrawny, the perfect picture-taking hipster, but hormones must have caught up with him. Defined cheekbones and a sharp jaw have replaced soft features, and his hair is shorter and a little spiky.

His trusty camera is strung around his neck, ironic buttons threaded through the strap. My favorite used to be one with a drawing of a sperm with the line "This is a very old picture of me," but a teacher made him get rid of it.

"Is he bothering you?" Brandon asks me.

"This isn't about you, punk," Declan says.

Brandon moves to stand beside me, not backing down. "Why don't you find someone else to harass."

"She's the one who took the damn picture—"

"Dec." Rev speaks slowly. "It's fine. Leave it."

"It's not fine."

"It better be fine," says Brandon. "Or I'll find a teacher to make it fine."

Declan whirls a finger in the air. "Woo-hoo. You're so tough."

Brandon's eyes narrow. "Don't you have a court hearing or community service to get to?"

Declan starts forward, but Rev grabs his sleeve and drags him back. "And we're done. Come on."

"Rev, I swear to god—"

"I wish you wouldn't." Rev keeps dragging him. "And the sad thing is, you *will* be late for community service. Come on."

Declan allows himself to be dragged, but he looks over his shoulder at me. "Delete it. You hear me? Delete it."

I watch him go.

I don't delete it.

I can't wrap my head around why it would bother him so much.

Brandon turns around to look at me. "Are you okay?"

My mouth is dry and my heart is pounding, but all this adrenaline is really quite pointless. "Yeah. Yes. I'm fine." I wonder if I should thank him.

He studies me, and I watch his eyes take in the camera. "I thought you'd given it up."

I half shrug. "Mr. Gerardi asked me for a favor."

"And you did it?"

I hold up the camera. "He bribed me."

Brandon's eyes light up. "Lucky."

I always used to find him irritating, but only because he was as good as I was—maybe better. His grandfather actually *did* win a Pulitzer for covering the war in Vietnam, and that connection helped Brandon land an elite internship with the *Washington Post* last summer. I had asked Mom to pull some strings for me, but she refused, telling me it would mean more if I earned experience based on my own merit.

Now I'm glad there was no internship. I spent the summer avoiding anything to do with a camera, instead crouching over a grave, writing letters.

Without any sense of competition, I realize Brandon is actually a nice guy. "Thanks." I look up at him. "You didn't have to do that."

"He shouldn't have been hassling you."

"Why was he so upset?" says Rowan.

I shrug and look at the picture again. There's nothing about it anyone could find objectionable. It's not like I set up a trick shot of the locker room. "I don't know."

Brandon snorts. "Who knows with him?"

Something in his voice makes me study him. "Do you know him?"

He looks at me like I'm crazy. "Declan Murphy? No. I know *of* him, like everybody else." He pauses and shrugs. "Maybe a little more. My dad reads the police reports out loud at the dinner table."

"Did he really steal a car?" says Rowan. Her voice is a little hushed.

"Yeah. He got loaded, stole a car, and ran it into an office building."

Wow. None of us say anything after that.

Brandon finally gestures at my camera. "Have you gotten pictures of anything else yet?"

"No," I admit. I hesitate. "I actually just started."

"It's nice to see you guys out again." His cheeks turn a bit pink, and he looks away. "I mean, I'm glad you haven't lost your touch."

"I'm just doing a favor."

Brandon looks back at me. "If you say so." He pauses. "Are you covering the dance tomorrow night, too?"

"No, just this."

"I am."

"Oh." I'm not sure what else to say.

"Are you going?" he says.

"To the dance?" I squint at him. "I don't think so."

"Oh." He hesitates and fiddles with his camera for a moment. "You can come hang out with me if you want."

I swear Rowan stops breathing. She nudges me with her hip.

"Are you asking me out?" I say, frowning.

"Well"—he glances up at me— "sort of. I mean, technically I'd be working. But maybe it could be fun." His eyes flick to Rowan. "It doesn't have to be a date. You could both come. If you want."

I take a step back. I'm so unprepared for this. The emotion of the camera in my hands and the interaction with Declan and then Brandon's sudden intervention. I don't know what to say.

No, obviously. He's not even expecting me to accept his offer, I can tell from the way he's already framing new shots.

A *dance*? What on earth would I do with myself at a dance?

I open my mouth to decline, but then I remember The Dark's email.

I followed your lead and did something unexpected.

You're right. It was terrifying.

Let's do it again.

"Sure," I say.

Brandon lowers the camera and looks at me. "Really?"

"Really." I swallow. "But only if Rowan comes, too."

Rowan grabs me around the waist and gives a little squeal.

I point at her. "I guess we're coming."

But if I'm honest with myself, I feel like squealing too.

Not much.

Just a little.

CHAPTER NINETEEN

From: Cemetery Girl <cemeterygirl@freemail.com>
To: The Dark <TheDark@freemail.com>
Date: Friday, October 4   10:23:05 AM
Subject: Unexpected

Are you going to Homecoming tonight?

I am.

I hope that's shocking. It's shocking to *me*, and I'm the one who agreed to go. Someone asked me and I said yes.

I blame you. I wouldn't even have said yes if not for you and your challenge to do something unexpected. Now I have to find a dress after school, and I'm not even sure I like the guy I'm going with. In fact, I've spent the last three years thinking he was kind of irritating.

Doing all these unexpected things is leaving me off balance.

When I told my father I was going to Homecoming, he looked like he was going to have a stroke. Then he handed me his credit card and told me to get whatever I want. I think he specifically said "Spare no expense," and it's not like we're made of money.

He seemed relieved to see me having some kind of a normal teen experience. I feel like I'm faking it, though. I'm a balloon, waiting for someone to stick me with a pin so I pop, leaving a torn pile of latex on the ground. I should be excited about the opportunity to go buy a dress and get my hair done, but I don't really care. My best friend asked if I'm disappointed that my mother isn't here to go shopping with us (because I'm going out with her and her mom), but that's not it. This isn't the kind of thing my mother would *ever* do—even if she were in town. The first glimpse she got of my junior prom dress was a week later, when she got the picture I'd emailed her. Even then, she never mentioned it.

When I think about her life, my worries about these insignificant things seem so petty. Mom was documenting something *real*. She was showing the effects of war to people who are content to flip the page to find out what's going on in Hollywood. She was making a *difference*.

What am I doing? Buying a dress?

I keep thinking she'd be disappointed in me. I'm worried I'm going to get to the dance and have a nervous breakdown.

Please tell me you'll be there. I know we don't know each other, but I'll feel a little better knowing I'm not the only person on the dance floor who's completely screwed up inside.

Especially since you're the one who showed me I could be normal.

At least for a little while.

My mouth is on fire. Kristin, Rev's mother, likes to experiment with the foods of different cultures, and this month she's on a Thai kick. The table has a platter of noodles in spicy peanut sauce, a bowl of curried beef stew, a plate of massaman chicken, and various roasted vegetables sprinkled with spices. I want a second helping of everything, but I'd like to have some sensation in my taste buds later.

I have dinner here every Friday. It started when Alan decided Friday nights should be family-dinner nights, and I wanted no part in that. Now Fridays are Mom-and-Alan-eat-at-home-while-I-eat-here nights.

Win-win as far as I'm concerned.

I haven't mentioned Cemetery Girl's email to Rev.

I've read it so many times I could recite it verbatim. I haven't written back. Yet.

You're the one who showed me I could be normal. Like this morning, her words light me with a little glow.

It's been a long time since anyone made me feel like I was good for anything more than taking up space until I could fill a prison cell.

Rev's parents are still fostering a baby, and the little girl sits beside the table in a high chair, picking at pieces of shredded chicken and cut-up noodles. Her name is Babydoll—for real. I know better than to make a comment about it. Kristin says kids can't help what they're named, and she never lets anyone speak negatively about the kids in her care, even when the kid in question doesn't have a clue what we're saying.

"You're quiet tonight, Declan," Kristin says.

"Just thinking."

My mind is wrestling with the idea of going to the Homecoming dance. I haven't gone to a single dance since school started, and until 10:23 this morning, I had no intention of altering that plan.

"Thinking about anything interesting?"

I shrug and force my brain to stay with safer topics. "I didn't know you could feed a baby Thai food."

Babydoll shovels a handful of shredded food into her mouth and swings her legs happily. She talks with her mouth full and half falls out. "Ah-da-da-da-da-da." There's a noodle in her hair, and Kristin reaches out to pull it free.

Geoff scoops some coconut rice onto his plate and tops it with a third serving of beef. "What do you think they feed babies in Thailand?"

I aim a chopstick in his direction. "Point."

Rev smiles. "Some kid in Bangkok is probably watching his

mom tear up a hamburger, saying 'I didn't know you could feed a baby American food.'"

"Well," says Geoff. "Culturally—"

"It was a *joke*." Rev rolls his eyes at me. Geoff is a college professor, but you'd think he'd been born with an encyclopedia in his hands. Once Kristin made a comment about seeing a robin early in the spring, and we spent a half hour listening to Geoff go on about the migratory patterns of birds.

"Take off the tweed blazer, dear," Kristin teases. "We're eating."

"We can't eat and learn?"

"How is your mom feeling?" Kristin asks me, ignoring him while tearing more chicken for the baby.

I blink at her. "Fine. I guess."

"I ran into her at the store last weekend, and she said she's been feeling run down. She thought she might be coming down with something."

"Nope." I scoop rice onto my chopsticks and shovel it into my mouth. "She and Alan had an exciting time power-washing the deck yesterday."

"Oh, good," says Kristin.

"We should power-wash our deck," muses Geoff. "Maybe I should rent—"

"Do you want to go to the dance tonight?" I say to Rev.

Both Kristin and Geoff stop short and stare at me.

Rev seizes a piece of chicken with his chopsticks. "Only if you wear that little red sequined number I like."

"Shut up. I'm serious."

Rev looks at me sideways. "You want to go to Homecoming?"

"With Rev?" says Geoff. His food still hangs suspended between the plate and his mouth. I can see the wheels turning in his head. It's almost comical. He's not homophobic at all. Instead, he's probably trying to determine if there are signs he's missed.

"Not *with* Rev." I cough to cover a laugh and stab at my plate, pushing food around. "A girl I know asked if I'm going to be there."

Rev raises an eyebrow. "Who?"

I hesitate, then pull my phone out of my pocket. I unlock the screen and hand it to him.

He reads for a minute, then hands it back to me. "Okay."

No hesitation. This is one of the reasons why I love him.

"What am I missing?" says Kristin. She puts a spoonful of rice on the high chair tray, and Babydoll immediately grabs a fistful and shoves it into her mouth.

"Are you allowed to go to a dance?" Geoff says.

There's no judgment in his voice, but it's another reminder of the rockiness of my own rutted path. "Yeah." I look back at my plate and poke at a piece of chicken. "If it's a school activity."

"Who's this girl?" asks Kristin.

I hesitate, and then to my horror, I realize I'm blushing. "Just a girl I've been talking to." I follow the baby's lead and push more food into my mouth. "It's nothing."

"Yeah," says Rev, rolling his eyes. "So much *nothing* that he's dragging me to the first dance of my high school career."

I study him, wondering if I'm missing a note of anxiety under the teasing. I make my voice serious. "Rev, you don't have to go."

He chews his food thoughtfully, then swallows. "I want to." He glances at my phone and smiles. "Maybe I'd like to do something unexpected myself."

CHAPTER TWENTY

From: The Dark <TheDark@freemail.com>

To: Cemetery Girl <cemeterygirl@freemail.com>

Date: Friday, October 4   6:36:47 PM

Subject: Homecoming

Don't worry, Cemetery Girl. I'll be there.

A blue-and-silver party factory exploded in the school gym. Balloon bouquets hang everywhere, along with crepe-paper rosettes and streamers crisscrossed in every direction. I don't remember a disco ball in here, but maybe they pack it away for dances. It's so cheesy, but I secretly like the way the tiny mirrors throw spots of light around the darkened gymnasium.

Brandon is going to have a heck of a time trying to get usable pictures in here.

We didn't drive together. He practically tripped over himself trying to apologize, but he'd already made plans to shoot candids of the dance planning committee while they were finalizing the setup, so he needed to be here ninety minutes early. He asked me if I wanted to join him, but that was a little too much intensity for my taste.

I had to get a dress anyway.

I haven't seen Brandon yet. Instead, I'm clinging to Rowan.

Well, I'm walking beside her. Mentally, I'm gripping her arm.

My eyes rake over the crowd. The music crashed over me when I walked in, but now my ears are used to it. The driving bass combined with the flashing lights make for a sensory experience that doesn't leave any room for my usual anxiety. Flares of light arc across unfamiliar faces, and I find myself searching the crowd for The Dark. He could be anyone.

Rowan leans in close. "Are you looking for Brandon?"

Not at all. "Yes. Have you seen him yet?"

"No. Let's go over by the food tables so he can find you."

Food tables. Perfect.

Along the back wall, six long tables have been set up. Alternating blue and white tablecloths hang over each, with more streamers accenting the fronts. Someone has turned on a row of track lighting behind the tables, so you can see what you're eating but not much else. One table has two punch bowls with a teacher left to stand guard, with three huge platters of cookies spread out.

The other tables have bottled water, candy bars, and bags of chips, but they all cost money, so I pick up a cup of punch. I lift it to my lips and turn, prepared to scan the crowd again.

I choke on the punch and almost cough it all over Declan Murphy.

My pulse goes from sedentary to cardio in the span of one second. I'm still keyed up over the way he acted about the photograph yesterday, and it's all I can do to keep from snapping in his face.

Or running.

I wish I could say he doesn't clean up well, but he does. He obviously spent time with a bar of soap and a razor, because he smells fresh and clean, and his face is probably the smoothest I've ever seen it. The dance has a dress code, and I wouldn't expect him to comply with something so conventional, but he did. He's wearing a white shirt, khaki trousers, and a blue-and-green-striped tie. The sleeves have already been rolled up his forearms and the top button unbuttoned, and his hair is a little too long to be stylish, but he's combed it. He looks like an errant boy whose mom dressed him up for pictures, and he was having none of it.

I do my best to get my heart rate under control. "Stalker much?"

"Yeah," he says, his rough voice low and quiet and full of sarcasm. "I'm stalking you at the food table." He moves to get past me.

"Looking to spike the punch?" I say.

He goes still in that way a dog will before it's about to bite. There's no growl, but the lips are drawn back, the muscles tensed to spring.

I shouldn't have said anything. Especially that. I already regret it. He leaves me so off balance, like I need to jab at him first, before he can poke me full of holes.

Declan shifts back to look at me again. His eyes are full of ice, but his voice doesn't change. "And what if I am? You going to stop me?"

"No," says Rowan, speaking up beside me. "We're going to tell a teacher."

"Go ahead." Then he moves past me again, throws two dollar bills onto the table to the left, and walks off with two bottles of water.

Rowan pulls close to me, and we watch Declan stalk off. "What is wrong with him?" she says, sounding completely mystified. "Why does he have to be such a jerk?"

I take another sip of my punch. It's too sweet, or maybe I feel too bitter. "I wasn't exactly nice, Ro."

"After the way he treated you yesterday? You think he deserves it?"

I'm still watching Declan walk away. He stops over in a shadowed corner. I see him give the bottle to someone else, but it takes me a moment to make out who it is.

My eyebrows go up. "His friend isn't wearing a hoodie."

"Well, look at that," says Rowan. "Rev Fletcher can look normal." She pauses, and her voice takes on a note of appreciation. "Better than normal. He's actually a decent-looking guy. Why do you think he chooses to dress like the Unabomber?"

"Who dresses like the Unabomber?" says a voice behind her.

I turn. Brandon stands behind Rowan, his camera ready in his hands. He's wearing the vest and slacks of a charcoal-gray three-piece suit, along with fluorescent-blue Chuck Taylors, a black button-down shirt, and a red bow tie. On anyone else, it would look ridiculous, but he can pull it off. Quirky-hot, I'd call it.

He gives us an appraising look, and appreciation lights in his eyes. "You guys look nice."

I blush. I can't help it. I'm almost ashamed of it. My dress is nothing special, just a strapless black sheath that stops above my knees, but considering his colorful look, I'm glad I went with something basic.

"So do you," I say.

"Are you actually wearing a pocket watch?" says Rowan.

"Why, yes, I am." Brandon lifts his camera to his face. "Get closer together."

"No way." I attempt to step out of range, but Rowan catches my arm and drags me back into the shot.

"We need to commemorate this," she says.

"Commemorate what?" I say. "The food table?"

"Senior year," says Brandon. "It's your last high school Homecoming. Don't you want a picture with your best friend?"

"I do," says Rowan.

And that's enough for me. I can do this for her. I force a smile onto my face.

Brandon takes a few steps back. "Try not to look like someone is killing you, Juliet."

I'm tempted to give him the finger, but his voice is light, teasing. Everyone here is having fun. I should be, too.

Maybe I can fake it. I put an arm around Rowan's waist and lean into her.

She puts her head against mine. "I'm proud of you," she murmurs. "I know you don't want to be here."

A wave of emotion hits me hard, and my eyes are welling before I'm ready for it.

Brandon lowers the camera. "Are you okay?"

A tear escapes. I grab a napkin to stop it before any more can damage my makeup. "I'm fine. I'm stupid."

"You're not stupid," Rowan says, getting a napkin herself and dabbing gently to get something I've missed. "You're amazing and brave and—"

I push her hand away and throw my arms around her neck to hug her. "Stop." My voice is broken. "Stop, Ro. I'm none of those things. And I'm sorry I've been a bad friend."

"You haven't been a bad friend," she says. "Not even once."

A camera flash flares, and I draw back, sniffing away the tears. "Great," I say to Brandon. "That's a moment I want saved forever. The time my makeup dripped off my face at Homecoming."

He presses a few buttons on his camera and turns it around to show me. "How about the moment two friends supported each other?"

Rowan and I look at the image on the screen. Brandon captured us with our eyes closed, midhug, and you can barely make out the fine line of tears on our lashes. Even on the small preview screen, emotion pours out of the camera. It's a great photograph.

"You're really talented," I tell him, meaning it. He was great last year, but this is miles ahead of what he was shooting last spring. "It's almost wasted on the yearbook."

"Thanks." He snorts. "And you're right. Half the guys in our class won't look past the fact that your boobs are touching."

"How about you?" I say. "Are you looking past that fact?"

He gives me a crooked smile. "Maybe."

He's flirting. I wish I could do the same in return. I'm smiling, but it's probably on par with the expression from earlier when he told me to stop looking like someone was killing me. I feel so hollow inside.

I wonder, if I keep faking it, will I eventually believe it? A part of me worries that I'll keep faking it and completely forget what's real at all.

"Do you have to shoot all night?" I ask him.

"I can take breaks."

"Do you want to dance?" The words are out of my mouth before I realize what I'm even saying. I was looking for something to do that wouldn't involve talking or taking more pictures.

His eyes widen, and then he smiles. "Sure."

I grab Rowan's hand. "Ro has to come with us."

"No, I do not," she hisses. "You're on a *date*, Jules—"

But then she sees my expression, and she allows herself to be dragged. "I hope you like threesomes," she teases Brandon.

"Do you hear me complaining?"

We dive into the crowd. The theme of the dance is Songs through the Ages or something else completely lame, and the songs range from current, floor-pumping hits to bubblegum pop from the sixties. They've got a good DJ, though, because even the oldies are undercut with bass, the tempo altered to give everything a modern vibe. Right now we're jamming to "It's My Party."

I'm not a great dancer or anything, but I can hold my own. I'm glad the music is fast so I don't have to press close to Brandon. My hair is pinned up on my head, but I must not have enough bobby pins, because some of it has come loose. I don't care. Now my hair can match my makeup.

The loud music is cathartic, and I begin to lose myself in the beat. Brandon has taken my hand a few times, but I've drawn away. He doesn't push, which I appreciate. He's also paying equal attention to Rowan, but she doesn't avoid his hand. He spins her until she laughs. Her dress is white and strapless with silver beading through the bodice. The skirt is chiffon and flows past her knees, but it flares when she moves.

He's a good guy. I wish I felt something.

Well, I do. Gratitude. He asked me out, giving me the opportunity to say yes.

Though he's not the one who gave me the *strength* to say yes.

My eyes flick around the crowd again. He said he'd be here. I'm surrounded by people—hundreds of them—but somehow I'm trapped in a sphere of loneliness. Knowing The Dark is here keeps it from collapsing around me.

Would he be dancing? I don't think so—though I don't really know for sure. I feel like I know him so well in some ways, but in reality, I don't know him at all.

The song is ending. This one is more modern, with a really peppy beat. Rowan and Brandon are doing some goofy move, and when the song ends, she collapses into giggles, almost crashing into him. He's got a grin on his face as he catches her and sets her upright.

Looking at the two of them, I think he asked the wrong girl to the dance.

I wave a hand at my face, fanning air at myself. "I need to get some punch. You guys keep having fun."

Brandon loses the smile. "Are you okay?"

"Yeah! Just thirsty."

Rowan comes after me. "I'm sorry. I got carried away. I'm totally crashing your date."

"No!" I put my hands on her arms. "I think he's really into you. I want to step out of the gravitational pull for a few minutes."

"But he asked *you* out—"

"Ro, trust me. I'm not into Brandon. I told you that all last year when you kept telling me I should date—" I stop short. "Oh my god. Ro, did you have a crush on him? Do you?"

Her cheeks are flushed, and the spinning lights make her eyes sparkle. "Oh! No. Well. Maybe. It's—we're having fun. He's really silly."

I turn her around and give her a firm push. "Go. Dance with him. You're actually kind of adorable together."

She goes, looking worriedly back at me over her shoulder.

Go! I mouth, making a shooing motion with my hands. I watch as Brandon looks concerned and then listens to whatever Rowan tells him, and his expression changes to indicate some kind of acceptance.

I step off the dance floor and move into the shadows by the bleachers. There's a gap in the risers here, backed by the emergency-exit doors. It's one of the few corners of the gym where the lights don't reach. I feel like I'm hiding in a cave, peeking out at the real world.

"I don't want to scare you . . . ," says a voice behind me.

I suck in a breath and whirl.

Someone moves from the shadows. The size and lack of sparkle tells me it's a guy, but I can barely see anything in this corner. He gives a soft laugh. "Well, I didn't *mean* to scare you." He pauses and then moves close enough for some light to find his features. It's Rev, Declan's friend. "I just didn't want you to think you were the only one standing in the dark."

"It's okay." I swallow, alerting my adrenaline to dial it back a notch. Again, I think of that moment on the quad when he and Declan looked like opposing angels. "Why are you hiding?"

"I'm not hiding." He glances at the crowd, then back at me. "I needed a moment to step away from the noise and the light."

"Me too."

"Yeah?"

"Yeah." I feel a draft and shiver.

Rev frowns. "Cold?"

"A little." I pause. "It's a weird night."

His lips quirk up. "Tell me about it."

He's got such a quiet, patient manner, and I think about Rowan's comment earlier, wondering why he always dresses like the Unabomber. He said he wasn't hiding here in the darkness, but maybe he hides every day, just in another way. His hair is way too long, and it falls across half his face, but it shines. Unlike Declan, he hasn't shaved, leaving his chin shadowed. His shirt is buttoned all the way up, his tie neatly knotted. He looks like a rock star who was told he needed to go on a job interview.

Rev wasn't being literal, but I tell him about my night anyway. "I told my best friend to dance with my date. I think I specifically told her they'd make a cute couple."

There's no malice in my voice, and his smile widens. "How did your date take that?"

"Pretty well, I think. I mean, he's still dancing with her." I pause. "You're not here with anyone?"

He hesitates. "I don't really date." He glances into the dark shadows behind him. "I'm playing wingman."

"For who? The darkness?"

Now he grins. "No. For Dec. He's outside, grabbing a cigarette."

I glance behind him again. No wonder there's a draft over here. The emergency-exit door is partially propped open. A sliver of dim light peeks around the door frame.

I look back at Rev. "He snuck out?"

"You think the faculty is going to let him smoke on the quad?"

I'm appalled at this flagrant defiance of the rules.

I'm also jealous.

I walk past Rev to the door and push through. Declan is standing beyond the emergency light, and he jumps a mile. He's stomping out the cigarette before he realizes it's just me.

His eyes ice over again. "Stalker much?"

He's throwing my own words back in my face. I tell my cheeks not to flush. They don't listen. "Hasn't anyone ever told you that smoking will kill you?"

"You're kidding. They should write that on the package." He shakes out another one and puts it between his lips.

"How did you even get out here? Doesn't the door set off an alarm?"

"Nah. Ricky Allaverde disconnected this one three years ago and no one's ever bothered to fix it." He takes a drag on the cigarette and blows a plume of smoke into the sky. "If you think you're going to say something about it, I'll know it was you."

The words aren't threatening in themselves, but the chill in his voice sends a shiver down my spine again. I have to fold my arms across my stomach. "I won't say anything. I'm not like that."

He laughs, but there's no humor to it. "Sure you are."

My face is still burning. I'm not entirely sure what drew me out the door. After the thumping beat inside the gym, the quiet behind the school wraps around us, making this interaction far more intimate than it needs to be.

"What are you doing out here?" he asks.

"I needed to get away from the noise."

He inhales, making the cigarette glow red. "Where's your friend?"

"Dancing."

"With that douchebag with the camera?"

My temper flares. "Brandon's not a douchebag."

Declan laughs. "Yeah, okay."

"You're one to talk."

He blows smoke through his teeth, and the intensity of his gaze traps me there. He's closer suddenly, his voice low and rough. "You don't know anything about me."

My mouth is dry, but his closeness sparks something in me, and I speak without thinking. "I know you're a loser with a record."

Any humor in his expression evaporates. I instantly regret the words. He drops the cigarette to the ground and stomps this one out, too. Without a glance at me, he heads for the door.

How can he make me feel so guilty without saying anything? How does he *do* this?

He's through the door so quickly that I realize he's about to let it slam in my face. I hustle to catch it, and then I'm thrust back into the spinning lights and pumping music, just barely broken by our square of darkness. The song switches to a heavy metal ballad from the eighties, and each strum of the guitars grates against my senses. Declan and Rev are heading into the light.

"Stop," I call.

He doesn't.

"Wait," I say, breathless and uncertain. "Let me—"

"What?" He turns, and his expression is fierce.

It steals all of my nerve. The apology stops in my throat.

"Better get back on the dance floor, princess." Declan's words are full of icy disdain. "Wouldn't want anyone to catch you slumming with the losers."

My eyes are burning. This is all going so wrong.

I never should have come here.

I turn around and burst through the emergency-exit doors and run into the night.

CHAPTER TWENTY-ONE

From: The Dark <TheDark@freemail.com>
To: Cemetery Girl <cemeterygirl@freemail.com>
Date: Friday, October 4   10:06:47 PM
Subject: You owe me, Cemetery Girl

I hope you're having a better night than I am.

The cemetery is a well of silence. Thanks to the overcast sky, darkness pools in the valleys between graves. I found my way to my mother's headstone in the dark an hour ago. It took very little effort—I come here so often I could find my way blind-folded.

At first, I thought I could handle the chill, but I'm freezing. Cool moisture hangs in the air, and rain is a heartbeat away. I'd kill someone for a sweater.

The irony makes me smile, considering I'm in the middle of a cemetery and the only people around me are *dead*.

Then I lose the smile. It's not very funny, really.

Most people would be freaked out to be in the cemetery this late at night. There are girls in the senior class who still won't walk into a dark bathroom because they're afraid of Bloody Mary.

I've spent so much time here that I don't think anything of it. Nothing is going to come crawling out of the ground—not even bugs, especially not this late in the year. There will probably be frost on the ground in the morning.

If I sit out here much longer, there will be frost on *me*.

I can't make myself leave.

I can't make myself talk to Mom, either. All I have in my purse is my phone, my license, and my keys, so I can't write her a letter. With a swell of guilt, I realize I haven't written her a letter in weeks—since I started writing to The Dark.

I tell the guilt to knock it off. It's not like Mom's around to be missing my handwriting.

I'm not sure what I'm doing out here. I started driving, and this is where I ended up. I texted Rowan when I got here, because I didn't want her to worry. A worried Rowan could easily end with parents being notified and cops being called. I told her I wasn't feeling well and asked if she could get a ride home from Brandon.

When she asked if I was home, I told her yes.

I mean, I'll get there eventually.

I brush my fingers across the gravestone, tracing the letters of my mother's name. *Zoe Rebecca Thorne.* I know her name was important to her, but now that she's gone, I wish we had even that in common. No one looking at this grave would ever connect her to me.

No one would have connected us in life, either. I felt lucky to catch wisps of her talent.

Sudden pain grips my throat, and I choke for breath. I miss her so much. I would give anything for one more conversation. One more moment.

I think of the email I just read. *I hope you're having a better night than I am.*

Well, I'm not sure how The Dark's night is going, but I'm about to be a sobbing wreck on top of a gravestone in a deserted cemetery. I should offer him the chance to see how his night stacks up.

I suck back the tears and drag my phone out of my purse. I open his email and begin to type.

Raindrops appear on the screen, skewing the letters. More strike my bare shoulders. I shiver again, swipe the phone on my dress, and try again.

Thunder rolls and the sky opens up. Cold pours down from the darkness.

I shriek and run, holding my purse over my head like it's going to do a darn thing. I fumble my car keys, and they go flying into the grass. Of course. By the time I have them in hand, my dress is soaked through. Hair is plastered to my neck.

Here I thought I was freezing before. I'm shivering so violently that it takes three tries to get the keys into the ignition.

And then the car won't start.

I think of Declan Murphy telling me to replace the battery, which I never did. I hate that he was right. I *hate* it. A fresh round of tears burns my eyes. If I call my father and tell him I'm stuck at the cemetery when I'm supposed to be spending the night at Rowan's house, he might actually have an aneurysm.

He was so happy I was going to the dance. I imagine shattering that.

My breath shudders.

Get it together, Juliet, I tell myself. *Think.*

Declan turned everything off before jump-starting the engine. Maybe that will help. I flip every dial I see, killing everything. Then I insert the key and give the ignition a try again.

The car gives a pathetic *rum-rum-rum* sound but then flares to life. Victory!

It causes me physical pain to leave the heat off, but I need the headlights and the windshield wipers, and I don't want to risk anything else draining the battery. I put the car in gear and turn onto the main road.

The rain must be keeping reasonable people home tonight, because the roads are mostly empty. I turn onto the two-lane highway that cuts through town, accelerating briskly because I need to get a blanket before I shiver myself out of this dress. I keep both hands on the wheel and peer into the darkness.

A loud *clunk* sounds from beneath the car. The vehicle lurches sideways.

I hit the brakes instinctively. The car begins to spin. The screech of metal on asphalt slices through the silence. All I see is darkness, with my headlights cutting a swath of sparkling raindrops. Somehow I'm moving at light speed, yet time has slowed down.

I can't think. I can't think. I can't think.

Help me, Mom.

From out of nowhere, my driver's ed instructor's voice intercepts my thoughts. *Steer into the skid.* I do my best to keep from jerking the wheel to the right. Instead, I steer into it. The car swerves and wobbles and makes it to the opposite shoulder. I ease on the brakes until the car rolls to a stop.

It's a miracle I haven't wet my pants. Dress. Whatever. My heart has never beat so hard. My hands still clutch the steering wheel, and I put my forehead against the leather. The smell of burned rubber is thick in the air. I'm breathing like I've run a marathon.

Adrenaline is a great ally: I'm not cold at *all*.

Did I hit something? A deer?

Something worse?

It takes me a while to unwrap my fingers from the steering wheel. I'm terrified to climb out of the car and into the darkness, to see what I hit.

Finally, I do. I kill the engine and climb out to inspect the damage.

To my surprise, there's nothing wrong with the front end of the car.

Except for the fact that my entire left tire is gone. The shiny steel rim rests against the pavement.

How is my entire *tire* gone? Does that kind of thing happen?

I climb back into the car and find my cell phone. Even if I knew how to change a tire—which I don't—I can't do it in a strapless dress on the side of the road during a thunderstorm. At least I'm away from the cemetery, and I can tell my father I was on my way home from the dance.

Well, I could tell him that if he'd answer the phone. It rings and rings and goes to voice mail. Twice.

I look at the clock again. It's after ten, and he expects me to spend the night at Rowan's. He's probably asleep already.

I try a third time. No answer.

I try Rowan. Straight to voice mail. I send her a text, but she doesn't respond right away. She's probably back on the dance floor, flirting with Brandon.

I can probably turn the car back on and get some heat going now. I don't need wipers and headlights if I'm stranded.

The car won't start again. No matter what I do.

This sucks.

Then I look back at my phone. I click on the Freemail app.

There's his message.

You think you're having a bad night? I think. *Beat this.*

CHAPTER TWENTY-TWO

From: Cemetery Girl <cemeterygirl@freemail.com>
To: The Dark <TheDark@freemail.com>
Date: Friday, October 4   10:22:03 PM
Subject: Upping the ante

Here's a recap of my evening:

I began the night coming face-to-face with the rudest, most abrasive person I know, and somehow I walked away from the interaction feeling like I was the bad guy.

Then I sobbed all over my best friend because I thought my mother might be disappointed in me doing something as silly and frivolous as going to a dance when there are more important things in the world.

A little later, I realized my date was more interested

in my best friend than in me (which is fine because I'd be more interested in dating a piece of wood than him, but *still*), so I left them on the dance floor to go sulk in the shadows.

And now? I'm sitting on the side of the road in a car that won't start.

I'm soaking wet.

I'm freezing.

My car is missing a tire.

My dad won't answer his phone.

And I don't know what to do.

Trump that, Dark.

Holy crap. I almost drop my phone.

I look at the time stamp on her email. She sent this five minutes ago.

I click back to the main screen of the app. The little green dot sits beside her name.

I don't even think about it. I send her a chat.

The Dark: Are you OK?

Cemetery Girl: That depends how broadly you're
     defining OK.

The Dark: Seriously. Are you in a safe place? Are you off
     the road?

Cemetery Girl: I'm on the shoulder of Generals Highway.
     It's raining hard, but I have my headlights on.

The Dark: Are you sitting in the car? Please tell me you're
   not standing on the side of the road.
Cemetery Girl: I am in the car. The doors are locked.

"Who are you texting?"

I glance up at Rev. He's been warning me about my eleven
o'clock curfew for the last half hour. We live less than ten minutes away, so it's not like we're in any danger of being late. Rev is
funny about rules, though. Breaking them makes him anxious.

"Cemetery Girl," I tell him.

"Is she still here? Is that why we haven't left yet?"

"No." I show him her message.

He reads through the whole thing. "Should we call someone?"

"Who? I don't even know who *she* is."

"You could ask her."

My fingers hover over the buttons. I don't *want* to ask her. I
like this anonymity. Once we know each other, that's gone.

Rev watches me, probably sensing my hesitation.

"Ask her if she wants your help," he says quietly.

The Dark: I'm still at the school. Do you want help? I can
   come to you.

For the longest time, nothing happens. No response, not even
the flashing message to tell me she's typing.

Maybe someone has already stopped to help. Maybe her father
called her back.

Then my phone flashes.

Cemetery Girl: Yes. Please help me. I don't know what to do.

Rain falls in sheets across the road. Rev and I got half soaked getting to the car, and the drops felt like icicles. I cranked up the heat as soon as I had the engine started. This weather is one of the worst things about Maryland: a warm day can be followed by a rainstorm followed by temps in the thirties.

"Do you want to call Alan?" Rev asks.

I'd rather slit my wrists. "Why the hell would I want to call Alan?"

"Because of your curfew."

"God, Rev, would you give it a rest? I'm not going to miss curfew. It's barely ten thirty."

"Do you think there's any chance this is a setup?"

I glance away from the road to look at him. In the dark, his eyes are hooded and serious.

"I don't know," I say honestly. I think about it for a long minute, turning the thought around to examine it from all angles. I'm the last person anyone would call popular, but I'm not hated. At least I don't think I am.

After a moment, I shrug. "I don't know who would do something like that. Or why."

"People don't always have logical reasons for doing what they do." He pauses. "You should know that better than anybody."

I don't have a response to that.

He's right, of course.

"Scared?" I mock him, to take the edge off the conversation.

He doesn't take the bait. "Prepared," he says seriously.

We make the turn onto Generals Highway, a two-lane road that stretches for miles all the way to Annapolis. Out here, the houses are few and far between, and the speed limit is high. In her email, she said she was missing a tire. Did that mean she'd had a blow-out, or had someone stolen it?

We come around a bend, and I see a car way up ahead, parked on the shoulder. Strips of rubber litter the road and make little bumps under my wheels. I take my foot off the accelerator, preparing to pull over behind her. My heart has picked up a staccato rhythm in my chest. I'm excited. I'm terrified. I want to throw myself out of my car, jump into hers, and say, "You. You understand me."

And after that, I want to sit in the car with her, breathing the same air, just being present with someone else who gets it.

Then my eyes register the color of the vehicle on the shoulder. The bright yellow side panel is like a beacon in the path of my headlights.

My heart stops. Freezes over.

I hesitate, just for a moment, still allowing my car to drift onto the shoulder.

Then I jerk the wheel back into the traffic lane and downshift into third to accelerate past her broken-down car.

Rev turns to me, eyes wide. "What are you doing?"

I can barely speak around the block of ice forming in my chest. "Going home."

"Why? What happened?"

"You were right. It was a setup."

"What? Who? How do you know?"

I don't answer him. I have to focus on the road, on remembering my best friend is seated beside me, because otherwise I might drive straight off a cliff.

"Dec," Rev says, his voice quiet. "Talk to me."

"That's her car."

He hesitates. "Right . . . ?"

I glance over. "Juliet Young's car. Don't you remember? We jumped her battery."

"Yeah, but—how are you sure it's her car?"

"Because I *looked* at it."

He's quiet again, studying me. "You genuinely think she's setting you up?"

"Yes. No." I run a hand through my hair, then punch the steering wheel. I'm halfway yelling, and I know I need to get my emotions under control, especially if I'm going to face Alan anytime soon. I clench my teeth and grit out the words. "I don't know, Rev. Just—I don't know. Forget it."

I know you're a loser with a record.

Everything I've felt has been an illusion. Everything. Juliet Young doesn't know anything about me. She sees the same thing everyone else does: a guy killing time until he'll be riding the government's dime, being told when to sleep and when to eat.

My throat feels so tight I don't think I can swallow. Heat is building in my chest, melting the block of ice. This feels like fury. This feels like betrayal.

I can't believe I told her about my father. I can't believe I told her about Kerry.

Thank god we kept it anonymous.

I jerk to a stop in front of Rev's house like an impatient taxi driver. I don't look at him. I don't even move. I keep my eyes fixed on the windshield.

"We could go back," he says.

"No." My voice is rough.

"Dec. She's stuck there. Anyone could—"

"Good for her."

"But we should call—"

"Rev." I swing my head around to glare at him. "Are you going to get out or what?"

He stares back at me. The judgment in his eyes is killing me.

I turn my eyes back to the darkness. My fingers are knotted around the steering wheel. "Get out, Rev."

He gets out, but he stands there looking at me.

"Where are you going?" he says.

"Home," I snap. I reach out, grab his door, and slam it.

Then I put the car into gear and drive.

CHAPTER TWENTY-THREE

INBOX: CEMETERY GIRL

No new messages

I've refreshed my inbox at least a hundred times. Maybe two hundred.

He told me he was on his way twenty minutes ago. I probably could have *walked* to school in twenty minutes. The rain has slowed, and now it's a steady *tap-tap-tap-tap* on the roof of the car. The headlights went dim a few minutes ago, which must be a sign the battery is getting ready to give up the fight. I kill the headlights, but I leave the parking lights on. The last thing I need is some half-drunk kid slamming into my parked car because he didn't see me sitting here. I already had a near panic attack when one car veered onto the shoulder, only to swerve around me and accelerate like a bat out of hell.

My dress has started to dry, and for some reason that makes me colder. I keep shivering intermittently.

I try my dad again. No answer.

I try Rowan again. Straight to voice mail. Her phone must have died.

I stare at the screen, willing The Dark to send me a message. Something. I'm going to have to call 9-1-1 in a minute. I don't know what else to do.

I've been sitting in my car for half an hour, not doing a thing to help myself. I try to imagine what Mom would do in this situation. She would have gotten out in the rain and flagged someone down. She would have ended up getting a ride from the ambassador to Australia, and his wife would have offered her a wrap, and Mom would have been invited to dinner at the embassy.

I'd get out, start waving, and end up under some idiot's tires.

Against my will, tears flood my eyes. Before I realize it, I'm sobbing into my hands. The emotion warms me up from inside, but not in a good way. My shoulders shake from the force of it, and I don't try to stop them. Why bother? There's no one here to see.

Knuckles rap on my window.

I gasp and jerk my hands down. A man stands in the rain beside my car.

He's here! Oh, he's here! I swipe at my face. My heart cavorts and prances and leaps.

But then my eyes process what they're seeing. Headlights shine behind us, lighting half his face and filling my car with light.

It's not The Dark. It's Declan Murphy.

Because my night didn't suck enough.

"Are you broken down?" he says loudly.

No, I'm fine, I want to yell back. *Go ahead and leave me here.*

I push the button to roll the window down, but the motor makes a sad little noise, and then nothing happens. I have to unlock the door manually to open it.

He backs away to give me room, then catches the door in one hand. Cold air streams into the car.

"Did your tire blow out?" he says. "I saw all the rubber in the road."

"I've already c-c-called someone," I say, hating how I can't control the shivering now. I wrap my arms around my midsection. "He should b-be here any m-minute."

His eyes are dark and inscrutable. "So you don't want any help?"

"No." I suck a shaky breath through my teeth. "I'm fine."

He studies me for a long moment, standing there in the rain, his eyes as ice cold as they were behind the school.

"Suit yourself," he finally says. He swings my door shut and turns away.

I can't believe my options are sitting here all night or asking Declan for help.

He's about to get back into his car. I can see him in my rear-view mirror.

Damn it.

I swing my door open and step out of the car. "Wait!"

He stops and looks at me across twenty feet of rain and darkness. His door isn't open after all, and he was already facing me. Was he coming back to my car? The thought throws me.

We stand there and stare at each other. Rain trickles into my dress.

"Is your battery dead?" he finally says.

I nod. "Yes." I hesitate. "I didn't replace it."

"Shocking." He jerks his head toward his car. "Come sit in mine so you can warm up."

I'm halfway to his car when I realize this could be a trick. *So you can warm up* sounds like the worst kind of double entendre. My steps slow as my instincts kick in, but it's so cold outside that the rest of me doesn't give a crap about innuendo.

His car is black—or gray. I can't quite tell. It doesn't shine at all, which makes me wonder if it's been covered in some kind of matte paint, or it's in desperate need of a paint job. From what I can see of the body, it's an older vehicle. A long, flat hood leads to a two-door body and a short trunk. Dropping into the passenger seat confirms the age, though the interior is in better shape. Leather seats that are too wide to be modern, no headrests. It's a stick shift. The radio is old, with silver dials and big white numbers. The windows have crank handles.

I expected the car to smell musty, like rotten foam padding and too many cigarettes, but he must not smoke in here. It smells like old leather with a faint undercurrent of some guy-brand cologne.

Declan slides into the driver's seat and starts the engine. It roars to life, and he spins a few dials. The center vents immediately shoot warmth at me.

I was sitting as close to the door as I possibly could, but when I feel the heat, I shift forward and press my hands over the openings.

Declan moves toward me, his hand reaching for mine. I jerk back and pull my hands against my stomach, sucking back into the seat.

He gives me a look, then finishes his motion, twisting a dial to flick open the vent closest to the door. "That one sticks," he says.

Oh.

I still wait for him to shift back to his own space before putting my hands over the vents again. We sit in silence for the longest time, listening to the thrum of the motor, hushed by the loud whisper of air through the vents.

"Are you afraid of me?" he asks suddenly.

I can't read his voice, and I'm not sure how to answer. His question makes me feel ridiculous—but it sounds like he might be genuinely curious, not cocky.

I chance a glance at him. He hasn't moved since opening the vents, and now he's lounging back in the driver's seat, lit by nothing more than the lights on the dash.

I have to clear my throat. "If I say yes, are you going to use it against me?"

"No." His voice is even. Almost a challenge.

I look at him. "Then yes. A little."

Headlights fill the car, a vehicle approaching from behind. I twist in the seat to look. The car doesn't even slow, sailing past on Generals Highway.

I sigh and rub my arms and put my hands over the vents again.

Declan turns the heat dial even farther to the right. "How long were you out here waiting?"

"I don't know. Awhile."

"Why are you all wet? Did you try to change the tire?"

I snort. "I don't know how to do that. I was just trying to figure out what happened."

"From the look of your tires, you're lucky it wasn't all four."

"You're kidding. I was so busy memorizing the latest copy of *Car and Driver* before showing up at Homecoming."

He looks amused. "I'm talking about basic maintenance. You're the one stranded on the side of the road. I'm scared to ask if you've ever bothered to change the oil in that thing."

I scowl—but he's right. I don't think I've ever had the oil changed. Headlights fill the car again, and I crane my neck around. Another car goes flying by.

Declan stares out the windshield. "What kind of car are we waiting for?"

I hesitate. "It's a friend from school. I don't know what kind of car he drives."

I expect Declan to give me a hard time about that, but he doesn't. His jaw looks set, and he keeps staring out the window.

I slide my finger across the screen of my phone, hoping The Dark has sent me a message.

Nothing. I sigh.

"What are you afraid of?"

I look at Declan, but he's still staring out at the rain. His voice has gone quiet, and he's not half as threatening as he was.

"I don't know," I say.

He gives me a look that reveals flickers of icy judgment. "Liar."

This is so bizarre. He's not as furiously angry as he was behind the school, but I'm not sure what to do with this line of questioning. I pull my hands away from the vents and fold my arms across my stomach. "You don't have the best reputation. That can't be a surprise."

"Oh yeah? Tell me about my *reputation*."

I hesitate. I don't know what to say. I know what Brandon told me, and I know about the rumors, but I don't know what's true. Not really. "You have a criminal record."

"So what?" He looks at me. "That's got nothing to do with you."

I swallow. "Brandon said you got high and stole a car, then wrecked it." I pause. "You've gotten into fights at school." Another pause, and I meet his eyes. "You're pretty confrontational."

"I'm *confrontational*?"

He doesn't bat an eye at accusations of car theft or physical fighting, but calling him *confrontational* gets a reaction. "Maybe you don't remember getting in my face and telling me to delete some stupid picture."

His eyebrows go up. "Maybe you don't remember accusing me of pouring liquor into the punch bowl."

My cheeks flare with heat, and I have to look away. "You're right. I'm sorry. I shouldn't have said that."

"It's not like you're the first." His voice hasn't changed tone, but he flicks a lever on the dash pretty hard. "You know what sucks? If you pick on someone weak at school, you end up suspended."

"And that's a bad thing?"

"No. But people can say whatever they want to a guy with a *reputation*, and no one cares. People actually *root* for it."

He's right. Like in the gym, guilt pricks at my senses. "You don't do much to help yourself. Did you ever consider *asking* me to delete the picture? Or not calling Brandon a douchebag?"

Declan glares at me. "You think he gave a second thought to what he said about me?"

No. Probably not. I don't know what to say.

We sit there in silence, listening to the rain rattle the roof.

Declan finally looks away. "Is that what people think?" he finally asks. "That I got high and stole a car?"

"You didn't?"

He shakes his head. He's not looking at me now. "I was drunk, not high."

He says it like it should make a significant difference. "That's it?"

"No." He pauses. "I didn't really steal the car, but my dick-head stepfather pressed charges anyway."

"It was his car?"

"No. It was my dad's truck."

"Why did you—"

"Does it matter?" Declan glances out the back window, agitated now. "How long are you going to wait for this guy?"

I'm thrown by his sudden shift. "Ah . . . I don't know."

"Give me your keys."

"What?"

"Give me your keys. I'm going to change your tire while we're waiting."

I fish in my purse and come up with a handful of keys. "You're going to—"

"Stay in the car." He grabs the keys and practically yanks them out of my fingers. Then he slams the door in my face.

I watch him in the path of his headlights, mystified. He opens my trunk, and, moments later, emerges with the spare tire. He lays it beside the car, then pulls something else from the darkened space. I've never changed a tire, so I have no idea what he's doing. His movements are quick and efficient, though.

I shouldn't be sitting here, just watching, but I can't help myself. There's something compelling about him. Dozens of cars have passed, but he was the only one to stop—and he's helping me despite the fact that I've been less than kind to him all night.

He gets down on the pavement—on the wet pavement, in the rain—and slides something under the car. A hand brushes wet hair off his face.

I can't sit here and watch him do this.

He doesn't look at me when I approach. "I told you to wait in the car."

"So you're one of those guys? Thinks the 'little woman' should wait in the car?"

"When the little woman doesn't know her tires are bald and her battery could barely power a stopwatch?" He attaches a steel bar to . . . something . . . and starts twisting it. "Yeah. I am."

My pride flinches. "So what are you saying?" I ask, deadpan. "You don't want my help?"

His smile is rueful. "You're kind of funny when you're not so busy being judgmental."

"You're lucky I'm not kicking you while you're down there."

He loses the smile but keeps his eyes on whatever he's doing. "Try it, sister."

I'm tempted. This bickering is somehow exhilarating. It's the first time in months that I've had an interaction with someone that didn't seem to be happening through a fog.

"Why did you want me to delete the picture?" I ask instead.

Whatever he's twisting hits the car with a metallic *thunk*, and he stops. He looks up at me. "Is your parking brake on?"

"Um . . ."

"Go. Check."

I go. I check. It's not. I pull the lever, then get back out in the rain. He's using the bar to loosen the bolts that hold the wheel onto the car.

"Thanks," he says. His voice is tight with strain.

I wait for more, but that's it. He doesn't answer my question.

"Are you deliberately not answering me?"

He nods.

"Don't you need to jack the car up before you can take the wheel off?"

"They need to be loose first. Otherwise pulling on them could push it right off the jack."

"And that would be bad."

"Yes. That would be bad." The muscles in his forearms stand out from the effort. He pushes wet hair off his face again. He attaches the bar to the metal object under the car and continues twisting.

"Is that a jack?" I ask, feeling foolish.

He glances up at me, and his expression makes me wish I'd waited in the car.

I wait until he goes back to the jack and ask, "What are we going to do about the battery?"

"I'll see if I can jump it again. Then I'll follow you home. And then you're going to get a new one tomorrow." He glances up at me. "Right?"

I nod quickly. "Right."

Everything about him is so unexpected. He's so prickly, and then he'll startle me with words that sound dangerously close to concern.

I watch him in silence, until he has the old wheel off and he's putting the spare in its place. No cars have gone by in a while, and it's very quiet out here with the faint whisper of light rain in the trees.

"Did you ever delete it?" he asks, his voice low.

I hesitate. I don't want to lie to him, but I'm afraid of his reaction. "No."

He doesn't look away from what he's doing. "Why not?"

"Because you were a dick when you asked me to."

He laughs softly, under his breath. Then he sobers. "It wasn't for me."

"What do you mean?"

He scoops a nut or a bolt or something off the pavement and looks up at me. "I didn't ask you to delete it for me. It was for Rev."

"Then why didn't *he* ask me to delete it?"

"Rev isn't like that."

No, he's not. I barely know Rev Fletcher, but I can already tell he's not the type of person to ask much of anyone. Declan Murphy isn't, either, now that I think about it. This knowledge tugs at my conscience, making me want to go back to the school right this second and delete the photos from Mr. Gerardi's memory card.

"Rev doesn't like having his picture taken?"

"No. If you look in the old yearbooks, you'll see he doesn't have a portrait in any of them."

I blink. "Really?"

"Yeah. Really."

"Why?"

Declan's hands go still, but he keeps his eyes on the wheel. "Because his father used to hurt him and then take pictures of it."

It's so far from what I was thinking that I nearly do a double take. I don't even know if my imagination is conjuring better or worse images than what really happened to his friend. I want to know more—but I don't. I'm not sure what to say. "Why?" I whisper.

"Because he was a sadistic bastard. If you ask Rev, he'll tell you he's glad it happened, because there was a record of everything that had been done to him."

Thunder rolls overhead, and I expect the rain to pick up, but it doesn't. "He was . . . glad?"

Declan shakes his head. "I don't mean he has a scrapbook. When Rev was taken away, there was no chance of him going back." He begins twisting the bolts into place. "He still doesn't like having his picture taken."

I swallow, and my throat is tight. Shame has me in its grip, and I don't see it letting go anytime soon. "How would he feel about you telling me this?"

"Fine." Declan looks at me, holding my eyes. "Rev would know I'm telling you for a reason."

I shiver. "I won't gossip about it."

"I know you won't." His voice has lost any trace of an edge. He begins lowering the jack, and I watch him.

I know you won't. There's trust in those words, and it's not something I expected to hear from him.

He tosses the keys to me. "I'll pull my car in front of yours and hook it up. Don't try to start it until I say so, okay?"

"Okay." I hesitate, my fingers wrapping around the keys until the teeth bite into my palm. "Thanks."

My car fires right up when connected to his battery. He sits in his vehicle and I sit in mine, and I'm surprised to find there's a small part of me that wishes our conversation hadn't ended right then. I feel like there's so much more to say—which is ridiculous because I don't know him at all.

After a few minutes, he unhooks the jumper cables and comes to my window. "You okay to drive?" he asks.

I nod.

"I wasn't kidding about the battery," he says.

My mouth is dry. "I know."

"Okay. I'll follow you home." He doesn't wait for a response. He turns around and walks back to his car.

I drive cautiously, glad his headlights are in my rear window. It's well after eleven now. I have no idea what happened in the last half hour, but I feel completely off-kilter. I replay our interaction about the photograph. Rev's hesitation makes sense now. So does Declan's vehemence about my deleting it.

It makes Brandon's insults seem all the more cutting. Declan was right, how it's all but a capital offense to say some things, but you can tear down someone like him without worrying about repercussions. I think back to that first moment in the hallway, when I crashed into him and spilled his coffee, but he was the one sent to the office. Even the teachers expect the worst from him. I know I did. If you'd asked me to name guys at school who'd get down on the ground in the rain to change a girl's tire, Declan wouldn't have made the list.

And tonight he was the only person to stop.

I suddenly want to apologize for the way all of our interactions have gone. The misunderstandings weren't entirely my fault, but I think he knows that, too. He's guarded, like I am. I can let a few links out of my armor—especially since he offered a small degree of trust, without asking for anything in return. It's so unexpected.

I remember that I'm supposed to be doing the unexpected, too.

I'm sorry, I'll say when we get to my house. *Maybe we can start over.*

I pull into my driveway and glance in my rearview mirror, expecting him to stop and wait for me to get out.

He doesn't. He doesn't even slow down. Declan zooms off into the night.

CHAPTER TWENTY-FOUR

From: Cemetery Girl <cemeterygirl@freemail.com>
To: The Dark <TheDark@freemail.com>
Date: Friday, October 4   11:32:53 PM
Subject: Home

I wanted to let you know that I made it home safely.
    I hope you're okay.

My house is mostly dark, which is a surprise. I half expect Alan to come charging out, screaming threats about curfew and Cheltenham and how I'm a good-for-nothing punk.

But no one comes out. I turn off the car and sit in the silence for a minute, reading her email again.

I should have told her.

Now I have no idea how to unravel this.

When I knocked on Juliet's car window, I thought she would figure it out immediately. I expected her to explode with fury, kind of the way I felt when I discovered she was Cemetery Girl.

I didn't expect to find her crying into her hands.

Even now, it pulls at something inside me, and my brain is struggling to reconcile the girl from my letters and emails with the girl who sneered at me about smoking and accused me of spiking the punch.

Better get back on the dance floor, princess. Wouldn't want anyone to catch you slumming with the losers.

Remembering my words makes me wince. Going to this dance meant something to her.

And then I had to crap all over it.

My phone *pings*, and I jump, expecting a message from Cemetery Girl.

Juliet, I think. I need to remember she's not some anonymous girl anymore. She's *Juliet*.

Either way, it's not her. It's a text from Rev.

RF: Did you go back and help her?
DM: Yes
RF: I knew it.

I turn off the phone and shove it in my pocket. He'll send more messages until he drags the whole story out of me, but I need some time to analyze it myself.

The house looks so quiet I wonder if Alan is waiting inside to drop the hammer. Anxiety chains me to the steering wheel. If he wanted to get into it, if he wanted to *fight*, I wouldn't hesitate. But Alan doesn't fight with fists and anger. He fights with court appointments and police officers.

The nights I spent in jail last May were terrifying enough. I don't want to go through it again—especially when there might not be an end point.

Finally, my unease about confrontation is eclipsed by my fear of doing nothing, of being found in the driveway, paralyzed with indecision. I get out of the car and walk up to the front door.

My key whispers in the lock, and the front foyer is dark. I wonder if fate has offered me the first stroke of luck I've seen in years. Only a small light at the base of the stairwell is lit, along with the night-light in the upstairs hallway. I stand in complete silence for a full minute. The house is hushed. They must be sleeping.

Tension drains out of me, leaving me a bit giddy. I smile in the dark. This is *awesome*.

Then I hear the cough. Two coughs. Then the clear sound of someone vomiting. I don't know what about the noise is feminine, but it's not Alan.

I follow the sound to the back bathroom, the one in the mudroom behind the kitchen. The door isn't even closed, but my mother is there, kneeling on the floor, heaving her dinner into the toilet. She's wearing one of Alan's T-shirts and a pair of stretch pants. A tissue is clenched in her hand.

"Mom?" I sound afraid. I can't help it. In a flash, I'm ten years old again, watching my father doing the same thing. This is different, though. She's not sliding off the toilet. The air isn't thick with booze. "Mom, are you okay?"

She nods with her eyes closed, then wipes at her mouth. She kneels there and breathes against the toilet for a long moment.

She's as pale as the porcelain beside her face. I go stand next to her, but I'm not sure what to do. "Do you want me to get Alan?"

"No." Her voice is raw. "No, it's fine. I don't think dinner agreed with me."

"Do you want more tissues?"

At first she shakes her head, but then she nods. I retrieve the box by the kitchen sink and set it beside her. Then I fill a glass with water and bring it back.

She flushes the toilet, then rises to sit on the lid.

"Water?" I hold it out.

She cringes like I'm offering her poison.

"To rinse your mouth out?" I suggest.

"Okay." She does, then spits in the sink. After another long breath, she washes her face and hands.

I hang in the doorway, feeling completely useless. "Do you want me to help you upstairs?"

She shakes her head. "I think I'll sit on the couch for a while until this passes."

"Okay." That sounds like a dismissal, but I'm not sure I should leave her.

She straightens and looks at me more fully. Her eyes widen. "You look so nice, Declan. I didn't realize this was a dress-up dance." She smooths the shirt over my shoulder, straightening my tie as if it matters.

I freeze under her touch.

She looks up at me. "Did you get caught in the rain?"

"I helped a friend change a tire." I hesitate. "That's why I was a little late."

"Is it late? I dozed off while I was waiting, and then . . ." She makes a face, then glances at the toilet. "Let's go sit on the couch. I need to sit down."

We go sit on the couch. She doesn't want the lights on, so we sit in the dark, barely more than shadows.

"Is Alan in bed already?" I ask.

"Yes. He's going into the office in the morning, and you know I don't mind burning the midnight oil."

I'm glad she was the one up, though finding her puking in the back of the house still has me unsettled. "Are you sure you're okay?"

"Oh, yes." She puts a hand on my arm and squeezes. "We picked up some steamed shrimp at the market, and you know what that does to you if it's even a little sour."

I can't remember the last time she's touched me, and now it's been twice in three minutes. I feel like I've walked into the twilight zone. "Kristin said you were sick last week, too."

"Oh!" Mom looks surprised. "That was a summer cold."

"It's October."

She gives me an exasperated look. "Declan."

"What?" I sound petulant. "I'm just asking."

"Tell me about the dance. Did you have a nice time?"

"No."

She sighs.

Way too much history exists between us for Mom and me to have a postmortem about Homecoming. "I didn't."

She puts her hands on my face, pushing my hair back from my forehead. I expect her to make some kind of dig about my haircut, but instead her hand stops there, her thumb stroking my temple. Her eyes are locked on mine.

I don't move.

"You're kind of freaking me out," I whisper.

She doesn't smile. "I feel like you're growing up and I'm not a part of it."

I don't correct her. I feel exactly the same way.

I jerk my eyes away and push her hand off my forehead. "I'm going to get out of these wet clothes."

She lets me go without protest, and the most microscopic part of me wants her to hang on. Instead, I'm halfway up the stairs before I even chance a glance at her.

I expected her to be fiddling with the remote controls, but instead, she's watching me.

I clear my throat and keep my voice down, because the last thing I want to do is wake Alan. "Do you want me to bring you a blanket?"

She smiles, and there's something uncertain about it. "That would be very nice. Thank you."

By the time I return downstairs with the white fleece throw from the guest room, she's stretched out on the couch, watching HGTV.

"Do you remember this?" she says. "We used to watch all the decorating shows together during your summer vacation."

Yes, I remember. We always did that while folding laundry. It was the worst kind of torture.

I think about her hand on my forehead. Maybe not the *worst* kind of torture.

I spread the blanket over my mother. "Do you want anything else?"

"No. Thank you, Declan."

I hesitate, and she looks up at me. "I'll be fine." She reaches out and takes my hand in her small one, then shakes it a bit. "Don't you worry about me."

CHAPTER TWENTY-FIVE

From: The Dark <TheDark@freemail.com>
To: Cemetery Girl <cemeterygirl@freemail.com>
Date: Saturday, October 5   01:06:47 AM
Subject: Tonight

I'm sorry I was late tonight. I had to drop a friend off first.
He was flipping out about curfew. By the time I got to
your car, I saw someone else had stopped. I didn't want
to make it awkward.

I'm glad you're okay.

And if I'm being totally honest, I'm glad we haven't
met yet.

By morning, the rain moved out, leaving even colder tempera-
tures. I dig a sweater out of my dresser and pull knee-high boots

over my jeans. Comfort clothes, which seem so necessary after my evening with Declan Murphy. I still feel a bit raw.

My father finds me eating cereal in the kitchen, and he stops dead in the doorway. "You're . . . up early."

I'm always up before he is, but I'm not usually home on Saturday mornings. I glance up from the magazine I've been flipping through. "Is that all right?"

"Of course." He moves to the counter and stops again. "You made coffee, too?"

"I needed a cup."

He fetches a mug from the cabinet and pours himself some. I flip another page in the magazine.

"How was the dance?" he asks. "I would have waited up if I'd known you were coming back here."

I lift a spoonful of cornflakes to my mouth and shrug. "It was fine. Rowan was having a good time with Brandon Cho, so I didn't want to be a third wheel."

Rowan had sent me a flurry of worried texts around midnight, when she must have plugged in her phone. I told her someone stopped to help and that I'd made it home without a problem.

I haven't mentioned Declan Murphy yet. I'm still trying to figure that out on my own.

Dad eases into the chair across from me. He's freshly showered and clean-shaven, wearing a polo shirt and jeans. He looks more alert than I've seen him in weeks.

"Are you going somewhere?" I ask.

"I was going to head to Home Depot to get covers for the

outdoor furniture. Then I was going to tackle the leaves." He pauses. "Feel like helping me?"

"Helping you rake leaves?"

He smiles, but it seems tentative. "I'm taking it that's a no."

I shake my head and take another spoonful of cornflakes. "I'll help. You shouldn't have to do it alone."

"Okay."

"Okay."

We sit there in silence for the longest time. He unfolds the morning paper and starts reading the business section. I see him glance my way several times, but he doesn't say a word. The perfume ads in the magazine are giving me a headache, but if I close it, I'll be forced to talk to him, and I have no idea what to say.

When he gets up for a second cup of coffee, he clears his throat. His voice is very careful. "You didn't feel like going to the cemetery this morning?"

"I can't." More cereal. "My car needs a new battery."

He turns and looks at me. "Since when?"

"Since . . . I don't know. A few weeks. It broke down last night."

"You broke down?" He looks appalled. "And you didn't call?"

"I did. You were already in bed."

"Jules, I'm sorry." He sits back at the table. "I wish you'd said something."

He hasn't called me by my nickname since before Mom died. It throws me for a second, and my mouth freezes around my words. I have to swallow before speaking. "It was okay. A friend from school jumped it and followed me home. I just don't want to take a chance with it anywhere else."

"I'll call the shop and see if they can take care of it today. You're sure it's the battery?"

"Um. No." I can feel myself blushing. I don't know what that's about. "My friend said the tires are bald, too. He had to change one."

"I'll call now. Home Depot can wait."

He calls and sets up an appointment for later this morning. I shift in my seat uncomfortably. The agreement when I got the car was that I would pay for all the maintenance and fuel myself. That was back when I'd planned to get a job over the summer, instead of blowing through my modest savings driving back and forth to the cemetery and school.

"Do you know how much all this will cost?" I say when he hangs up.

He hesitates. "A new battery and four new tires? A lot."

My heart sinks. "Maybe we can ask them if the tires are really that bad."

"If you need them, you need them. I don't want you driving if it's not safe."

"Okay." I do some mental calculations, trying to remember how much I have left in my savings account. It's not a whole lot. "Can you give me a ballpark guess on how much?"

"At least an afternoon of leaf-raking. Maybe mowing the lawn, too."

I look at him to see if he's serious. "But you paid for my dress last night."

"It's okay," he says quietly. "I can help you out." He pauses. "Is that all right?"

"Yeah." I sniff and shovel cereal in my mouth before emotion can get the best of me. "Thanks."

"You're welcome." He stirs his coffee idly, then turns another page in the newspaper. "Ian called me again."

Mom's editor. I freeze. "Why?"

"He said he had someone looking for a Nikon F6 and wanted to double-check whether we were interested in selling that one."

The F6 was Mom's film camera. The body alone cost a couple thousand dollars, so it's not a light offer. Mom normally used her digital cameras for field work because everything could be uploaded quickly from anywhere, and she didn't have to worry about film getting damaged. She loved the permanence of film, how you couldn't just delete an image and try again.

One shot, she used to tell me. *Sometimes that's all you get.*

"No." My voice comes out husky, and I try again. "Not yet."

He nods. "That's what I told him."

"Thanks, Dad." On impulse, I get out of my chair and hug him. I can't remember the last time I did this, but I need the connection right now.

If he's surprised, he doesn't show it. He hugs me back, like we've been this hugging family unit all along.

"Never is okay, you know," he murmurs.

I draw back a bit. "What?"

"You said 'not yet.'" He looks at me. "I'll leave it up to you. But 'never' is okay, too, Jules. Never is always okay."

‹‹ ››

Rowan and I sprawl on the swings on opposite ends of her front porch. Late-afternoon sunlight has turned the street gold, and the breeze is strong enough to make me glad for the sweater.

My swing is still, my feet propped on the armrest at the end. I'm tired from raking with Dad but glad for my new battery and four shiny new tires. Rowan has a foot on the ground, and she gives herself a solid push every few seconds. Her swing creaks with the effort.

Cartoon hearts and flowers are oozing from every pore of her body. She hasn't shut up about Brandon since I got here.

I'm happy for her, though. I haven't seen Ro crush this hard on a boy in . . . ever.

"Tell me again how he kissed you," I say. "You must have left out *some* detail."

She giggles and chucks one of the throw pillows at me. "Shut up."

I catch the pillow and hug it to my chest, reveling in the warmth there. I've seen Rowan almost every day since Mom died, but it's like her death created an invisible wall between my best friend and me. We've been struggling to find a way to break through it. Last night didn't tear down the wall—but it knocked a few bricks loose.

I wish I could figure out how to tear it down the rest of the way. This small crack is barely wide enough to join hands through, but maybe that's enough.

Out of the blue, I say, "I need to tell you something."

My voice must sound more serious than I intended. She sits up straight on her swing. "Tell me."

I turn my head and look at her. "It's not a big deal."

"Yes. It is a big deal. I knew there was something. Spill."

I frown. "You knew there was something? What something?"

"Jules! Oh my god! Just tell me!"

Now I'm self-conscious. Any confidence vanishes. "It's silly. It's stupid."

"Is it something about Brandon?"

I laugh. "You *are* obsessed." I pause. "No. It's nothing about Brandon. It's about another boy."

"I'm listening."

I pull my phone out of my pocket. "I don't know his name. We've been emailing." I should have planned this better. "This is going to sound ridiculous."

A frown line appears between her eyebrows. "You met him online?"

"No. Not really." I hesitate. "I met him in the cemetery. Sort of. He wrote back to one of my letters."

The frown line deepens. "Your letters?"

My cheeks feel hot, and I look away. "I was writing letters to Mom. He wrote back to one of them. At first it pissed me off, so I wrote back to him. But then . . . something happened." I shrug a little. "He's lost someone, too. I think . . . I think we understand each other. A little. Last night, when I was stuck on the side of the road, he offered to help, but someone else got there first."

"What's his name?"

"I don't know." I click through my app until I find the latest email, where he's apologizing for taking too long to help me. "In his email address, he calls himself The Dark. So that's how I think of him."

She scans the email quickly. "I can't decide if this is the most romantic thing I've ever heard or if this is creepy as hell."

I grab my phone back from her. "This is not *creepy*!"

She gives me a look. "Are you disappointed or relieved that he didn't show up last night?"

Well, that's a direct question. "Both. I think." I pause, considering. "But I'm more relieved because knowing who he is would ruin some of the . . . openness." I fiddle with the phone, rubbing at the edges. "I've told him a lot about Mom. He's told me a lot about his family. His sister died a few years ago. Something to do with his dad . . . I don't know all the details yet."

Rowan gives me a leveled look. "When you do meet this guy, make sure it's in a public place, okay?"

"I'm not stupid, Ro."

"You asked a complete stranger to help you when you were broken down on the side of the road, Jules."

Right. I did do that.

I make a face. "You're right. I wasn't thinking."

"Who *did* help you? You never said."

I wonder if my answer is going to be better or worse than the fact that I asked a complete stranger to help me on a dark, deserted road in the middle of the night. "Declan Murphy."

"No, seriously."

"I am being serious."

She throws herself back into the swing, making it rock violently. "I am never leaving you alone again."

I think of Declan, how he seemed almost affronted that I was afraid of him. Heat returns to my cheeks. "He was . . . okay."

"I'm glad you're here to talk about it instead of lying in a ditch on the side of the road." She turns toward the street and makes a face. "Look. There's his weird friend."

I follow her gaze, and there's Rev Fletcher, pushing a pink-and-white baby stroller down the sidewalk on the other side of the street. He's back in a hoodie, leaving his face in shadow, but out in the sunlight, there's no disguising his height or the breadth of his shoulders. It's a shame he spends so much time hiding, because he's built like a quarterback, and when you actually get a look at his face, he's not too hard on the eyes.

I remember what Declan said about the photograph. "He's not weird," I say under my breath.

"What?" says Rowan.

"I said, he's not weird. He's actually a pretty nice guy." While Rowan starts scraping her jaw off the floor, I raise my hand and call out to him. "Hi, Rev!"

He looks up in surprise and almost seems to shrink into himself until he locates me waving at him. His whole frame relaxes, and he changes course to push the stroller across the street and up Rowan's driveway.

"Hey," he says.

The baby in the stroller squeals and swings her legs. She's got a cookie in one hand, but she's gummed it to where bits of shortbread cling to her chubby fingers.

"Are you babysitting?" I ask him. It's somehow both unexpected yet unsurprising.

"Sort of. Mom had a client call and Babydoll wouldn't nap, so I figured I could get her out of the house for a half hour."

"Her name is . . . Babydoll?" says Rowan.

"Yeah," he says, like it's nothing.

Her eyebrows go up, but she doesn't say anything further. My eyes flick between Rev and the dark-skinned baby. "This is your . . . sister?"

He smiles. "Not exactly. She's a foster kid."

"And your mom had a *client*?" Rowan says. Her tone makes it sound like his mother is doing something unsavory, and I think of what Declan said about how some people seem to be fair game for hostility.

Rev blinks at her. "Yeah. My mom's an accountant."

"Oh." Rowan seems thrown by that.

I want to elbow her to stop being so rude. Is this how I came across a week ago?

"Can I hold her?" I say to Rev.

"Of course." His movements are quick and efficient, and he hoists the baby from the stroller in a practiced motion. She's wriggly at first, but my shirt collar seems to fascinate her. She rolls the fabric between the fingers of her free hand, mouthing the cookie in the other. Her eyes are large and dark and guileless.

"She's so cute," I say.

"She likes you," he says.

"She doesn't know me."

"She's a good judge of character." Rev pauses, then says, "How's your car?"

Declan must have told him. "It's okay. My dad let me trade yard work for new tires and a battery."

His eyebrows go up. "Your dad sounds like a nice guy."

He is, I realize. Maybe it's been buried for a few months, but at his core, Dad is thoughtful. Compassionate. Somehow I'd forgotten.

"I'm glad I saw you," I say. Beside me, Rowan is silent but fidgety.

"Yeah?"

"Yeah. I wanted to tell you . . ." I hesitate, but Rev is patient. There's nothing hurried about his expression. I shrug a little. "I'll delete that picture on Monday. The one I took at the Fall Festival."

His expression takes on a sudden stillness, which I only partially understand. I don't want to make him uncomfortable. "Could you tell Declan?" I say quickly. "I know it was important to him."

He nods—but then he hesitates. "I don't think he really cares that much. You don't have to delete it."

"I don't?"

"No. It's . . . okay."

The baby must feel the tension in the air, because she begins to fuss. I bounce her a little and she settles. "Are you sure?"

"Yeah." He reaches out to take Babydoll from me. "I should probably keep her walking. I don't want her to lose it."

I watch him buckle her back into the stroller. She doesn't protest one bit. In fact, I think he must be making faces at her, because she giggles a little.

"You're really good with babies," I say.

Rev smiles, but his expression is a little hollow, like he's still trapped in our exchange from thirty seconds ago. "I get a lot of practice."

"Seriously," says Rowan. "What's with you and the hoodies?"

He straightens. "What?"

"Are you trying to make a statement?"

I can't figure out her tone. It's not bitchy—she sounds genuinely curious. I am, too, really.

"Yeah. A statement that it's cold." Rev starts pushing the stroller down the walkway. After a moment, he looks back. "I'm glad you got your car taken care of. Dec said it was in pretty bad shape."

"It was." I hesitate. "Tell him thanks. If you see him. You know. No one else stopped."

Some of the tension leaks out of his expression. He nods once. "I will."

Then he doesn't say anything else—and I'm not sure what to say, either. We both have a secret tragedy in our pasts, and not for the first time, The Dark and Rev occupy the same space in my thoughts.

"I didn't mean to make you uncomfortable," I say.

"You didn't." But he hesitates, like he wants to say more.

"Come on, Jules," says Rowan. "We need to go inside for dinner."

"One sec," I say.

But when I look back, Rev is on the sidewalk, moving away, heading toward home.

CHAPTER TWENTY-SIX

From: Cemetery Girl <cemeterygirl@freemail.com>
To: The Dark <TheDark@freemail.com>
Date: Sunday, October 6   11:22:03 AM
Subject: The guy who stopped

So . . . remember how I told you about the guy who gave
me a hard time at the dance? The one who was such a
jerk that I left?

He's the one who helped me with my car. That's who
you saw.

His name is Declan Murphy. Do you know him? Don't
answer that. Maybe that's too close to us figuring out
each other. But even if you don't know him, I'm sure you
know of him.

He's kind of notorious.

When he knocked on my window in the pouring rain, I was terrified. I thought he was going to steal my car or murder me or use me to smuggle drugs or something I don't even want to imagine.

Okay, I almost went back and deleted that last sentence because I feel so terribly guilty about thinking those things. Now, in retrospect, those assumptions feel ridiculous. You want to know what kind of egregious crime he committed after knocking on my window? He let me sit in his car and warm up while he got down on the ground in the rain and fixed my car. Then he followed me home to make sure I got there safely.

Mom used to tell me how her goal with photography was to tell a whole story in one picture. I'm not sure if Mom ever felt she accomplished that. She came close—I know she felt pride about much of her work, and in many of her pictures, you really *can* see several different layers of what's going on. It's all in the details, like with her Syria photo. The joy in the children, the fear in the men. The sweat and the blood, the motion of the swings. Something terrible has happened, but the children can still find joy. But is that the whole story? Of course not.

The more I think about it, I wonder if that was a crazy goal altogether. Can a picture ever tell the *whole* story?

When I was sitting with Declan, he said something that I've been thinking about all weekend. He made a comment about how vulnerable people are protected by rules and guidelines, but people like him can be attacked without question, because people assume he deserves it.

Do you think there's any truth to that? If a rich kid taunts a poor kid for wearing old hand-me-downs, that's obviously cruel. If a poor kid mocks a rich kid for failing a test, is it a lesser cruelty because of their stations in life? Is *everyone* a one-dimensional target in some way?

And if we are, is there a way to show more of ourselves? Or are we all trapped in a single photograph that doesn't tell the whole story?

Notorious. Her words jab at my pride and tug at my heart simultaneously.

I wish I had told her.

I'm glad I didn't. Maybe.

This space, with one of us knowing, feels uncomfortable. I don't like keeping a secret from her. It feels wrong, like now I'm tricking her. Before we had a level playing field. Now I don't know what we have.

What *I* have.

I remember her sitting in the rain, crying behind the steering wheel of her broken-down car. At the dance, I'd seen another beautiful, spoiled girl with nothing better to do than sneer at me, the lowlife who might tarnish her shine and sparkle. In the letters, I know a girl who peeks from beneath a glitter overlay, hiding the torment. It's hard to reconcile. It's hard to wrap my head around it.

I know what it's like to need to strike first. I wish I'd seen through her bravado when we were standing by the punch bowl. I wish I'd known it was just a front.

Rev has this saying that he likes, something about how a gentle tongue can break a bone. Knowing him, it's from the Bible. This is the first time it's ever made sense to me.

What did she say to me in the car last night? *You're pretty confrontational.*

I wish I'd been more patient with Juliet. How could I have missed the turmoil that simmered just below her surface?

How could she have missed mine?

Alan is alone in the kitchen when I come downstairs around lunchtime. He's reading something on his tablet while eating a sandwich. Sunlight pours through the window behind him, and I'd say he looked like a normal suburban dad if he were any other guy.

We both stop and look at each other. If we were wolves, there'd be raised hackles and cautious circling every time we interact, but we have to do the human thing and glare.

Alan looks away first, which is usually the case. He's not intimidated by me, though. That would be too easy. Instead, he looks away like I'm not worth his time.

We weren't always like this. I can't imagine Mom marrying him if we were. He made a few attempts to play the father figure in the beginning, but we must have been operating on different frequencies because I missed the signals. More likely, I ignored them. He'd try to have man-to-man conversations about school and responsibility and—well, I really have no idea. I'd plug in my headphones and tune him out. I basically thought he was another transient boyfriend who'd be sent packing sooner or later, so why waste the time?

Now I feel like Alan skipped stepfather and went straight to warden.

Really, I can't decide which bothers me more: that he plays the heavy or that Mom lets him.

I head for the cabinet and dig around, looking for cereal. Mom is on this new health kick, so everything is organic and full of fiber. Maybe protein. I would kill someone for Froot Loops, but instead I grab a box of strawberry Power O's.

When I open the refrigerator for some milk, I realize Alan is still watching me.

I don't like him watching me.

I think about Cemetery Girl's line—*Juliet's* line, I remind myself—about being trapped in a single photograph. That's how I feel right now. Alan saw one side of me, one moment of my life, and that's all I'm reduced to now. That's all anyone sees. Declan Murphy, drunk driver, family ruiner. My snapshot, captured forever in time.

It's a depressing thought, and my hackles go down. "Where's Mom?"

"Taking a nap."

I hesitate with the milk poised to pour. "In the middle of the day?"

"That's when naps usually happen." His voice is sharper than it needs to be, more acerbic.

My hackles go up again—but the image of my mother getting

sick in the back bathroom is still fresh in my mind. I wonder if he has any idea. He should have been the one taking care of her. He should be the one worrying about her *now*. "You don't have to act like such a prick, Alan."

"Watch your language." He points a finger at me.

I slam the milk back into the refrigerator, then whirl, ready to get into it.

He's not even looking at me. He's looking back at his tablet.

I want to flip the table and send everything flying. I want to get in his face and scream, *Look at me! Right now! Look at ME!*

My cell phone vibrates against my thigh, and I jerk it out of my pocket. I press it to my ear without looking at the screen—the only person who ever calls me is Rev.

"Hey," I say.

"Hey, Murph."

The voice is thickly accented, and it takes me a second to place it. Melonhead. I haven't been able to break him of the nickname, but I've found I prefer "Murph" to the overenunciated *DECK-lin* that turned out to be the alternative. He's never called me. I have a panicked moment thinking I'm supposed to be at community service right now, but then I remember it's Sunday. My heart sputters and finds a normal rhythm.

I still have no idea why he's calling. "What's up?"

"I was wondering if you were doing anything this afternoon. I was thinking maybe I could use your help. Well, my neighbor could."

I am so confused, and I can't think past the work we do on Tuesdays and Thursdays. "You need me to mow today or something?"

He laughs like I've said something truly funny. "No. My friend needs help with his car. You said you're good with engines, right?"

I frown. "Sometimes. I mean . . . if it's something modern, he should probably take it to the shop. Newer cars have computers—"

"It's not new. He's restoring it. It's a—" He pauses and must put his hand over the phone to talk to someone else, but I hear him say, "What is this?" A dog barks in the background.

After another pause, he comes back on the line. "A 1972 Chevelle. He thinks it's the carburetor."

I grunt noncommittally and take a spoonful of cereal.

People *always* think it's the carburetor.

"Do you know about carburetors?" Frank says.

"A little."

"So you want to see if you can come help or what?"

It's been months since I've worked on anything more complicated than Juliet's old Honda, but my hands itch for the chance to get at something challenging. I glance across the kitchen at Alan. If I walk out of here without clearing it first, I guarantee you he'll be on the phone with someone in law enforcement, and I'll be in handcuffs fifteen minutes later.

He's still sitting there, staring at the tablet, ignoring me but listening to every word I say. Tension hasn't left the kitchen, and it's turned to a haze between me and him.

I wish I could ask Mom.

She's taking a nap.

Fear twinges inside me. I don't want to think about it too

hard, and I don't want to bother her if she needs the rest. I put my hand over the phone. "Hey, Alan. My community service supervisor wants to know if I can help with something today."

His eyes flick up. For an eternal moment, he regards me with an unreadable expression, and I'm certain he's going to say no, just to jerk my chain.

Then he swipes at the screen. "Go ahead. Make sure you're home before dinner."

I almost drop my spoon.

Frank Melendez doesn't live far, but I'm surprised how much his neighborhood looks like mine, another older, middle-class suburb with short driveways, occasional sidewalks, and fenced yards. For some reason I expected him to live in the projects. Juliet's email digs at me, reminding me I'm just as guilty of judging people on one snapshot of their lives.

It's easy to find the right place because I can see the glistening orange Chevelle from down the block. This guy had to have paid a fortune for the paint job, because that shade of orange looks custom-matched. Two men are standing in the driveway, staring down at the engine block. A massive German shepherd sprawls on the pavement between them, ears pricked and alert. When I park, the dog trots over, tail waving.

I put out my hand and wait, hoping I'm not about to lose it.

"She's all right," calls the man standing with Melonhead. "Skye's the welcome wagon."

The dog confirms this by pressing her face under my hand. I rub her behind the ears and walk up the driveway.

"Hey, Murph," Melonhead says. "This is my neighbor, John King."

The man is middle-aged with graying hair. He's wearing a lime-green polo shirt, and he looks like the kind of guy who'd go golfing with Alan. I want to dislike him for that alone, but he gives me a warm smile and holds out a hand—not the kind of reaction people usually give me. "Murph, is it? Frank says you're an expert on engines."

"Declan Murphy." I shake his hand. He's got a firm grip, but it's not overpowering. "And I don't know about 'expert.' Frank only saw me fix a lawnmower."

His smile falters the tiniest bit, but then he glances at my car. "Did you have a hand in rebuilding that Charger?"

"I did most of it myself."

He gives a low whistle. The full smile is back. "You're a lucky kid. I know guys who would kill for one of those."

So do I. I shrug. "My dad lucked out and found the body and half the engine in a junkyard. He started it when I was young. I finished it." I wince, thinking of the air-blasted body. "Well, not the paint. Not yet."

"Saving up for custom?"

"Sort of." I had been, yes. Until Alan told my mother that every penny in my savings account should be used to pay for my legal defense. I don't like where this line of questioning is going to lead, so I nod toward his Chevelle. "This is beautiful. What's going wrong?"

He rubs the back of his neck and sighs. "I put a new Holley carburetor on her, and I can't seem to get it adjusted."

I lean in for a closer look. The engine is spotless. I bet this guy takes better care of this car than he does of his wife. "Yeah? What's it doing?"

"The idle is all wrong, and I was looking for speed, but now it's gone sluggish. I've been tinkering with it for two weeks, and I was telling Frank I was ready to give in and take it to a shop, but that feels like cheating." The men chuckle.

I can already see the problem, but I need to hear it to be sure. "Can I turn it on?"

He hesitates, and I can see him trying to figure out whether letting me turn the key is a good idea. "Sure. Keys are in it."

The interior is as stunning as the outside. You can smell the leather of the seats. The engine roars when I turn the ignition, and I listen, breaking down the sounds coming from under the hood. He's right about the idle. After a minute, I can smell burning fuel, and I turn it off.

John is watching me expectantly, and there's a light of challenge in his eyes. "What do you think?"

"I think your Holley is too big."

He chuckles again, but it sounds strained. "What are you talking about?"

"That's a seven-fifty, right? I think it's too big. When you were talking, I thought maybe it was the choke, but then I got a listen. I bet you'd do better with a six-fifty. I could probably get it to run a *little* better, but—"

"Wait a minute." The smile is completely gone. "I just put that in. All it needs is some tuning."

He reminds me more of Alan every minute. "You wanted my opinion. I gave it to you."

"You're telling me to get a whole new carburetor?" He looks like I told him to eat a fistful of sand.

"Well. Yeah. You're drowning your engine. Like I said, I can try to adjust it—"

"No. It's okay." He looks pissed, but I can't tell whether it's at himself or at me. "I'll have the mechanic look at it tomorrow."

I bristle. I can feel the familiar tension crawl across my shoulders, travel up my neck, and settle into my jaw.

Frank is watching this interaction, and his expression has lost the good humor, too. "Nothing wrong with a second opinion, right, Murph?"

"Sure." I shrug, but it feels forced.

A little girl's voice speaks from somewhere, sounding tinny. "Papi? Papi? Can I get up?"

Melonhead pulls a baby monitor from his pocket. "I've got to get back inside, John." He claps his friend on the shoulder. "At least you've got some ideas when you call the shop tomorrow, eh?"

"Yeah. Sure." John's jaw seems tight, too. "Thanks for your help, kid."

He might as well be saying *Thanks for nothing*.

Before I can say anything, Melonhead waves me along. "Come on, Murph. I'll get you some lemonade."

It's bizarre to be inside his house. The aged brick front and beige siding look like every other house on this street, but the interior is open, with few walls, and very neat and tidy.

"Just let me get Marisol," he says, leaving me in the living room.

The fireplace doesn't have a mantel but is instead surrounded by varying shades of gray stone. A collage of photos hang in silver frames above it. Most of the pictures are of a baby girl who must be a younger Marisol, but one picture features a younger Melonhead with a beautiful woman hanging her arms around his neck.

From their expressions in the photograph, you can tell that time stops when they look at each other.

"Declan!" A little girl shrieks with excitement, and then I have almost no warning before she tackles my legs. "You came to play with me!"

If only girls my own age would react this way when I walk into a room. "Sure," I say. "We can play the lemonade game."

Her nose wrinkles. "The lemonade game?"

"Yes. I drink some, and then you drink some, and then you win."

She giggles. "I like this game."

Melonhead is watching us. "You're very kind to her."

"I figure I can't piss her off by telling her she spent five hundred bucks on a worthless upgrade."

"'Piss me off'?" she parrots. "What's 'piss me off'?"

Her father's face darkens, and I wince, chagrined. "Sorry."

"It's okay. Come sit down."

When Marisol is settled with crayons and we're sitting with

sweaty glasses on the table between us, Melonhead gives me a leveled look. "Do you really think he needs a new carburetor?"

I shrug and take a sip from the glass. "I know he does."

Melonhead nods. "Before you got here, he said he might have made a mistake. I think he was hoping you'd tell him he was wrong."

My eyebrows go way up. "So he knew?"

"I don't think he wanted to admit it to himself. He tinkers with that thing every weekend, but he's just a hobbyist." He pauses. "You could really hear the problem?"

I trace lines in the condensation along the glass. "It's not a big deal when you're used to it. I'm out of practice, but his was pretty obvious."

"You said your dad was a mechanic?"

I nod. "A good one. He used to own a custom shop, did restorations, hot rod upgrades, those kinds of things. I was in the shop with him almost every day. I could practically rebuild a transmission before I could walk." I don't want to think about my father, but my brain is happy to supply me with memories. I remember getting into a heated argument with one of the shop guys over the correct ignition timing on a Chevy Impala, and Dad could barely stop laughing long enough to tell the guy I was right. I was eight years old. "He taught me to drive as soon as I was tall enough to work a clutch and see over the steering wheel at the same time. I would move cars in and out of the shop without a thought."

Darker memories slide in there, too. The times I had to drive a lot farther than the distance from the back lot to the front of the garage. The times I would put on a ball cap and stretch to make myself as tall as possible because I was worried the cops would spot me and figure out a kid was driving.

In retrospect, I wish a cop *had* caught us. Maybe Kerry would still be here.

"Where's your dad now?" Melonhead asks.

His voice is just a little careful, and normally I'd dodge the question because there's too much pain and guilt wrapped around these memories. But Melonhead doesn't judge me—if he did, he wouldn't have asked me to help out his neighbor. He wouldn't let me be around his daughter. This feeling of sanctuary is almost foreign, and it's something I usually only feel at Rev's.

"He's in prison," I say quietly, my eyes on my glass. "He was drunk and he wrecked his car. My sister died."

Melonhead puts a hand over mine. "Ah, Murph. I'm sorry."

The touch takes me by surprise, and it's so unfamiliar that it's almost uncomfortable. I pull my hand away and rub the back of my neck. "It's okay. It was a long time ago."

"Do you ever see him?"

I shake my head. "Mom never goes, so I never do, either."

"Your mom's remarried, yes?"

"Yes."

"How's that going?"

I look at him and give him a half smile. "What, are you my court-appointed therapist now?"

"No, I'm just trying to figure you out."

I take a drink of lemonade. "There's not much to figure out."

"You work hard. You don't give me much grief. You're smart. I don't get kids like you through the program much."

"I just don't want to be hassled."

"I don't think that's it." He pauses. "You have a drinking problem, Murph?"

"Obviously." I snort and drain more lemonade. "I mean, you know my record, right?"

"Yes. I do. Do you have a drinking problem?"

I shrug, then shake my head. I can remember the burn of the whiskey as if it happened yesterday. I don't remember much after that, but I still clearly remember the burn. "No."

"Did you?"

I shake my head again. "It was just one day. One stupid day." The second-worst day of my life, in more ways than one.

"Do you want to talk about it?"

The room shrinks incrementally, and sweat has begun collecting between my shoulder blades. He's going to push, and I'm going to explode out of here, leaving a Declan-sized hole in the drywall. "Not really, no."

"Hey." He puts a hand on my shoulder and gives me a gentle shake. "Take it easy. I didn't mean to ramp you up."

I take a breath and let go of the glass. I didn't realize how tightly I was gripping it until I let go. "Sorry."

Marisol bursts into the kitchen with papers in her hands. "Declan! I draw you!"

She thrusts it in front of me. It's a colorful stick man with brown hair.

"This is amazing," I tell her. Somehow my voice is steady. "Can you draw me another one?"

"Yes!" She runs out.

The kitchen falls silent again. My eyes fix on my glass.

"Can I tell you one thing?" Melonhead says.

I swallow. "Sure."

"One day isn't your whole life, Murph." He waits until I look at him. "A day is just a day."

I scoff and slouch in the chair. "So what are you saying? That people shouldn't judge me on one mistake? Tell that to Judge Ororos."

He leans in against the table. "No, kid. I'm saying you shouldn't judge yourself for it." He pauses. "Do you *have* a court-appointed therapist?"

I give him a look. They'd have to drag me in handcuffs. "No."

His eyebrows go up. "You think there's something wrong with having someone to talk to?"

"I don't need someone to talk to. I'm fine."

"Everyone needs someone to talk to, kid." He hesitates. "Do you have anyone at all?"

I trace another finger through the condensation on my glass, then lift my eyes to meet his. "Yeah. I do."

CHAPTER TWENTY-SEVEN

From: The Dark <TheDark@freemail.com>
To: Cemetery Girl <cemeterygirl@freemail.com>
Date: Sunday, October 6   11:58:35 PM
Subject: The whole story

With your mom, does it ever feel like you've buried all
kinds of memories in a box, but when someone tugs at
one, they all break free? That happened today. Someone
started asking about my father, and now I can't stop
thinking about him.

My mom used to think my dad hung the stars. She
wasn't alone. He could do no wrong in my eyes—in a
lot of people's eyes. He was a friendly guy, always had
a smile. Got along with everyone. He could talk about
sports, he could talk about politics, he could make my

sister laugh at the dinner table, even when she was in a mood. He would gallop around the backyard with my sister or me on his back, chasing whoever was still on the ground. He owned his own business and made good money. Everyone thought we were the perfect family.

They didn't know he drank alcohol like it was water.

A lot of people put drinking on a shelf beside anger and violence. They don't realize that happy drunks can be just as dangerous as the crazy, violent ones. More dangerous, really, now that I think about it. People ask Mom why she didn't leave him sooner, like he was beating the hell out of her on weekends or something. He never laid a hand on her. He wasn't that kind of drunk. He loved my mother. He loved us kids. That was never a problem.

We all loved him back. Maybe *that* was the problem.

When I was really little, I thought that because Dad was happy, everyone was happy. It took awhile for me to understand the strained expression on my mother's face when he'd come home lit. Around the time I turned nine, I began to figure it out. His voice would turn different. He was too permissive, too forgetful. I lost track of how many times he forgot to pick me up from school, and I started walking home just so the teachers would stop asking questions. I used to go to work with him on the weekends, and sometimes he'd forget to take me home with him. Mom would come and fetch me later, shaking her head to the other guys about her "scatterbrained" husband.

They all knew, I'm sure of it, but they never did anything. She didn't, either.

Like I said, happy drunk. Everyone loved him. Harmless, right?

I'm sure you know what's at the end of this road. I told you he killed my sister.

When I was thirteen, I started driving him home on the weekends. I know that sounds crazy, but he'd taught me to drive young. It's kind of like how kids on a farm can plow a field when they're seven or kids who grow up hunting can fire a rifle as soon as they're strong enough to carry one. We were always the last to leave the shop, to lock up, so it was easy.

I was always so scared someone would catch me—but I didn't have any alternative. I'd learned that dad's swerving on the road wasn't a game. It was a threat. One time, he hit something and kept going. I still have no idea what it might have been, but sometimes I have nightmares that we hit a person. I remember asking him over and over again if we should go back and check, but he wasn't even aware we'd struck anything. I told Mom about it, and she shook her head and told me that I was overreacting.

So one Saturday afternoon, I made a decision. I hid his keys.

He stumbled around his office, slamming doors and checking pockets, getting agitated. I hung in the corner, the keys trapped in my pocket, almost shaking with the tension of what could happen.

"Maybe we should call Mom?" I said.

He grunted. "Your mother's working."

"What are you going to do if you can't find your keys?"

I hoped he'd say that we'd call a cab, or he'd call one of the guys back to drive us.

No, he swept everything off his desk—*everything*, making a mess—and yelled, "Damn you people. I'll tear someone a new one for stealing my keys."

It was the first time I'd ever seen him turn the corner to mean drunk.

I started "helping." I "found" his keys real quick. I was shaking, and I didn't want him to drive, especially now. I kept my voice light, like I was joking, "Maybe I could drive home. See if anyone catches us."

For half a second, I thought he was going to snatch the keys out of my hand. He didn't. He laughed and patted me on the back and said "Good boy."

That was the beginning.

I never told anyone then, not even my best friend. I loved my father, and I knew this was the only way to keep him out of trouble. I was tall for my age, and I'd wear a baseball cap, so no one ever glanced twice. It's amazing how many people will look the other way when they don't think something is a big deal.

My sister was clueless, and we kept it that way. She wouldn't have figured it out anyway. Dad had long since given up trying to teach anything mechanical to Kerry—she was a girly-girl in every sense of the word. She was a kid, a baby in my eyes. I was in eighth grade, and I stupidly thought I was special. I wasn't breaking the law! I was a man, taking care of my family. I was *helping*.

I think Mom started to count on my driving.

I know she did.

She asked me to take care of my father on the day my sister died. That was our code. *Take care of him* meant, "Drive him wherever he needs to go."

I was supposed to be on an overnight trip for Scouts that weekend. I'd been looking forward to it for weeks, but then Mom got called into work. Dad had gone through half a six-pack by 9 a.m. Mom didn't want anyone to see Dad show up with me at camp smelling like a brewery. So my trip was canceled.

I sulked around the house for hours, slamming doors and heaving big breaths of disappointment. I'm sure you can imagine. When Dad asked me to drive him to his shop, I slammed my door in his face and told him to get there himself if he wanted to go so badly.

I thought he'd stay home. In such a short amount of time, I'd grown used to being his chauffeur, and I assumed that if I weren't driving, he would stay home.

I was wrong. He went out.

He took Kerry with him.

Only one of them came home.

The stormy weather from Friday night has returned, forcing everyone to hang out in the cafeteria before classes start.

Today's breakfast special is pancakes and hash browns, so the place is packed. Rowan skipped the pancakes in favor of a fruit cup. I can't remember the last time we had an opportunity to sit down and actually *eat* before school started. Breakfast isn't a quick affair when hundreds of other people have the same idea.

The rain kept me out of the cemetery this morning, though, and I'm feeling the need for some comfort food. A stack of pancakes sits on my tray, untouched.

Now that they're in front of me, I haven't been able to take a bite.

"What's up with you this morning?" says Rowan, popping a blueberry into her mouth.

I can't stop thinking of The Dark's letter. I can't repeat a word of it to Rowan. He didn't say I needed to keep his words a secret, but he didn't need to.

I poke at the pancakes, but they look like a big, sticky mess. "Just thinking."

"About your mystery guy?"

I narrow my eyes at her. "Don't mock it."

She shrugs equably. "I'm not mocking it. Why don't you try to find out who he is?"

"I've thought about it." I hesitate, considering his letter. "I don't think we have that kind of relationship. I think it only works because we *don't* know who the other person is."

"What do you talk about?"

I look away and prod at the pancakes again. I'd be lying if I said I weren't desperately curious about him. I wonder what would have happened if Declan Murphy hadn't shown up Friday night. I've never been able to speak so openly with someone. With The Dark, I'm not some girl who had it all together before veering off the rails. I'm just . . . me. He's just . . . him.

Rowan is still waiting for an answer. I shove a forkful of pancake into my mouth. "Nothing. Just . . . stuff."

"Oh my god, Jules. You are blushing!"

This is appalling. She's right. I can feel it. "I am not!"

She leans in and teases me. "Do you need a mirror? You're bright red."

"Stop it. It's not like that. We talk about . . . heavy things." I don't want to say "death." Even that much feels like breaking a confidence. "We're not flirting."

"So he hasn't sent you a picture of his manhood yet?"

I burst out laughing. "Has Brandon sent you a picture of his?"

"No!" Now she's blushing.

"Knowing him, it would be artfully framed, with perfect lighting and specifically placed shadows—"

"Shut up!" But she's giggling.

I have missed this so much. I didn't realize how much until we were doing it again.

Rowan's laughter stops, her eyes fixed on someone behind me. "I think Mr. Gerardi is looking for you again."

I wait for the instinctive need to hide to overtake me, but this morning it's missing. I turn in the seat and look for my old photography teacher. When he sees me, his face lights up, and he maneuvers his way through the cafeteria to where we're sitting.

"Juliet," he says, "I'm glad I caught up with you this morning. I had a chance to download the pictures from Thursday afternoon, and you got some amazing shots. Really nice use of light."

"Most of those were probably the ones I took," says Rowan.

His eyebrows knit together. "What?"

"She's being silly." I hesitate. It's weird to be complimented on photographs after so long. "Thanks."

"I was wondering if you'd have an opportunity to help me edit some for the yearbook."

I freeze.

He speaks into the silence, and his voice is gentle, accommodating. "Only if you have time. I don't want to tamper with your work if I don't have to."

A familiar tightness begins wrapping around my chest, and I look away from him. I'm glad I took the photographs, but going back to the photo lab means putting another foot closer to rejoining that world. "I don't know." I peer up at him. "Can I think about it?"

"Of course." He begins to turn away but then pauses. "There's one in particular that I'd like you to do on your own, if you wouldn't mind. I think it would be a perfect wrap shot for the cover."

My heart stops and stutters back to life. Every year, they do a shot that wraps around, from the back of the yearbook to the front. It's a big deal, and it's usually a planned thing. I don't know if it's ever been a photo taken by a student. "Really?"

He nods. "Really." The first bell rings, and he looks at the clock. "I need to get back to my classroom. Let me know, okay?"

"Okay." My voice trails after him as he fights his way through the swarm of students.

"Jules!" Rowan hits me in the arm. "This is awesome!"

A year ago it would have been a dream come true. Now I'm not sure how to feel about it. I stepped away from photography for a reason. I'll never have the talent she had. My thrill at Mr. Gerardi's praise is so minor compared with what Mom could have captured with a camera.

"I have to go to homeroom," I say. "I don't need another detention."

She must pick up on my mood shift. "Are you okay?"

"Yeah. Fine." I storm past her to pitch the unfinished pancakes into the trash can, then whirl to rush to class.

I end up in the path of Declan Murphy. He's got an empty container in his hands, so he must have been headed for the trash can as well. I consider ducking away and losing myself in the stream of students, until I realize that he seems to be considering the same thing.

For a moment, we both freeze—but then he completes his motion, tossing the container into the trash before stopping in front of me. He's as tall and imposing as ever, but after the way he helped me in the rain, he's not nearly so frightening. I keep thinking about what we talked about, how people are judged on one snapshot of their lives, and I will myself to look up at him.

"Hey," I say.

"Hey." His voice is quieter than I expected, and his presence has created a pocket of space between us. I'm going to be late for homeroom, but for a heartbeat, I don't want to move.

"I got new tires," I announce. "And a new battery."

"I noticed."

I blink. "You noticed?"

"Well, I noticed the tires." He lifts one shoulder. "Your car is hard to miss."

"Oh." Is he insulting me? I don't know what to say, and I can't read his expression.

He moves a little closer, and for the first time, he looks less guarded. Almost hesitant. "Hey, I wanted to ask you something."

I look into his eyes. This is so different from when we were in the car, when I was nearly pressed against the door to stay away from him. The rush of students makes me step closer, too, getting out of their way. I never thought I'd be this close to him, exchanging words like we're not at opposite ends of a spectrum.

A breathless Rowan catches my arm. "Jules, what are you doing?" Her eyes flick dismissively at Declan. "I thought you didn't want to be late."

"Just a sec," I tell her as the second bell rings. We have three minutes to be in our seats, but my subconscious is telling me to play this out. I look back at Declan, but I can already see his expression shifting, shutting down. "What did you want to ask me?"

He looks down at the two of us. "Nothing. Don't worry about it." He moves away, sliding into the throng of students making their way to the door.

"Wait!" I call after him, but he's already gone.

CHAPTER TWENTY-EIGHT

From: Cemetery Girl <cemeterygirl@freemail.com>
To: The Dark <TheDark@freemail.com>
Date: Monday, October 7   09:12:53 AM
Subject: Rage-y thoughts

I've been thinking about your email since I woke up.

We've spent a lot of time talking about guilt and blame and intersecting paths and single defining moments, but right now I want to punch someone. It's obvious you feel responsible for what happened to your sister, and that makes me so angry. I want to find your parents and beat them senseless. I hope you don't hate me for saying this, but I'm glad your father is in jail. I think your mother should be, too. Who lets a thirteen-year-old kid drive around town to protect a drunk? WHO DOES THAT?

I just snapped at a teacher who told me to put
my phone away. I'm so angry I'm going to end up in
detention.

I can't believe your parents put you in this position.

I can't believe your mother let it go on.

I can't believe I don't know who you are, because right
now I want to wander the halls of this school until I find
you, so I can grab you and shake you and tell you THIS IS
NOT YOUR FAULT. Do you understand me? THIS IS NOT
YOUR FAULT.

Does anyone else know about this?

You do know who I am. Find me. Grab me. Shake me. Please.

I want to type the words so badly. I'm practically shaking myself. Not even Rev knows the whole truth, and now I've dumped it all on a girl who might still think the real me is a worthless waste of space. I almost told her this morning, but now I'm glad I didn't. Would she still feel this way if she knew it was me?

Her hurt for my alter ego pours off the screen, though, and my chest swells from the pressure. I can't remember the last time someone other than Rev spoke in my defense. Emotion gathers steam in my head, and my eyes feel hot.

Yeah, I need to shut this down. I close the app and shove the phone deep in my backpack.

I immediately want to pull it back out and read her words again.

I know my parents were wrong to let me keep driving. I know it.

But I had alternatives, too. I could have told someone. I could have called a cab that first time. I never had to volunteer in the first place.

I could have driven the car on the day Kerry died. I was selfish and stupid, and I could have stopped it.

I was stupid and selfish last May, too, when I drove my father's car into that building. No one made me do that, either.

I wonder how Cemetery Girl would feel if she put those two events together.

"Declan, would you mind reading the first two lines?"

The air is heavy with expectation. I look up and realize everyone else has textbooks open, notebooks and pens ready. I'm still sitting here with a closed book, and no pen or paper anywhere.

Mrs. Hillard is watching me. Her voice doesn't change, and I don't detect an ounce of impatience. "Page seventy-four. The first two lines."

I could heave and sigh and act like this is a huge imposition, but she's not hassling me, so I can return the favor. I flip the cover and find the page, then read without really caring about the words. My mind is still trapped in that email, in Juliet's hot temper on my behalf.

"'There's not a joy the world can give like that it takes away, when the glow of early thought declines in feeling's dull decay.'"

The words click in my head, as if my brain was waiting for them. Paper rustles somewhere behind me, but otherwise the room is quiet.

"What do you think that means?" asks Mrs. Hillard.

The words of the poem echo in my head, over and over again, though now it's a memory. I'm remembering this same poem read on a different day. My head buzzes with the sound of my mother's voice, reading that exact verse.

Mrs. Hillard is studying me, waiting to hear what I have to say. "Read it again to yourself," she suggests. "Everyone, read it again. Give it a moment. Let it sink in."

My eyes read the line again as if they're pulled to the ink on the page.

Time stops, just for a heartbeat. My brain is too tangled up in death and guilt, and I can't read another word of this poem. My chest is going to explode, or maybe my head. Blood roars in my ears, deafening me.

I slam the book closed and shove it in my backpack. I've never walked out of class before, but I'm walking now.

Mrs. Hillard comes after me. "Declan!"

"I'll go to the office." My voice is rough and broken, and I don't even care.

"Stop. Tell me what just happened."

"I hate this!" I'm loud and furious, and I round on her in the hallway. "Would you leave me alone?"

She doesn't react to my anger, and she doesn't try to calm me down. "Why?"

A door farther down the hallway opens, and another teacher pokes his head out. He sees me in the hallway, fists clenched and shoulders up, and he looks back at Mrs. Hillard.

"Do you want me to call security?" he says. Of course.

"No. No one needs security." Mrs. Hillard takes a step away

from her doorway, until she's right in front of me. The other teacher doesn't move, but she ignores him. "Go to the office," she says to me. "Will you wait there for me?"

My body feels ready to rattle apart, held together by nothing more than the way my fingers are biting into my palms, but I manage to nod.

"Good," she says. "I'll be down after class."

Hamilton High School was built over thirty years ago, and you can see the age in areas that haven't seen much of an upgrade. The main office is one of those places. Countertops are bright orange, peeling in spots, and the paneled walls have been repainted a glossy white so many times that they still look wet. The administration has done a decent job trying to make it inviting for students, with a small area off to the side featuring plush chairs, a round table, and racks of college brochures and guidance pamphlets.

When I walk through the main doors, I want to ask for the sick room—but the only thing worse than waiting on a teacher would be waiting on my mother. One of the secretaries glances up at me. Her name is Beverly Sanders. Her hair is bleached blond this year, and she has a penchant for floral sweater sets. She's going through a divorce.

You could say I visit the office a lot.

The air conditioning is blasting in here this morning, and I'm freezing. My body feels like it's shrinking in on itself. Everything around me seems huge. My breathing sounds loud in my own ears.

Ms. Sanders doesn't stop typing. "I'll let Mr. Diviglio know you're here."

Mr. Diviglio is the vice principal. He deals with student issues. We're great friends.

By which I mean I would rather slam my hand in a door than sit in an office with him. Especially right now.

I clear my throat, but my voice is still rough. "I don't need to see him. Mrs. Hillard told me to wait for her here."

Her fingers go still, and she looks up at me more fully, then glances at the clock above the door. "The bell won't ring for another twenty minutes."

"I know."

"Take a seat."

I drop into one of the chairs and try to get my thoughts to settle. They refuse. I read Juliet's email again. I wonder what it would feel like to hear her say those things to my face.

I wish I could talk to her right now.

Please, I want to say to her. *Please figure me out.*

It's you? she'd say. *Ugh. You big freak.*

"You're not supposed to be using a phone during class time," says Ms. Sanders.

My eyes flick up. "I'm not in class."

Her lips purse. "Please put it away."

I sigh and shove it into my backpack.

By the time the bell rings, my anger has burned itself out, leaving me anxious and twitchy. It's the first lunch bell, and students pour into the office for various reasons. No one looks at me. I wait, my elbows braced on my knees.

I count each minute, until I start to wonder if she's forgotten.

Mrs. Hillard comes bustling in five minutes after the bell, a bag slung over her shoulder and a harried expression on her face.

When she finds me sitting in one of the armchairs, she lets out a long breath. "You waited."

"You told me to." And then I feel like an idiot for waiting.

"I'm glad you did." She nods to the left, toward one of the doors. "Let's go into one of the conference rooms."

The conference rooms are where you go when they want to call your parents, or someone wants to have a *serious* conversation, which generally means something that's going to go on your record. But she's not grabbing an administrator, so I follow her, and we sit.

Her voice is calm, but she doesn't screw around. "What happened in class?"

I pick at a spot on the table. The room is too bright, and it reminds me of the holding cell at the police station. Now that I've had some distance from it, I can't re-create the fury that drove me out of her classroom. "I don't know."

"What was so upsetting?"

Everything. "Nothing."

"Lord Byron just sets you off?"

Her voice is dry, which takes me by surprise. Luckily, I'm fluent in sarcasm. "Something like that, yeah."

She sits back in her chair, then pulls a book from her bag. "Would you read it now? Tell me what you think?"

Sweat is collecting between my shoulder blades again. "It's a stupid poem."

She raises her eyebrows. "Then it shouldn't be a big deal."

She's right. They're just words. They have no power over me. I can do this. I pull the book closer to me, then read the first line again.

There's not a joy the world can give like that it takes away.

I slam the book closed. Breath rushes in and out of my lungs like I've won a race.

Mrs. Hillard doesn't say a word. She's patient, and she doesn't react.

I sit without moving for the longest time. My hands are slick on the edge of the table.

She waits.

Eventually, my breathing slows, but I can't look at her. My voice is so low that it's a miracle she can hear me. "My mother read that at my sister's funeral. I don't—I don't want to read it again."

"Okay." She's quiet for a moment, and she slides the book away from me. Then she shifts her chair closer and puts her hand over mine. "You're a smart kid, Declan, so I'm about to tell you something that's going to sound pretty obvious."

I'm frozen in place, trapped by her words. *You're a smart kid, Declan.*

And she didn't make me talk about Kerry.

"Next time," she says, "if you're having a problem, you can just *tell* me."

I snort and pull my hand away. And here I thought she had something meaningful to say. "Yeah. Okay."

"You think you can't?" Her expression is challenging. "It worked just now, didn't it?"

Well. There's that.

I think of Juliet in the car, telling me how I could have just asked her to delete that picture.

Mrs. Hillard is still sitting patiently, but the intensity in the room is almost tangible. She's not going to let this go. "You don't need to give me details, but you don't need to run out of the classroom, either. If there's a problem, you can just tell me."

I don't say anything to that. I don't know *what* to say to that.

"Do you trust me?" she says.

No. Yes. Maybe. "I don't know."

"Fair enough." She turns to her bag again and starts rifling through a folder packed with worksheets and student compositions. "If you want to stay away from Lord Byron, I'm going to give you something else to work with."

I hold very still. If she pulls another poem about death out of her bag, I'm out of here.

She slaps a photocopied piece of paper on the table in front of me.

Invictus, it reads. *By William Ernest Henley.*

"My AP students are reading it," she says, "but I think you can handle it."

I'm scared to read the first stanza. I want to crumple it up and bolt out of here.

I'm such a wuss. I look at the corner of the paper so I don't have to read any more. "You want me to read it now?"

"No. Take it home. Write me two paragraphs about what he's going through." She pauses. "I think you'll identify with it."

"Sure." I shove it into my bag. "Whatever."

"Declan."

My name is weighted, but not with warning. It makes me hesitate. "What?"

"Give me a chance. Okay?"

"Sure." Then I yank the zipper on the bag, throw it over my shoulder, and walk out of the room.

CHAPTER TWENTY-NINE

From: The Dark <TheDark@freemail.com>
To: Cemetery Girl <cemeterygirl@freemail.com>
Date: Monday, October 7   2:15:44 PM
Subject: Poetry

Have you ever read "Youth and Age" by Lord Byron? It's the worst poem in the world. It's all about the decay of death.

My mother read it at my sister's funeral.

I wanted to rip it out of her hands. I mean, who reads something like that at a funeral? I would have preferred a passage from the Bible, and if you know me, that's saying something.

We read the poem in English this morning. Well, I didn't read it. I walked out.

So I can relate to your near miss with detention.

You asked if anyone else knows the whole truth about what happened with my family. My best friend knows most of it. I don't think he knows how long it all went on, but that doesn't really matter now, does it?

I appreciate all the vehemence on my behalf, but you're wrong. It might not have been *all* my fault, but some of it was.

It's absolutely killing me that I don't know who he is. I take AP English, but we're not reading Byron, so that only eliminates about fifteen guys.

I try to think of who in the senior class could use a word like "vehemence" but still be defiant enough to walk out of class. The obvious answer is right in front of me: I could just ask him. But that would mean ending this. I don't know if I'm ready for that. Maybe the mystery is part of what's so attractive about him. Maybe I'd meet him and he'd be horrible.

He wouldn't be. I just know.

But still.

He said once that Mom probably wouldn't like him much, but he's wrong about that. I think she'd like him a whole lot. She'd find him fascinating.

I find him fascinating.

Mr. Gerardi has a group of students at his desk when I find him after the final bell. I linger in the back of the classroom, looking at the photographs stapled to the wall. These must be from the beginner photography elective, because I remember the assignment. The photographs are all simple shots of nature, but a few stand out with creative use of light. One in particular, a shot of an ant crawling through grains of sugar on wood, catches my eye. I love the composition, with a torn-open sugar packet blurred in the background.

"I love that one, too," says Mr. Gerardi behind me. "I hope she sticks with it."

"Freshman?" I ask.

"Junior. She was trying to fill an elective, and discovered she has a flair for it." He pauses, and I keep my eyes on the photography exhibit. I don't want to look at him, because I'm still so uncertain about what I'm doing here. He speaks to my shoulder. "Did you want to see the photo I had in mind for the yearbook cover wrap?"

Being here after staying away for so long feels like I'm somehow betraying my mother's memory, but curiosity keeps driving me forward. I wet my lips. "Sure."

He turns, leaving me to follow him, and I do. At his desk, he turns the monitor around so I can see.

I stop breathing. There on the screen is the first photograph I took on Thursday. Declan and Rev sitting on the quad on one side, the cheerleaders practicing a routine on the other.

I knew. Somewhere inside me, I knew it would be this one.

"I love it," Mr. Gerardi says in a rush. "I think it'll make a perfect cover, because of the negative space in between. The cheerleaders symbolize school spirit and togetherness, and their half of the photo could be on the front, while the boys could be on the back, symbolic of friendship, of the isolation everyone occasionally feels in high school—"

"I don't know." My voice comes out as a croak.

"You don't know?"

"I'll have to ask them."

"The girls? Do you know them? Parents sign a disclaimer at the beginning of each school year. We don't need individual permission for yearbook shots—"

"No." My voice cracks again. Rev said I didn't need to delete the photograph, but that doesn't mean he'd be okay with it splashed across the cover of the yearbook for our graduating year. I have no idea how many yearbooks are produced on an annual basis, but there are over eight hundred graduating seniors alone. "No, the boys."

"Okay." He sounds puzzled. "Do you think it would be a problem?"

I keep thinking of my conversations with The Dark about our roads in life and whether they're predestined. Fate seems determined to send me careening through the paths of Declan Murphy and Rev Fletcher. "I don't . . . I have no idea."

Mr. Gerardi hesitates. "Is there something you're not telling me?"

His words are guarded, and it pulls my attention off the screen. "What?"

"This seems like it's a big deal. I'm trying to figure out why."

"I just . . . I want to make sure it's okay."

He studies me. "Do you want *me* to ask them?"

I let that scenario play out in my mind. A strange teacher asking if a photo they didn't want taken could be used as the cover for the yearbook.

I imagine Declan's reaction after the way he acted Thursday afternoon.

"No," I say quickly. "I'll ask."

He gives me an encouraging look. "And then you'll edit the photo yourself?"

"Yes. Sure." I suddenly need to get out of here. "Later this week, okay?"

I don't even wait for an answer. I flee the room like a bomb is counting down.

The parking lot is only half full by the time I make it out of the school. The only cars left are students with sport or club obligations, of which I have none.

Oh, and Rev and Declan.

They're standing behind Declan's car, which is exactly as I remember it, only in more need of a paint job now that I'm looking at it in the sunlight. They're leaning on the tailgate, and Declan has a cigarette between his fingers.

I stop under a small copse of trees in the middle of the parking lot. I didn't anticipate seeing them *right now*, but I'm not surprised that they're still here, just like they were *still here* last Thursday, when I took the picture in question. I have to walk past them to get to my car, and the look in Declan's eyes reminds me of his temper, so different from his attitude when he approached me in the cafeteria this morning.

Hey, I wanted to ask you something.

What?

"Stalker much?" Declan calls.

But his voice isn't cruel. Is he teasing?

I sheepishly step out from under the tree but stop in the middle of the parking lot, about fifteen feet away from them. "I didn't want to get in the middle of . . . whatever."

"Whatever?" Declan takes a drag on his cigarette. "We're killing time."

"You know you're not allowed to smoke on school property."

He takes another drag and blows smoke rings. "You seem awfully concerned about my smoking habit."

"I hate it. It's disgusting."

The words are out of my mouth before I really consider them, and I brace myself for him to launch into nastiness—or to flick the cigarette at me.

He does neither. If anything, he looks startled, and he tosses it to the ground, then stomps it out. "Sorry. I didn't know."

He could sprout wings and I'd be less shocked right now. I mock-gasp to cover my surprise. "But however will you maintain your badass façade?"

"I'll manage."

Rev does a slow clap, then bows his head in my direction. "Thank you. I hate them, too."

Declan shoots him a glare. "Shut up, Rev." His eyes return to me, and he gives me a look up and down. "Still afraid of me?"

"No."

"Then why are you standing way over there?"

I don't know if that's an invitation to join them or what, but I take a few steps closer. "Why are you killing time?"

Declan shrugs and leans back against his car. "There are maybe three places I'm allowed to be. This one isn't within shouting distance of my stepfather."

I can't stop looking at him, and it's almost to the point where

I can't even listen to what he's saying. He looks good in the sunlight because it brings out red in his hair and brightens his face no matter what expression he's wearing. I could study him all day and not get bored. "And here I thought you were posing with your vintage Mustang."

Declan's face goes still, and I can tell I've said the wrong thing.

Rev lets out a low whistle. "Those are fighting words."

"This is not a Mustang," Declan says. He sounds more offended about the car than he did about the cigarette.

"Okay, then what is it?"

"It's a Dodge Charger." He snorts. "I don't know why I'm surprised."

"They all look the same to me."

He points across the parking lot at my late-model Honda. "*That* doesn't look like *this*"—he jerks a thumb at his own car— "any more than those two cars look alike." He points at two cars across the row, one a minivan, one a four-door sedan.

"If you say so."

He pulls his phone out of his pocket and unlocks it. "Here. I'll show you what a Mustang looks like."

Rev grabs the phone. "No. We're not starting this." Then he looks at the screen and must notice the time, because he says, "We have to go anyway."

I take another step forward. "Where are you going?"

I don't know what made me ask, but I know I don't want him to leave. Like every time life throws us together, this moment seems destined to end before I'm ready.

Rev exchanges a glance with Declan, then smiles at me from under his hoodie. "Babysitting. Want to come?"

"For Babydoll?"

He nods.

"Scared?" taunts Declan, his eyes challenging.

"Not at all," I lie. "Let's go."

Rev's house is the mirror image of Rowan's: a modified split-level with a sprawling lower half, and a long stretch of grass leading to the street. His house features blue siding with white trim instead of beige siding with brown trim, but it's a pretty generic middle-class neighborhood. I could walk into half the homes on this street and know my way around. Nothing about his house is surprising.

No, what throws me for a loop is that I see his mother and realize Rev must be adopted.

Facts about Rev click into place in rapid succession, like my brain needs to connect all the dots before I'll be coherent. Declan said something about Rev being taken away from his father. I just hadn't played that out all the way.

Rev said his mother would be working for the afternoon, and this, combined with the knowledge that she's an accountant, had me imagining someone harried and wearing a pencil skirt. Not a woman with short-cropped hair and voluptuous curves, dressed in a flour-speckled red T-shirt and jeans. She has a bright, welcoming smile, radiating so much warmth that I feel lucky to be invited inside.

She whispers hellos and embraces each of us like we've all been coming here after school for years. It's kind of weird, but also kind of nice to be welcomed so openly. She smells like vanilla and sugar and baby powder. When she gets to me, she whispers, "It's so nice to meet you. Call me Kristin," and ushers me into the house.

I'm confused by all the whispering, but I whisper back, feeling foolish. "Hi. I'm Juliet."

Declan leans close enough to speak low. "The baby must be sleeping."

"Oh." His breath brushes against my ear, and heat flares on my cheeks. "I'll be quiet," I say.

"Nonsense," whispers Kristin. "Just go downstairs if you're going to make any noise." She presses a baby monitor into Rev's hand. "I'll bring some cookies down, but then I need to go into my office."

"Thanks, Mom." He glances at me, and his voice is dry. "Want to come downstairs and make some noise?"

I know he's teasing, but my cheeks practically catch on fire because it just *sounds* suggestive.

Kristin swats him. "Go on downstairs, you. I have work to do."

It's so normal, so unassuming. My mother was never like this—she wasn't around enough to see my friends come over all that often. Regret seeps into my chest, but the boys are going down the steps, leaving me to follow.

The lower level is covered by hardwood floors, and the entire space is wide open. One corner has a television mounted on the wall and a sectional sofa. Another corner has two doors that probably lead to a laundry room and a bathroom. The third corner has colorful mats, a play chalkboard, and boxes of toys stacked neatly along the wall. The final corner, half enclosed by the stairs, has thick black mats on the floor, a weight bench, and some kind of punching bag suspended from the ceiling. Free weights sit racked along the wall, under a row of mirrors.

Rev glances at Declan, and some kind of unspoken message passes between them, but I can't identify it before he looks back at me. "Do you want something to drink?"

I inhale to answer—but my throat catches. Being in the presence of a loving mother reminds me of how much I've lost. My brain locks up as grief tangles up the gears inside my head.

I should be at the cemetery—I haven't visited her in *days*. Not since I ran from the dance. And now I'm . . . what? Hiding?

Yes. I'm hiding. Hiding behind their normalcy, their lack of sorrow.

They're not even my *friends*.

Guilt punches me in the chest. Hard. I feel myself caving in from the force of it.

What would I tell her? *Sorry, Mom. I was intrigued by a boy.*

Kristin comes down the stairs, and the pressure on my chest snaps. I take a moment to turn away, inhaling deeply, blinking away tears. She sets the plate on a table behind the couch, and half tiptoes back up the stairs.

Thank god. I don't think I could have handled maternal attention right this second. My body feels like it's on a hair trigger.

I need to get it together. This is why people avoid me. Someone asks if I want a drink and I have a panic attack.

"You're okay." Declan is beside me, and his voice is low and soft, the way it was in the foyer. He's so hard all the time, and that softness takes me by surprise. I blink up at him.

"You're okay," he says again.

I like that, how he's so sure. Not *Are you okay?* No question about it.

You're okay.

He lifts one shoulder in a half shrug. "But if you're going to lose it, this is a pretty safe place to fall apart." He takes two cookies from the plate, then holds one out to me. "Here. Eat your feelings."

I'm about to turn him down, but then I look at the cookie. I was expecting something basic, like sugar or chocolate chip. This looks like a miniature pie, and sugar glistens across the top. "What . . . *is* that?"

"Pecan pie cookies," says Rev. He's taken about five of them, and I think he might have shoved two in his mouth at once. "I could live on them for days."

I take the one Declan offered and nibble a bit from the side. It *is* awesome.

I peer up at him sideways. "How did you know?"

He hesitates, but he doesn't ask me what I mean. "I know the signs."

"I'm going to get some sodas," Rev says slowly, deliberately. "I'm going to bring you one. Blink once if that's okay."

I smile, but it feels watery around the edges. He's teasing me, but it's gentle teasing. Friendly. I blink once.

This is okay. I'm okay. Declan was right.

"Take it out on the punching bag," calls Rev. "That's what I do."

My eyes go wide. "Really?"

"Do whatever you want," says Declan. "As soon as we do anything meaningful, the baby will wake up."

Rev returns with three sodas. "We're doing something meaningful right now."

"We are?" I say.

He meets my eyes. "Every moment is meaningful."

The words could be cheesy—*should* be cheesy, in fact—but he says them with enough weight that I know he means them. I think of The Dark and all our talk of paths and loss and guilt.

Declan sighs and pops the cap on his soda. "This is where Rev starts to freak people out."

"No," I say, feeling like this afternoon could not be more surreal. Something about Rev's statement steals some of my earlier guilt, to think that being here could carry as much weight as paying respects to my mother. I wish I knew how to tell whether this is a path I'm supposed to be on. "No, I like it. Can I really punch the bag?"

Rev shrugs and takes a sip of his soda. "It's either that or we can break out the Play-Doh."

We head to that corner of the basement. Rev straddles the weight bench and sits down while Declan sits on a yoga ball and leans against the corner. They fall into these positions so easily that I wonder if this is their *space*, the way Rowan and I claim her room or the plush couch in my basement.

I'm not a violent person, but hitting something sounds really good.

I draw back a hand and swing, throwing my whole body into it.

Ow. *Ow.* The bag swings slightly, but shock reverberates down my arm. I think I've dislocated every joint of every finger, but I can *feel* it, and it's the first thing I've truly felt in weeks. It feels fantastic. I need one of these in my basement.

I grit my teeth and pull back my arm to do it again.

"Whoa." A hand catches my arm in midswing.

I'm standing there, gasping, and Declan has a hold of my elbow. His eyebrows are way up.

"So . . . yeah," he says. "I don't want to be sexist here, but after the way you talk about cars, I didn't expect you to throw a punch like that."

I draw back and straighten, feeling foolish. "Sorry."

"What are you apologizing for?" He looks at me like I'm crazy. "I just don't want to watch you break a wrist."

"Here." Rev half stands, holding out a pair of black padded gloves. He's pushed back the hood of his sweatshirt, and I wonder if he's grown more comfortable around me—or if he's just warm. "If you really want to beat on it, put on gloves."

The baby monitor squawks, and he straightens. "She's up. I'll be back in a few."

Once he's gone, the basement falls completely silent, and Declan and I are alone. I'm left holding a pair of gloves, feeling a little silly, a little embarrassed, and a little badass.

"You going to put them on or what?" His voice is as edged and challenging as ever.

It takes me a second to figure out the Velcro straps at the wrist, but I quickly slide them over my fingers. They're like a cross between boxing gloves and fingerless mittens, with thick padding around the hand.

If I think about this too hard, I'm going to bolt out the front door, so I close my eyes and swing.

I feel the shock again, but I'm glad for the gloves. My finger bones don't feel like they're splintering inside my skin, and the straps keep my wrists stable. I strike harder. Again. And again. The shock travels through my body, a warmth that settles in my belly. I lose count.

"Open your eyes."

I open them, and he's right there, holding the bag from behind so it doesn't swing. I wonder how long he's been there.

"Get closer," he says.

I shift closer, staring up into his blue eyes.

"Closer," he says again.

I move close enough to hug the bag. I'm breathless, but I don't think it's entirely from the exertion. "Close enough?" I say softly.

His eyes study mine. "You don't want to reach for it."

I want to be coy, but my voice comes out serious. "Am I stronger than you thought I was?"

"You're exactly as strong as I thought you were."

The words carry more weight than they should, and I'm not

entirely sure why. Maybe every moment is meaningful, but this one feels more so.

I bounce on the balls of my feet and tap the bag, like I'm Muhammad Ali or something. I probably look ridiculous.

He inclines his head. "Go ahead. Hit it."

I throw another punch, but now my eyes are locked on his. I don't hit anywhere near as hard. I feel so torn, like being attracted to him is some kind of betrayal to The Dark. And yet . . . I can't help myself. Declan is prickly and explosive and sharp, but buried deep below all that is a boy who's caring and protective and loyal.

I want to see more of that side of him.

His cell phone rings, and he jerks it out of his pocket. After a glance at the screen, his expression darkens, and he shoves it back in his pocket.

"My stepfather," he says when he sees my questioning glance.

"You don't have to answer it?"

"I'll tell him I had my ringer off."

His phone rings again almost immediately. He doesn't even bother to take it out of his pocket this time.

"He'll give up eventually," he says.

I remember meeting his stepfather in the street, the way the man provoked Declan—though Declan sure provoked him right back. "You don't get along."

He snorts. "Have you ever heard of male animals in the wild killing the existing offspring of a new mate? Alan would probably be okay with that."

His phone rings again, sounding insistent.

"He must really want to talk to you," I say.

Declan actually does turn the ringer off now.

We stand there in silence for a moment, breathing at each other.

"Were you looking for me?" he says. "When you came out of school?"

His quiet voice is rich and full and gentle, revealing nothing of his temper. Something about it is so reassuring—maybe because I've seen the fierceness on the other side of it. I want to put my forehead against the bag and close my eyes and beg him to talk to me for five minutes.

I look at the bag and throw a solid punch, just to give myself a moment to figure out how to answer. "You remember that picture I took of you and Rev?"

"The one I 'should have asked' you to delete?"

I stop and look at him. "Are you making fun of me?"

"No." His expression is penitent. "You were right. I should have asked first."

Oh. I remind myself to breathe. Another punch. "Rev said I didn't have to delete it."

"Oh, he did?"

I hesitate and look at him over the gloves. Some of my hair has come loose, and it hangs in my eyes. "Yeah. He did."

"So what did you do with it?"

I have to hit the bag again. "Mr. Gerardi wants to use it for the cover of the yearbook."

"No, seriously."

"I am serious." I hesitate. "He seems really excited about it. I told him I wanted to ask you if it would be okay."

Declan looks incredulous, and not in a good way. Quiet and gentle is gone. "He wants to put a picture of me and Rev on the cover of the yearbook."

"Well. Sort of. You'd be on the back." His expression darkens as I babble, but I can't stop. I'm rambling, trying to get in front of Declan's temper before the train leaves the station. "It's a wrap, so the cheerleaders would be on the front, and it would stretch around the spine to show the friendship yet isolation of—"

"Are you insane?" The words grind out in a growl. His eyes are fierce.

I have to force myself to keep from shrinking back. "I don't know what you're so upset about—"

"I don't belong on that cover. I don't need an eternal reminder of this year, and I sure as hell don't need it wrapped around the yearbook for everyone else." He hits the bag so hard that it bounces off my gloves, but I refuse to step away. "This is the worst year of my life. Do you understand me?"

The bag is swinging now, and I use its momentum to slam it right back at him. "How do you think I feel?" My voice breaks, and I don't care. "I'm the one who took the picture."

He freezes, catching the bag.

My breathing is loud in the sudden silence, and I can't figure out his expression. Still furious, but there's something else. Shock. Shame? Regret, maybe.

I can't take it. "What?" My words are fractured. Hot tears sit on my cheeks. "You think you're the only one having a horrible year? You don't know anything about me, Declan Murphy. Get over yourself."

"Hey, Dec." Rev jogs down the basement steps, carrying the baby and a cordless phone. His voice sounds urgent, more than a plea for us to stop arguing. "It's Alan."

I take a second to swipe the tears from my cheeks.

Declan takes the phone and puts it to his ear. "What."

After a moment, his expression goes still. "What happened?" Another pause. "I'll be right there." Another pause, shorter this time. "I don't care, Alan. I'm coming." Then he pushes the button to turn the phone off.

His eyes return to mine, and any hint of kindness or empathy has vanished. "Do what you want, Juliet. I don't care." Then he fishes his keys from his pocket and turns away.

"What happened?" says Rev. "Dec, stop. Where are you going?"

"The hospital. Mom collapsed while she was making dinner. Alan called an ambulance." He doesn't wait, just heads up the stairs.

"Wait," Rev says. "Dec, wait. Let me get Mom. I'll come with you."

"I can't wait."

Now I can hear it. The fear in his voice.

I remember it well.

He's through the door.

"Give me the baby," I say to Rev. "Go. Go with him."

CHAPTER THIRTY

INBOX: THE DARK

No new messages

I don't know why I keep refreshing the app. I left Juliet an hour ago, and Rev left her with the baby. It's not like Juliet's going to sit down and send me a letter while a toddler destroys the place—especially when she doesn't know that Declan Murphy and The Dark are one and the same.

At the same time, I wish she would.

I rub the back of my neck. The waiting area in the emergency room is crowded and stifling. I haven't seen Alan, and he hasn't answered my texts or my calls.

I keep thinking of the three times he called me at Rev's house, how I ignored him.

The cynical side of me thinks he's doing this to piss me off.

The terrified side of me worries that Mom's in such bad shape that he can't even look at his phone.

Did she ever tell him about how sick she was Friday night? Maybe he didn't know. Maybe I should have said something.

She collapsed. What did that mean? A heart attack? Wouldn't Alan have said she had a heart attack? Maybe she just passed out.

But why would she pass out in the middle of the kitchen?

She was cooking dinner. Did she hurt herself? What happened?

I rub my hands down my face and blow out a breath. Music pours from some overhead speaker, but it's tuned to a station no one in their right mind would listen to. It's some kind of croony old-timer's music, and every time the singer hits a long note, the speaker crackles with static. I keep bouncing my leg. My nerves are shot.

When I look up, my eyes stop on a poster across the room about the warning signs for breast cancer.

Would that make you pass out? I have no idea. I look away. My eyes stop on another sign that talks about heart disease.

I jerk myself out of the chair. "I'm going to ask again."

"Dec." Rev's voice is steady, settling. "You asked ten minutes ago."

He's right. I've asked every ten minutes. They tell me that only one family member is allowed back at a time, and I'll have to wait for Alan to come out.

He hasn't.

The woman behind the counter keeps glancing at me, and I can tell I'm beginning to wear on her, too. If they throw me out of here, I don't know what I'll do.

I slam back into the seat. My pulse roars in my ears, making me very aware of every heartbeat. I drag my hands through my hair. My shoulders are so tense I'm going to have to hit something to release the pressure.

Rev puts a hand on my shoulder, and I freeze. For a minute, I'm worried he's going to say something biblical about God's will, and I'm going to have to punch him. Or he's going to say something empty and meaningless, like, *She'll be fine* or *I'm sure it's just low blood sugar. They're probably giving her a soda right now.*

But he's Rev and he's my best friend and he doesn't say any of those things. He sits there in silence, his hand on my shoulder.

In a way, it's reassuring, to know I'm not here alone. But we sit for the longest time, until fear is pressing down on me.

I text Alan again.

No answer.

I call him and it goes right to voice mail.

He's turned his phone off.

My chest tightens. Every breath is a struggle, and my throat doesn't want to work right. I can't sit here in silence anymore.

"I think she's sick."

Rev leans in. His tone is low, matching mine. "Why?"

"I found her throwing up after Homecoming." My voice almost wavers. My eyes feel wet, and I keep them locked on the carpeting.

He's quiet for a moment. "That was only Friday. It could be the flu."

I shake my head. "It wasn't like that. And she was fine yesterday." I freeze, and a tear slips down my cheek. I hastily swipe it away. "No. She wasn't fine yesterday. She was taking a nap. In the middle of the day."

Then I remember something else. Kristin's comment at dinner before Homecoming, asking if Mom was feeling better. "Kristin said she was sick last weekend, too."

Rev doesn't say anything to that. He remembers the comment.

Maybe Mom's been sick for a while.

Every moment is meaningful. Sometimes Rev's words feel like a premonition when I play them back in my head.

Each moment I sit out here, I'm not with her.

Rev's phone vibrates, and I'm sitting close enough that I can hear it. He fishes it out of his pocket and checks the screen. "Mom will be here in a minute. Juliet is staying with Babydoll until Dad gets home."

Kristin is coming. I don't know why, but that makes this feel more serious.

I can't stop the next tear that rolls down my face. I drag my sleeve across my cheek and inhale a jagged breath.

She could have been dying all this time. She could be dying right now, and I don't even know it because Alan has turned his phone off.

Rage is a new pressure in my chest, but I prefer it to the fear. I understand anger, and I welcome it, even as it crawls across my back to dig into my shoulders.

I want to kill him.

And just like that, as if my murderous thoughts summoned him, Alan walks through the double doors and appears in the waiting room. He looks tense and exhausted and afraid.

Just like me, really. It should dial back my anger, but it doesn't.

I want to put him through the wall.

"Alan." My voice could cut steel, and I'm halfway across the room before he registers that I'm barreling down on him. "Where is she? What's going on?"

"Keep your voice down." He glances between me and Rev and looks surprised that we're here.

"Where is she?" My fists are clenched so hard that my nails are leaving little half-moons on my palms. "I want to see her."

"Easy," Rev murmurs beside me.

"You can't." Alan turns weary eyes to me. "She's—"

"You've been with her for two hours," I growl. "I want to see her."

Frustration clouds his expression. "I told you not to come here, Declan. This is very personal, and it's between your mother and me right—"

I shove him.

No, *shove* doesn't do the movement justice. Alan is lucky there's a wall behind him, because he slams into that instead of slamming into the floor.

Rev grabs me, so I can't go after him.

Alan's hands are in fists, and he's going to come after *me*, though. I'm ready for it. I *welcome* it. There's fire in his eyes, and I know he's been wanting to hit me for *months.*

He doesn't move, though. He stands there, breathing hard, glaring at me. The way Rev has a shoulder against me suddenly feels like overkill.

Every pair of eyes in the waiting room is on us. A nurse behind the desk is on the phone, and I can hear her speaking quickly. ". . . may have an incident in the ER waiting room."

Juliet's words smack me in the face. *You're pretty confrontational.*

"Rev." My voice sounds like I've been chewing gravel. My eyes are locked on Alan. "Let me go."

He doesn't. "You're still on probation."

"I know," I grit out. "I'm fine."

"Grow up," Alan snaps. "Your mother doesn't need this. Not now."

Somehow all the fight has drained out of me, and I twist free of Rev's hold. I'm a heartbeat away from slamming through the double doors myself, and security be damned. Or maybe I'm a heartbeat away from curling up in a ball on the floor.

"Rev." Kristin appears beside us, concerned eyes going between me and Alan. "What's going on?"

"We don't know," Rev says. He's glaring at Alan, too. "We can't get anyone to tell us anything."

Alan looks at Kristin, and he seems relieved to have another adult here to help with the delinquents. "Can you take them home? I'm going to spend the night with Abby."

"Sure," she says, glancing at me and Rev and then back at him. "Is everything all right?"

I fight very hard to hold still. There's a security guard by the desk now, and while he hasn't approached us, it's pretty obvious he's here to make sure no one gets rowdy. "I'm not going home until you tell me what's going on, Alan."

A nurse comes through the double doors behind him with an iPad in a thick case. "Mr. Bradford, we're taking her upstairs now. An obstetrics nurse will meet you on the seventh floor—"

Kristin gasps. She puts a hand over her mouth. "Alan."

Rev and I both look at her. I don't know what that gasp means, but it's something big. The floor drops out from beneath me. "What?" I demand. Now I can't keep the fear out of my voice. "What's an obstetrics nurse? Is it cancer?" My voice breaks. "Is she sick? Can I see her?"

"No, Declan. Honey." Kristin takes my hand and pats it like I'm six years old. "Obstetrics is for pregnancy." She doesn't let go of my hand, but she turns to Alan. "Is Abby all right?"

I can't move. I can't breathe. My hand goes slick in Kristin's. *Pregnancy.*

Alan is nodding. "She's very dehydrated. They've put her on an IV. The baby is fine."

The baby.

The baby.

My mother is going to have a baby.

CHAPTER THIRTY-ONE

From: The Dark <TheDark@freemail.com>

To: Cemetery Girl <cemeterygirl@freemail.com>

Date: Monday, October 7   10:22:44 PM

Subject: The whole story, part 2

Marriage laws are funny. If you want to get married, you can go down to the courthouse, sign a few papers, and be married in less than fifteen minutes.

If you want to get divorced, you have to wait a year. Even if your husband is in prison.

My father was sentenced to ten years, and some naive part of me actually thought that my mother was going to wait around for him. Like he'd get out of prison one day, we'd go out for a soda, and good ol' Jim and Abby would pick up where they left off. As if he hadn't killed my sister and put us all through hell.

To my knowledge, my mother has never visited my father in prison. I definitely haven't. I asked to see him once, when the shock and numbness had worn off, and our lives were beginning to fall back into some kind of regularity. Mom looked like I'd said the filthiest, foulest thing that could ever come out of someone's mouth. She looked like she wanted to slap me.

Then she said, "We are never seeing him again."

And then she went into the kitchen and smoked a cigarette while standing over the sink.

I felt like I belonged in prison with him.

A year later, she started dating. I'd just started sophomore year, so I was a little oblivious at first. She didn't go wild or anything. I really didn't even know she was *dating* until she started bringing them home.

At first, this seemed like a great idea. After Kerry died, Mom was constantly in my face. Wanted to know where I was going, who I was with, what was going on with school. You can imagine how I reacted to this kind of treatment. A new boyfriend meant she could dote on someone else.

What came as a surprise was that my mother's taste in men *sucked*.

After my dad turned out to be such a winner, I probably should have figured.

The first one didn't last too long after he met me. Maybe he was fine with the idea of a stepchild in theory, or maybe he thought kids should be like dogs, locked in a crate when you didn't want to deal with them. Either way, he didn't like the fact that I wasn't a trained poodle. He would come over for dinner, and he always seemed irritated that I dared to eat at the table.

Eventually, Mom picked up on it, and he was history.

The second lasted a little longer, but not by much. Only because he didn't come to the house very often. He was super strict, super religious, and the way he watched me always made me nervous. My best friend wouldn't come in the house when he was around. I don't know what happened to break them up, but Mom was talking about him on the phone to a friend, and she called him a "near miss."

Number three was gay, something I noticed when I first met him, but for some reason it took Mom a few weeks. Number four was secretly unemployed. It ended when he asked to borrow a credit card for a little while. Not because he asked—because she *gave* it to him, and he racked up seven thousand dollars in charges before leaving town.

You might be noticing a trend.

Number five was still married. Mom found out when she tried to surprise him at home and ran into his wife. She cried for days, telling me she felt like such a fool.

She kept bringing these men into our lives, and they were all wrong. *Anyone* could see that. Sometimes I wonder if there's something broken in her head, the way she trusts people who are destined to disappoint her.

Then again, she trusted me, and look where it got us.

By the time she introduced me to number six, I was primed to hate them all.

Unfortunately, Mom was head over heels, as usual. He was a businessman, so a far cry from the dirty fingernails and blistered palms of a guy who works on cars all day. Number six actually got pedicures, if you can believe that. I mocked him to his face, hoping to speed along the inevitable breakup. Mom loved it, though. He took her to fancy dinners, wore shoes with a shine, and swept her off her feet.

He tried to win me over at first. He'd hit me in the shoulder and say something like, "Hey, pal, I've got skybox tickets to the O's game tonight. I thought maybe you and I could check it out."

Yeah, because everything about me screams "baseball fan."

I turned him down. I always turned him down.

When that didn't work, he tried to play the father figure. A teacher would call home, and *he* would try to deal with it. He'd accuse me of acting out, of deliberately hurting my mother to spite him. He started hating me. I could feel it.

Not like it mattered. It was only a matter of time before we'd learn the truth. Maybe this guy would turn out to be a meth addict. Whatever. I knew it wouldn't last.

Unfortunately, it did. They got engaged. They set a date.

He asked me to be his best man. I refused.

He said, "Ungrateful punk. Figures."

Figures.

I'm so angry now, remembering it. The disdain in his voice, the complete and total lack of regard. I'm glad the phone is autocorrecting because my fingers are all over the place. *Ungrateful punk. Figures.*

I was supposed to be grateful that yet another guy was swooping in to ruin my mother's life? Apparently so. I didn't fawn all over him like she did, so he wrote me off. He'd built that snapshot of me in his head, and that was it. That's how he saw me. How he *sees* me.

After that, I couldn't do anything right. I used to mow the lawn, but he started doing it while I was at school, and he'd do it in some stupid diamond pattern that made her gush. He took out the trash without being asked, and she'd make comments about how nice it was to have a man around to take care of the house. Mom used to take me places, but now she goes everywhere with him. After the best man incident, I didn't want to go anywhere with him—but they never asked anyway.

Sometimes I wish I had died in that car with Kerry. I think it would have been easier on my mother. She had a chance for a new start, but I was still around, getting in the way.

They got married last May.

I celebrated by trying to kill myself after the ceremony.

I didn't succeed. Obviously.

> But right now, after what I just found out about my
> mother, I wish I had.

I'm sitting in the dark, staring at his email. Five minutes ago, I was lying in the dark, waiting for sleep to steal my thoughts about Declan and Rev and what might be happening to them tonight, and then my phone lit up.

Now my heart is pounding and I'm wide awake.

The green dot still appears beside his name. He chatted with me once. Could I do the same?

> CG: Do you want to talk about it?

I wait, but he doesn't respond.

Adrenaline is still kicking along in my veins. I don't know what to do.

"Come on," I whisper.

I wish I had a way to call him. I wish I knew of another way to get in touch with him.

> CG: I know you're still online. Please let me know you're
> OK.

Nothing.

> CG: You're really worrying me. We don't have to talk, but
> please let me know you're there.

You're there. Because I can't type, *Please let me know you're alive.*
Nothing.

I glance at my clock. It's half past ten, and Dad's in bed, but I don't know what else to do. I'll have to wake him up.

I throw my blankets back, and the phone lights up.

TD: I'm here. Sorry. Was brushing my teeth.

CG: I want to punch you.

TD: ???

CG: I was really worried.

TD: I'm not having a good night.

CG: Do you want to talk about it?

TD: No.

Well. I don't know what to do with that.

My phone lights up again.

TD: My mom is pregnant.

CG: I sense that "Congratulations" isn't the right thing to say.

TD: She's four months pregnant. They've known for four
    months and they haven't told me.

CG: Maybe not that long. You can't tell right away.

TD: Fine. But they didn't find out today.

CG: Is she happy?

TD: I have no idea. I found out by accident. They weren't
    even going to tell me.

CG: They would have had to tell you eventually.

TD: Is this supposed to be making me feel better?

CG: I'm sorry. I've had a weird night, too.

TD: Why? What's going on with you?

CG: We don't have to talk about me. I wanted to make
sure you were okay.

TD: I'm fine. I don't want to talk about it. Why was your
night weird?

CG: I don't know if I want to talk about it, either.

TD: Why not?

Because it feels odd to talk to him about Declan. Which is ridiculous. But at the same time, it's not. It feels like talking to one crush about another, which seems to border a line of betrayal. At the same time, The Dark is anonymous, and I feel like he understands me in a way no one else has. It feels odd *not* to talk about Declan.

This whole thing is odd.

Odd and addictive. I bite at my lip and type slowly.

CG: Remember when I was telling you about Declan
Murphy?

TD: Yes.

I hesitate, staring at the screen. I'd been thinking Rev could be The Dark, but when I met his parents, I realized that didn't fit at all. But Declan . . .

My phone flashes.

TD: Are you still there?

CG: You never told me if you know Declan or not. I'm just
now realizing you have a lot of similarities.

TD: What kind of similarities?

CG: You both have stepfathers that you don't get along
with. You know your way around a car, and so does he.

TD: Way to crack the case, Sherlock. Half the guys in our
school have stepfathers they don't get along with,
and there are at least sixty kids in the senior class
alone who take some variety of auto shop.

CG: You share an attitude, too, I see.

TD: Quit beating around the bush. Do you want me to tell
you who I am?

I stop breathing. *Do I?*

I try to reexamine every interaction with Declan through this
new lens. None of it fits cleanly. It's all square pegs and round
holes. He showed up after Homecoming, so maybe that works
out—but why wouldn't he admit who he was? Why keep up this
charade?

And The Dark knows how difficult photography is for me.
Tonight, in Rev's basement, Declan seemed genuinely shocked
when I told him that taking the yearbook picture affected me,
too. The Dark has never mentioned any trouble with the law or
probation or any kind of community service, but I know Declan
is court ordered to do *something* after what he did last spring.
I don't even know all the details of his case, I realize, not any
more than what he told me in the car. And I've never heard
Declan mention a sister—and Rev hasn't, either. There's enough

pain in The Dark's words that I know she weighs heavily on his heart.

Then again, I don't think I've mentioned my mother to Declan.

All that aside, do I *want* to know who The Dark is?

If he's Declan Murphy, is that a good thing? I can't even lie to myself about the flickers of attraction in Rev's basement earlier—and then the flickers of anger and irritation and exasperation and worry.

I can still hear the rasp in his voice. *You're all right*.

I put my head down on my pillow. Oh, if this is Declan Murphy, what would that mean? My heart flutters wildly, and I don't even bother to tamp it down.

Then another thought tamps it down for me.

If this *isn't* Declan Murphy, what would *that* mean?

My phone lights up.

TD: I sense a hesitation.

I giggle. It's been almost five minutes since the last message.

CG: You must be psychic. We could probably ditch the phones.

TD: I actually thought maybe you'd fallen asleep.

CG: Still here.

TD: You didn't answer my question.

CG: I don't know. I don't know if I want to know who you are.

TD: Fair enough.

CG: Do you want to talk about your mom?

TD: No.

CG: Do you want me to let you go to sleep?

TD: No.

CG: Do you want to keep talking?

TD: Yes.

I smile and blush and nestle down under my blankets.
He sends another message.

TD: Tell me about your night with Declan Murphy.

I hesitate. Am I talking about Declan *to* Declan?
My head hurts. I type.

CG: There's not much to tell. Mr. Gerardi asked me to shoot
    the Fall Festival last week, so I did. One of the pictures
    captured Declan and his friend on one side of the shot
    and some cheerleaders doing a routine on the other side.

TD: Go on.

CG: Mr. Gerardi wants to use it as the cover of the
    yearbook. I told Declan and his friend, Rev, and
    Declan flipped out.

TD: Why?

CG: I don't know. He got in my face and said he didn't
    want a memory of this year.

TD: He sounds like a real prick. I'm wondering if I should
    be offended that you think I'm him.

CG: Sometimes he is a real prick. But I didn't take it well, either.

TD: Because of your mother.

CG: Yeah.

TD: Don't you think she'd be proud, that a picture you took would be on the cover of the yearbook?

CG: No. She'd be proud if I took a picture of the Baltimore riots that ended up in Time or something. She said photography was a way to show what the world is really like.

TD: Yeah, but in snapshots, right?

CG: Yes . . . ?

TD: A snapshot is one moment. When I was looking up your mother's photographs, I clicked around and looked at some other stuff. I found one from the Vietnam War, where a man is shooting a prisoner in the head. Do you know it?

CG: Yes. It's a famous photograph.

TD: Which man is the bad guy?

I blink and sit up again. I know exactly what picture he's talking about because it's fairly graphic. A man's *death* is captured in the image. I'm ashamed to admit I don't know the history surrounding the shot, just that it was pivotal in turning public opinion against the Vietnam War. I've always assumed the "bad guy" was the man with the gun, because—well, because he was killing someone else. But I don't know anything beyond that moment in time.

CG: I've always thought the man with the gun, but now I'm not so sure.

TD: The man with the gun was the chief of police. He was executing the other guy for killing more than thirty people in the street, some of them children.

CG: I don't even know what to say. I feel like I should have known that.

TD: Don't feel too bad. I'm reading from Wikipedia right now.

CG: I don't understand what any of this has to do with a stupid photo in a yearbook.

TD: I mean a photo is just that: a moment in time. We don't know what's really going on with the people in the picture. And we don't know what's going on with the photographer. What makes it important is what we bring to the photo: our assumption of who is the bad guy and who is the good guy. What makes it important is how we feel when we look at it. And a photograph doesn't have to be about riots or death or famine or children at play in a war zone to make an impact.

CG: So you're saying it shouldn't bother me that it's going to be on the yearbook.

TD: Yes.

CG: Okay, then.

TD: And I'm saying you should be proud of it.

CG: You haven't even seen it.

TD: Send it to me.

CG: I can't. It's at school.

TD: Well, it has to be pretty good if they chose your photo over making all the seniors stand in lines to spell out the school initials.

CG: Thank you.

TD: It's okay to succeed at something your mother did. Even in a different way.

Those words hit me so hard that I fall back on the pillow. My chest aches with pressure. I want to cry. I *am* crying.

You're okay.

I sniff and hold myself together.

CG: It's okay to be mad that your mom is pregnant.

TD: I'm not mad. I'm . . . extraneous.

CG: You're not extraneous.

TD: I am. She took this douchebag's name when she married him. Now there's nothing linking me to her, and only something linking me to a man stuck in prison.

CG: There's no name linking me to my mother, either, but I'm still connected to her. I feel it every day.

He doesn't say anything to that. I wait for a while, until the suspense is killing me.

CG: Did I say the wrong thing?

TD: No.

CG: Are you okay?

TD: I don't know.

CG: Does she know how you feel?

TD: My mother?

CG: Yes.

TD: No.

CG: Maybe you should tell her.

TD: I don't think so.

CG: Take it from someone who can't tell her mother anything anymore. You should tell her everything you can.

CHAPTER THIRTY-TWO

From: Cemetery Girl <cemeterygirl@freemail.com>
To: The Dark <TheDark@freemail.com>
Date: Tuesday, October 8   06:22:23 AM
Subject: Mothers

My mom was always on assignment, so we never had much opportunity for "girl talk." My best friend is very close to her mother, and they talk all the time. I envy that.

    Mom and I could have talked by email, and sometimes we did, but when I was young and learning to write, she encouraged me to send her letters. I did, and she would write back. When I was nine years old, getting a letter with a bunch of foreign stamps would be the highlight of my week. I did a project in fifth grade where I tried to collect stamps from as many countries as possible just because I already had two dozen in my desk at home.

Even after I had an email account and a phone, the letter writing stuck. I started writing several times a week. I told her everything.

Now I'm going to tell you something I've never told anyone.

This is so hard to type, I'm tempted to delete this whole email.

In my letters, sometimes I lied.

I know you won't get the full effect, but I deleted and retyped that line seven times.

Now eight.

I am forcing myself to keep going.

I lied to my mother.

Her letters were full of these grand adventures. She'd tell me about warlords or peace treaties or ballistic missiles or brushes with death. Nothing in her letters was false—she had the photographs to prove it. "Ian is sending me to Malaysia this week," she'd say. Or, "I'm going to be another few days in Iran. Ian wants me to see if I can get some shots of the protesters."

Ian is her editor, and sometimes I'd be tempted to write back and ask if Ian could assign her to spend a few weeks at home.

So I'd lie. I'd tell her that a photograph of mine was up for an award from the city council. Or I'd tell her I'd written a piece for the school paper that launched an investigation of some sort. Anything to get her attention.

She'd say the right things, but I could read between the lines.

It was all meaningless.

It's even more meaningless now, looking back. They weren't even *interesting* lies.

I wish I'd just told her the truth.

I wish I'd told her in real time, instead of in written letters that would take weeks to arrive.

I wish I'd told her how I felt, and how much I missed her, and how her being home, just a little bit, would have meant more to me than all the Pulitzer Prizes in the world.

I think that's why I wrote her so many letters after she died.

I'd give anything to tell her one true thing, any true thing, right now.

So. Talk to your mother. Tell her how you feel.

Report back.

I wish I could. Mom was still in the hospital when I left for school.

I had to spend the night at Rev's. Not like it was a hardship, but I'm seventeen years old. I could have spent the night alone. I don't need to crash on his couch because no one trusts me to stay away from the matches.

Then again, considering my mental state when we left the hospital, maybe staying with Rev was a good thing.

Sleep kept its distance last night, for various reasons.

Texting with Juliet—worth it.

Plotting with a sleepy Rev about how I want to disconnect Alan's fuel line—worth it.

Listening to Babydoll scream at 4 a.m.—not worth it.

Worrying about how my mother is re-creating a family without me—not worth it.

I'm practically crawling between classes this morning.

When I get to English, Mrs. Hillard is taking papers from students as they walk through the door. I didn't do the class assignment, because I wasn't there to get it—but I didn't look at the other poem she gave me in the conference room, either.

I move past without looking at her and drop into my seat.

"Declan," she says, "what did you think of 'Invictus'?"

I don't need this hassle. I don't need it.

I stab my pencil at my notebook. "I didn't read it."

Students continue filing past her, and she keeps taking their papers, but her eyes are locked on me.

"Why not?"

Because I'm extraneous. I don't need to be here.

I can't say that. I can't say any of it.

I look down at my notebook and begin doodling a line in the margin. The motion is casual, but tension begins coiling in my belly, and I know it's only a matter of time before it snaps, sending me careening into the hall, leaving rage in my wake.

She slaps a blank Post-it onto my notebook, and I jump. I didn't see her walk over.

"Tell me why," she says.

I pick up my pencil, but I stop with the point against the paper.

I can't tell her. I could barely tell Juliet, and that was without being stared at in the middle of a crowded classroom.

Mrs. Hillard doesn't move.

I wish she'd leave me alone. Like a stupid poem is going to make a bit of difference in my life.

She still hasn't said a word, but I can feel her waiting. Hell, at this point, the whole class is waiting.

She asked me to give her a chance. What would this cost me?

I scribble quickly, fold it in half, and hand it to her.

Panic grips me for an instant because I didn't consider that she might read it out loud.

But she doesn't. She reads what I wrote—*My mom was in the hospital last night*—and taps her fingers on my notebook. "I understand. Thank you. We're going to move on to a new poem in class, but I think I'd like for you to complete last night's assignment independently, if that's all right with you."

The coil of tension unspools a little, leaving me off balance. I have to clear my throat. "Sure."

"Good," she says. Then she moves away and calls the class to order.

I pull the photocopied sheet out of my bag. "Invictus." It's a little crumpled around the edges, but I can still read the poem.

I heave a sigh. I can come up with two paragraphs, easy. At least it's short.

Ten minutes later, I've read it three times.

I feel like I can't *stop* reading it. The words feel as though they were written just for me. One line in particular keeps drawing my eye.

"*Under the bludgeonings of chance, my head is bloody but unbowed.*"

In other words, life has a solid right hook, but it's not going to take me down.

The final lines are what really get me, though.

"*I am the master of my fate, I am the captain of my soul.*"

I can't remember the last time I felt like the master of my own fate.

Yes, I do. Last May, when I got behind the wheel of Dad's truck. When that bottle of whiskey burned a path down my throat.

I have never really cared about an assignment before, but all of a sudden, I need to write.

I dig in my bag and find a pen. I start writing, and it's like writing to Juliet. Thoughts pour out of me.

I end up with a lot more than two paragraphs.

CHAPTER THIRTY-THREE

From: The Dark <TheDark@freemail.com>
To: Cemetery Girl <cemeterygirl@freemail.com>
Date: Tuesday, October 8   11:42:44 AM
Subject: RE: Mothers

I think your relationship with your mother is a lot different
from mine.

But I'll think about it.

I read his email on the way to lunch, and it's so short that
I'm not sure what the vibe is here. Is he pissed? Genuinely
contemplative? Frustrated? Closed off?

I wonder how much I can tell Rowan about this. I need another
girl's analysis.

My phone pings, and it's her.

RF: Need to skip lunch. Meeting with teacher for Hon
    French project. You OK?

Well, there goes that. I text back that I'm fine.

Lunch is grilled cheese, green beans, and Tater Tots. I can already feel my pores clogging, but I didn't bring anything, and the alternative is ice cream on a stick.

I head toward the back of the cafeteria, intending to go outside to sit on the quad and obsess over The Dark's emails, but I spot Rev and Declan sitting at a table in the corner. Well, I assume it's Rev. It could be some other broad-shouldered guy in a hoodie, but I doubt it.

The remaining six feet of table is empty.

The last words Declan said to me are still stinging my ears.

Do what you want, Juliet. I don't care.

I walk over, smack my tray down, and drop onto the bench beside Rev, across from Declan.

"Hey, Juliet," says Declan, his voice as dry as ever. "Why don't you join us."

"I will. Thanks." I study the array of food between them. There must be ten separate plastic boxes, each packed with a different type of food. The offerings run the gamut from sliced fruit to rolled deli meat. "What is all this?"

"Mom's obsession," says Rev. He plucks a raspberry from one of the boxes, then nudges it toward me. "Help yourself."

I spy tomato and mozzarella. "Is that a caprese salad?"

Rev nods and slides it over. "She always packs enough to feed an army."

I pour a little onto my plate, and Rev shakes his head. "Have it all."

I move the grilled cheese and dump out the whole box, very aware of Declan's presence. He hasn't said anything since I sat down, but his shadowed eyes track every move I make. He looks tired.

I spear a tomato. "How's your mom?"

He twists a water bottle on the table in front of him. "She's coming home this afternoon."

"So it was just dehydration?"

"That's what they're telling me."

I'm not sure what to make of that, so I glance up. Just like last night, I try to realign what I know of The Dark with what I know of Declan Murphy, and not all of it fits. He meets my gaze and holds it. I can't decipher his expression, some mix of challenge, frustration, and intrigue.

I have no idea what my own face looks like, but my pulse quickens, just enough.

I have to clear my throat. "So you'll get to see her when you get home."

"Maybe. I have community service on Tuesday nights."

I still can't figure out his mood, but it's obvious he doesn't want to talk about his mother. "What's that like? Do you make license plates or something?"

"No." He looks like the question bothers him, but he doesn't want to let it show. "I ride a lawn mower. Sometimes, if I'm really good, they let me carry a WeedWacker."

"How long do you have to do it?"

He snorts. "For . . . ever."

"Ninety hours," says Rev.

"It would have been a hundred," says Declan, "but I got credit for time served."

"I don't know what that—"

"Maybe I should put you in touch with my probation officer," he says pointedly. "He can answer all your questions."

Oh. I put down my fork. "I'm sorry."

He frowns and pushes his food away. "No, I'm sorry." He rubs at his eyes. "I didn't get a lot of sleep. I'm being a dick. You can ask."

I stab a cube of mozzarella cheese and wonder how honest he'll be in the middle of the cafeteria. "Did they put you in jail?"

"Yes."

"Was it scary?"

"No." He pauses, then takes a drink from his water bottle. He shakes his head, and his voice is low and raspy. "Yes. Especially once I sobered up and realized no one was bothering to get me out."

Beside me, Rev goes rigid, but he doesn't say anything. He silently picks raisins out of a container, each movement very deliberate.

I look back at Declan. "How long were you there?"

"Two nights. I had to wait for a bail hearing. They were going to charge me as an adult."

My eyebrows go way up. "Your mom left you there?"

"Yes." He gives a little shrug. "Maybe Alan made her. I don't know, and I'm not sure which would make me feel better: that she made the choice to leave me there or that she let someone else make it for her."

I don't have anything to say to that.

Declan's intense eyes are still trained on me. "So you can see why I don't want a permanent memory of this year."

He's referring to the photograph. "I'll tell Mr. Gerardi that you don't want it on the cover."

"Don't pin it all on me," Declan says. "You don't want it there any more than I do."

"No," I agree. "I don't."

"Fine."

"Fine."

"I want it there," says Rev.

We both look at him.

"What?" he says. It's the first time I've ever heard him sound irritated. "I don't get a say?" He stands and flings the containers into his neoprene lunch sack, including one Declan was eating from.

Declan straightens, looking nonplussed. "Rev?"

Rev looks like he wants to flip the table. "No one bothered to get you out?"

"What?"

"Do you even hear yourself sometimes?" Rev leans down. "I would have gotten you out. Kristin would have. Geoff. But you don't get to sit in a jail cell feeling sorry for yourself, calling no one, and then act like a martyr."

Declan's hands tighten on the edge of the table. "What is your problem?"

"You made the choices that put you there," Rev says. "Stop acting like such a damn *victim*. You want to hate the whole year? Fine. But May twenty-fifth was one day. There are three hundred sixty-four other ones."

He turns to storm away from the table.

Declan looks like thunder. "I'm the victim?" he calls. "Who's the one hiding in sweatshirts when it's eighty degrees outside?"

Rev doesn't stop. Declan glares but doesn't go after him. His breathing is quick.

I'm frozen in place, my heart tripping along. My brain is stuck three sentences back.

It takes me a moment to get my voice to work, and when it does, it's a hoarse whisper. "What's May twenty-fifth?"

That pulls Declan's attention back to me. "Juliet—"

"What's May twenty-fifth?" I demand.

I don't think I'm that loud, but we've already drawn the eyes of the surrounding students, and the hush spreads.

Declan swallows. "The day I wrecked my father's truck."

"The day you got drunk? The day you blacked out and crashed into a building?" I'm screaming, yet I can't catch my breath. "The day you barely remember?"

He doesn't say anything. I feel like my chest is caving in. The room starts spinning.

A hand catches my arm. "Juliet. Juliet." A familiar male voice is speaking to me, but my vision has tunneled to nothing.

May 25.

The day my mother was killed in a hit-and-run crash.

CHAPTER THIRTY-FOUR

From: Cemetery Girl <cemeterygirl@freemail.com>
To: The Dark <TheDark@freemail.com>
Date: Tuesday, October 8   03:21:53 PM
Subject: I need to know

Are you Declan Murphy?
    If you are, I don't know if I can ever talk to you again.

I'm going to lose my mind.

She must have sent me the email as soon as school let out, because the final bell rings at 3:20.

She must have driven straight to the cemetery, too. She's sitting in front of her mother's gravestone, writing something longhand.

I know this because I'm watching her do it.

She can't see me. I'm not standing out in the open. I'm not that brave. No, I'm by the equipment shed, lurking in the shadows like a complete and total stalker. Melonhead is puttering around in there, and he hasn't seen me yet, either.

I don't know what she did for the rest of the school day, but I know what I did: I sat in the back of each class and replayed that night in my head. The wedding. The whiskey.

The impact. The cops.

I was only in the car for fifteen minutes. That's documented. I left the wedding at 8:01 p.m., and I plowed into the pillars of the office building at 8:16 p.m.

Fifteen minutes.

That doesn't seem like enough time to destroy someone else's life along with my own.

The cops aren't stupid, right? They would have put two and two together, right?

I knew the date. I *knew* it. That's how this started! I read the letter sitting on the woman's gravestone.

I keep thinking about those paths and wonder if ours—mine and her mother's—were set to intersect that perfectly. To collide that perfectly.

This makes me no better than my father. This makes me *worse* than my father.

Why didn't I succeed? My path was supposed to end. That was the whole reason I got in the truck after all. It'd worked for Kerry. It should have worked for me.

It would have been so much better for everyone.

I need to get out of here. I need to go home. I can't go home.

I didn't hit anyone that night. I didn't hurt anyone.

I know I didn't.

I'm pretty sure.

I'm not sure at all.

I feel sick. I'm going to be sick, right here in the grass.

Did I kill someone? Did I kill her mother?

I need Rev. I need to talk to Rev.

BUT HE WON'T ANSWER HIS PHONE.

I try again anyway. My fingers are sweaty, and I can't get the screen to work. A noise escapes my throat, and I fling the phone in the grass.

I'm losing my mind. I press my fingers into my eyes. My hands are shaking.

"Murph?" Melonhead is in front of me, peering at me, his eyes concerned. "What's going on with you, man?"

"I need to go." My voice sounds like I'm choking. "I can't do this."

"What's going on?"

I turn away and head toward the path that leads to the employee parking lot. Each step feels as though I'm moving through quicksand, but instead of pulling me into the earth, I'm being towed back to Juliet.

I need her. More than anything right now. I need her.

And because of everything between us, I can't have her.

Melonhead is still beside me. "DECK-lin. Talk to me."

I find my car and fumble with the keys. Twice. The steel prong refuses to slide into the slot.

I yell and punch the car with the handful of keys. Steel teeth bite into my palm and I hear metal *screek*.

"Hey. Hey." Melonhead catches my arm, and he's stronger than I expect. "Talk to me. Are you high, kid?"

"God. No." I put my forehead against the roof of the car. I wish I *were*. "I need to get out of here, Frank. Please let me go."

He inhales, and I'm ready for warnings about not fulfilling my community service, about calling the judge, about getting thrown back in jail.

"Okay," he says. "You drive. I'll listen."

I drive, but I don't talk. There's something soothing about being behind the wheel of a car, and I'm able to settle into the rhythm of the clutch and the hum of the road. At first, I do a few loops through the neighborhood where the cemetery sits, because I'm certain Melonhead is going to tell me that's enough, that I need to get myself together and go back.

He doesn't.

So I head farther east, merging onto the highway, until we're approaching the bridge over the Chesapeake Bay. I'm going to have to shell out six bucks for the toll, because I don't want to stop.

"Take the Jennifer Road exit," he says.

We've been driving for twenty minutes, and it's the first word either of us has said. "Why?"

"I want to stop at the hospital."

My hands grip the steering wheel more tightly. "I don't need a hospital."

"Who said anything about you? We're down here, I'm going to say hello to my wife."

That cuts through my self-obsession. My eyes flick over. "Your wife is sick?"

He shakes his head. "She works here. I want to surprise her."

It's not like I have a planned destination in mind. I hit the turn signal and take the exit.

When I've parked in the garage, I don't kill the engine.

Melonhead unbuckles his seat belt and hits me in the arm. "Come on, Murph."

"I can wait."

"Too good to meet my wife? Get out of the car, kid."

My nerves are shot, and I glare at him. "I'm not in the mood for this."

"What are you in the mood for?"

I'm in the mood to crawl under this car and hide there forever.

Rev's words keep echoing in my head. *Stop acting like such a damn victim.*

The words hit me like a bullet to the vest, and I'm still sore from the impact. I don't think I've ever heard him swear.

I pull the brake and turn the key and climb out of the car. "Whatever. Lead the way."

The hospital is as busy as it was yesterday. We go in through the main entrance, and people walk in every direction. The people in scrubs and white coats all walk a little bit faster. There's a guy sleeping on one of the waiting room sofas, and a hugely pregnant woman leaning against the wall by the elevator. She's swirling a drink in a plastic cup. That baby is giving her T-shirt a run for its money. A toddler is throwing a tantrum somewhere down the hallway. The shrieking echoes.

We move to the bank of elevators, too, and Melonhead isn't one of those guys who insists on pressing a button that's already lit. He smiles and says "Good afternoon" to the pregnant woman, but I can't look away from her swollen belly.

My mother is going to look like that.

My mother is going to have a baby.

My brain still can't process this.

Suddenly, the woman's abdomen twitches and shifts. It's startling, and my eyes flick up to find her face.

She laughs at my expression. "He's trying to get comfortable."

The elevator dings, and we all get on. Her stomach keeps moving.

I realize I'm being a freak, but it's the creepiest thing I've ever seen. I can't stop staring.

She laughs again, softly, then comes closer. "Here. You can feel it."

"It's okay," I say quickly.

Melonhead chuckles, and I scowl.

"Not too many people get to touch a baby before it's born," she says, her voice still teasing. "You don't want to be one of the chosen few?"

"I'm not used to random women asking me to touch them," I say.

"This is number five," she says. "I'm completely over random people touching me. Here." She takes my wrist and puts my hand right over the twitching.

Her belly is firmer than I expect, and we're close enough that I can look right down her shirt. I'm torn between wanting to pull my hand back and not wanting to be rude.

Then the baby moves under my hand, something firm pushing right against my fingers. I gasp without meaning to.

"He says hi," the woman says.

I can't stop thinking of my mother. I try to imagine her looking like this, and I fail.

I try to imagine her encouraging me to touch the baby, and I fail.

Four months.

The elevator dings.

"Come on, Murph," says Melonhead.

I look at the pregnant lady. I have no idea what to say. Thanks?

"Be good," she says, and takes a sip of her drink.

The elevator closes and she's gone.

Melonhead is striding away, and I hustle to catch up to him. We're on a patient floor now, and the walls are white and conversations are hushed. Monitors beep everywhere. I'm still in my school clothes, so I'm not too dirty, but he's been at the cemetery all day, and I keep waiting for someone to shoo him out of here.

A slim, dark-haired doctor is tapping keys on a computer built into the wall, and Frank walks right up to her, turns her around, and doesn't even wait for her to express surprise before planting a kiss right on her lips.

Clearly, it's a day for people to make me uncomfortable in all kinds of ways.

I turn away, trying to find something else to look at. The nurses. The crayoned pictures taped up along the wall of the nurses' station.

They're speaking in Spanish now, and I glance over awkwardly. I imagine their conversation.

What are you doing here?

Nothing really. I was in the area.

Who's the freak?

Just a murderer who hasn't been caught yet.

My stomach balls up in knots again. I shouldn't be here.

I just don't know where else I should be.

"DECK-lin. This is Carmen."

I snap back to reality and put a hand out, running on autopilot. "Hi," I say.

"Hello, Declan." She smiles at me. Her white coat reads *Dr. Melendez* over the right breast, but when she speaks English, her voice has no trace of an accent. "So you're the boy Marisol keeps telling me she's going to marry."

I cough. "Well. You know. We're taking it slow."

Her smile makes her eyes twinkle. "Frank tells me you're giving him a ride in the car you rebuilt? I'm impressed. I really thought that was a dying art."

"Nah. I don't think it's going anywhere."

"My neighbor said you picked out the problem with her

husband's car in less than thirty seconds. That's quite a talent."

I shrug, unsure what to say. "I guess I have an ear for it."

A nurse walks by and puts a hand on Dr. Melendez's shoulder. "Excuse me for interrupting," she says quietly. "You asked me to let you know when the test results for two-twenty-one were in."

Melonhead clears his throat. "We'll let you go."

"I'm glad you stopped by." She gives him another kiss, less impassioned this time. "It was nice meeting you, Declan."

"It was nice meeting you, too."

And then we're back in the elevator. Walking to the car. Pulling onto Jennifer Road.

"We went through all that for you to give her a kiss?" I say.

He shrugs. "What else do we have to do?"

Mow half the cemetery. But I don't say that. I glance over. "We spent more time with the freaky pregnant chick."

"Maybe one day you'll love a woman enough that a kiss will be worth all that trouble."

The thought draws me up short. I'm not sure why, but I'm caught between scowling and blushing. I expect him to tell me to head back to the cemetery, but neither of us says anything else.

I don't know where else to go, but I do know I'm not ready to head back there, especially if Juliet hasn't gone home. When I get to the stoplight by Route 50, Melonhead glances over. "Hungry?"

"No."

"Are you sure? My treat."

I look at him. "What is this? You give me hell if I check my phone when I'm supposed to be mowing, but now you want to stop for dinner?"

He shrugs. We drive.

"Who's the girl?" he says eventually.

"What girl?"

"The girl you were watching."

He might as well have punched me in the side. My chest caves in a little, thinking of Juliet. "No one. I know her from school."

"She used to come all the time. Now I don't see her much."

Juliet. Oh, Juliet.

I can see her first letter in my head, the words so full of pain that they inspired me to write back.

You can see it on her face. Her reality is being ripped away, and she knows it.

Her mother is gone, and she knows it.

There is agony in that picture.

Every time I look at it, I think, "I know exactly how she feels."

Did I cause that?

"Her mother died." My throat is closing up, and my words sound thick.

"Ah. So sad."

My vision blurs and fogs, just a little, just enough. I'm glad I'm not on the highway. "She died in a hit-and-run crash. The same night I got drunk and crashed my father's truck."

His voice is quiet, and I see him making the same connections we all did this afternoon. "Were you involved?"

My chest is so tight that I can't speak. I hit the turn signal hard, and we pull into a parking lot in front of a strip mall. Once I pull the parking brake, I can't look at him.

I fold my arms tight against my stomach, as if I can somehow ease this pain. "I don't know."

"And you're worried you were?"

"I don't know. I don't know what I am. I can't figure anything out."

He's quiet for a little while, and I listen to my breathing, trying to keep it steady.

When he speaks, his voice is low. "You don't have to figure it out on your own, you know."

"There's too much. It's too complicated now."

"My wife might be the doctor, but I'm not stupid, Murph. Give it a shot."

I inhale to tell him off—but instead, I tell him everything.

I start at the beginning, with the letters against the gravestone, how we started writing back and forth to each other. I tell him everything I told Juliet and everything I haven't told her, and describe how difficult it's grown to maintain separate storylines of my own life. I tell him about the night I found her on the side of the road, and how she seemed so convinced that I wasn't there to help her—and my willingness to let her keep on believing that.

I tell him everything about my father, and the auto shop, and secretly driving him around. I tell him about Kerry and how she died.

I tell him about my mother and Alan, and how I've turned into an outsider in my own home. I tell him about the pregnancy they've hidden from me, how every action they take ties her closer to someone else who will let her down.

I tell him about their wedding day. About the bottle of whiskey. About the crash and the jail cell and Alan's muttered comments about how I'm turning into my father. I tell him how badly I wanted to end it all, right there.

Frank is a good listener. He doesn't interrupt, and he doesn't say anything except for the occasional question to clarify a point.

Finally, I tell him about sitting around the lunch table, about how Rev told me off, and how Juliet needed to be taken to the nurse's office after learning the date I wrecked the truck.

When I'm done, darkness has begun its crawl among the buildings along Route 50. I feel wrung out and exhausted.

"That's a lot," he says when I fall silent.

I nod. "I knew the date," I say, finding it easier to speak now that I'm speaking to the darkness. "It was the first thing I noticed about her gravestone. But . . . I didn't know how she died. That came later. A lot later. And I didn't put those together until today."

"But you don't remember striking another vehicle?"

"I barely remember getting in the car."

His shadowed expression is thoughtful. "Do you know where her mother died? Or when?"

"No." I hesitate. "I know she was on her way home from the airport. In the evening."

"Where did you wreck? Would you have crossed paths?"

"I wrecked on Ritchie Highway. I have no idea."

"But it all happened in the same county?"

"Yeah. I guess."

He rubs at his jaw. "Well, the police aren't incompetent, Murph. If you wrecked in the same county, anywhere near the same time, I'm sure they would have investigated you playing a role in a hit-and-run. Especially if a woman died."

"The truck was destroyed. They had to cut me out of it. Mom said the only thing that saved my life was the seat belt because of the way the brick pillar collapsed onto the air bag. Maybe they couldn't tell if I'd hit someone else."

"There are still ways to tell. Paint marks, things like that. Don't you ever watch crime shows?"

For the first time all evening, some of the weight on my chest eases. "Really?"

"Yes, really." He pauses. "You could probably look up the mother. A fatal hit-and-run would have been in the news. They might have said what kind of car caused the crash, or at least what color."

His explanation is so reasonable, so matter of fact, that I want to sob all over the steering wheel and then do cartwheels across the parking lot.

But I don't.

There's still the rest of it.

"Do you mind if I give you a few thoughts about everything else?" says Frank.

I shake my head.

"Start heading back," Frank says. "I'll talk."

I shift into gear.

He doesn't make me wait. "I think your mother and her husband were wrong to keep a pregnancy from you this long, if they were doing it intentionally. But from what you tell me about the adults in your life, I'm not too surprised."

"I don't know what you mean."

"I mean your parents let you down when you were young, and they seem to keep doing it."

I spare a glance at him while I turn back onto the main road. "I still don't know what you mean."

"Damn, kid." For the first time, he sounds righteously angry. "You shouldn't have been driving your father around. Your mother shouldn't have let it happen. She shouldn't be letting you think it's your fault. I can't imagine expecting Marisol to cover up something like that. And even if I did, I can't imagine Carmen letting it continue. You said you don't know how to apologize to your mother for what you did on her wedding night—has she apologized to you for what she did?"

I shake my head forcefully. "She didn't—it was complicated."

"No. It is not complicated. It was a crime, and as far as I'm concerned, your mother bears as much responsibility as your father did." His accent thickens as his anger grows. "You're lucky you weren't killed. You were a child, Murph. And you're *still* a kid, but she's letting you walk around with this kind of guilt. You know why I think she doesn't visit your father? Because she doesn't want to face her own responsibility. As far as I'm concerned, she should be right there next to you mowing." He breaks off and swears in Spanish.

I keep the car between the lines on the highway, but inside I'm spinning out. No one has ever spoken up for me like that. Ever. I'm used to people holding me back, not stepping up in my defense.

Even if we're alone in the car, that makes a difference.

"It's not all her fault," I finally say. "When Kerry died—I think it killed something inside her."

"She still had you."

"That's not exactly a prize. I'm not easy to live with." I pause. "And I ruined her wedding. I don't think they'll ever forgive me for that."

Melonhead grunts. He's still pissed off.

That makes me smile, just a little.

"Thanks," I say.

He nods, but more like he's still thinking. "Does your stepfather know everything you told me?"

I snort. "Probably."

"But you don't know for sure?"

"What difference does it make?"

He looks at me, his expression hard. "That's an important question, Murph."

I open my mouth to go off—but then I realize that he's right. I try to realign everything I know about Alan, imagining all of our interactions without him knowing my part in our family's history. Mom and I have never talked about it. Not even once. I remember struggling for better grades, as if getting an A on a test would somehow make up for my failure to keep Kerry and my father safe. Keeping my room perfect. Doing every chore. Staying out of her way.

I remember how she didn't notice. How I stopped bothering.

By the time Alan entered our lives, Mom and I orbited different planets. I have no idea how much she told him about what happened.

Either way, I'm not sure it matters. I can't undo what I've done. None of us can.

"I agree with your friend," Melonhead says. "I think you should talk to your mother."

That strips the smile from my face. "I don't know what to say to her." I glance at the clock on the dashboard. "I'm probably going to catch hell for being out past the time my community service ends."

He pulls his phone out of his pocket. "Give me their number. I'll call them and explain you're working late."

Another ounce of weight lifts from my chest. He calls, and that's that. I'm not in trouble.

It's so simple. I think of Mrs. Hillard staring down at me. *If there's a problem, you can just tell me.* Or the way she accepted my explanation and let me complete the assignment in class.

"It *was* just one day," Frank says when he hangs up. "But you can't fix things with your mother or her husband if you continue on this path, right?"

At the mention of Alan, my thoughts darken. "I never wanted to fix things with them." I pause, and my voice is very quiet. "I wanted out. I screwed up."

"I don't know, Murph." We make the turn into the cemetery, and he hesitates, as if unsure of his next words. "I wonder if you're just telling yourself that."

I frown. "What?"

"I don't think you wanted to kill yourself."

I pull next to his car in the now-empty employee lot. "Didn't you listen to everything I just told you?"

"Yeah. I did. Maybe you wanted to *try* to kill yourself, but I don't think you wanted to actually do it."

"What's the difference?"

He opens the door and gets out, standing there, looking down at me. "You wore your seat belt."

I lock my eyes on the darkened windshield. I don't know what to say to that.

"Feel like helping me tomorrow night?" he says. "I'll have to work double to get those two sections done."

I like how he's asking me. He's not ordering me. I'm free to refuse.

I nod. "I'll come right after school. We'll get it done."

"Thanks, Murph." He swings the door shut, closing me in with a little less darkness than I started with.

CHAPTER THIRTY-FIVE

From: The Dark <TheDark@freemail.com>
To: Cemetery Girl <cemeterygirl@freemail.com>
Date: Tuesday, October 8   09:12:44 PM
Subject: DM

What happened? Are you okay?

Dad knocks on my door at half past nine, and I'm tempted to pretend I'm asleep instead of sitting here, staring at my phone, deliberating.

My light's still on, and if I don't answer, he'll come in here to check on me.

"Come in," I call.

He opens the door a few inches. "Do you feel like company?"

No. I feel like crawling under my bed and sleeping there for a month. I sat in front of her grave for hours, trying to write a letter.

The words wouldn't come.

I couldn't figure out the right way to say *I'm sorry for having a crush on someone who might have killed you.*

My throat tightens before I'm ready for it. If fate were a person, I'd punch her in the face.

Dad peers in at me, his eyes concerned. "Juliet?"

I rub at my eyes. I know he means well, but I can't do the father-daughter thing tonight. My emotions are shot, and my voice is, too. "I'm really tired, Dad."

"Okay." He nods. "I thought it might be too late. I'll tell them you're sleeping." He begins to slide the door closed.

Them?

My first thought is Declan and Rev, and my heart skips to quadruple time. "Wait!" I scramble forward on my bed. "Someone is here?"

He frowns. "What did you think I meant when I asked if you wanted comp—"

"I didn't understand." I can't get the words out of my mouth fast enough. I feel like I've taken a shot of adrenaline and espresso simultaneously. Maybe Declan is here to explain. To apologize. To convince me that there's some plausible way his criminal record is unrelated to my mother.

I shouldn't be this excited at the thought of him coming here, but I can't help it. Guilt is stabbing me, but so is intrigue.

I am the world's worst daughter.

I push the hair back from my face. It's a tangled mess from

the way the wind wove through the cemetery. "Who is it? What do they want?"

Now my father is looking at me like I'm nuts, and he's not too far off the mark. "It's Rowan, and she's here with a boy. I think he said his name is Brendan . . . ?"

"Brandon." Air rushes out of my lungs, deflating me before I have a chance to figure out whether I was enraged or excited at the thought of confronting Declan Murphy. "You can send them up."

"Darn right we're coming up," Rowan yells from somewhere downstairs. "You can ignore my calls, but you can't ignore Nachos BellGrande."

They clomp up the steps, and Dad gets out of their way. Rowan is ethereal and glowing in a white gauzy shirt that hangs over yoga pants. She's carrying a massive bag from Taco Bell. Brandon is wearing skinny jeans and an unbuttoned plaid shirt over a tee that reads *Bacon Is Meat Candy.*

They look like they've stepped out of the pages of a novel, an angel and her hipster sidekick.

I'm wearing pajamas, and I'm pretty sure makeup has dried in streaks on my cheeks.

Rowan drops the bag beside me on the bed, then climbs in next to me. "Oh, Jules. What happened? They said you fainted in the cafeteria. Why didn't you call me? How did you get home?"

"I didn't faint." I rub at my cheeks, which feel a little crusty from tears. "Vickers said it was a panic attack. She let me do independent study for the afternoon." It's the most sympathy I've gotten out of Vickers since the school year started.

Brandon starts pulling food out of the bag. He hasn't said anything, but he's making himself useful. I like that he's avoiding the fact that I'm basically a train wreck wrapped up in a comforter.

Considering which, I should probably put on a bra.

I swipe at my eyes and extricate myself from Rowan and the blankets. "I'm going to go put some real clothes on. I'll be right back." In a wave, the scent of the food finds me, and I realize that I haven't eaten dinner—on the heels of barely eating lunch. "Thanks for bringing food. I'm starving."

In the bathroom I wash my face and brush my teeth and twist my hair up into a clip. I grabbed clothes haphazardly, so I end up in jeans and a tank top, but it's better than looking ready to do Ophelia's mad scene.

When I return to my room, Rowan has made my bed, and they've got a buffet spread across the comforter. Soft music spills from my radio. Dad has brought up sodas.

I'm so blown away by their kindness that I want to burst into tears again. It's been so long. I don't deserve any of this.

"Your phone lit up a few times," Rowan says.

I pick it up and press the button.

TD: Seriously. Are you okay?

I unlock it and type quickly.

CG: I'm okay. Friends over. I'll write back later.

Then I lock the phone and shove it under my pillow.

Rowan has a plate of nachos, and she's watching me. "What was that all about?"

"I don't know."

"You don't know?"

I grab a plate and start piling it with chips and beef and cheese. "I don't know."

"Mystery boy?"

"There's a mystery boy?" says Brandon. He's taken my desk chair in the corner, and four tacos are piled in front of him.

"Sort of." I shovel a chip into my face. The Dark didn't answer my question from this afternoon—is that an answer in itself? Or was he just concerned and didn't feel the need to answer?

Declan is so confrontational that I can't imagine him dodging the question. When we were sitting in the cafeteria, he didn't back down from the question about the date—why wouldn't he face it head-on now?

Why wouldn't he tell me?

Unless The Dark isn't Declan Murphy at all. Which would also make sense. Sort of.

We all sit there eating quietly for the longest time. My radio continues cranking out tunes.

Finally, I speak into the solitude. My voice comes out very small but steady. "Declan Murphy wrecked his car on the same night my mother died. That's why I got upset at lunch. I think he might have been involved. He was drunk, and he blacked out."

Rowan stops with a chip halfway to her mouth. "Did you tell your dad? Did he call the cops?"

"I haven't told anyone." I hesitate. "I don't . . . I don't have all the details. What if it's not the same time? What if—"

"Do you have a computer?" says Brandon. "I could look it up."

I straighten. "You could look what up?"

"I have the password to the local beat crime feed."

Rowan leans into me and stage-whispers, "He is so handy to have around sometimes."

"You do?" I say. "How?"

"From my internship. I thought they'd change it or whatever, but they never did." He shrugs. "It's interesting. Sometimes I look. We could check it out. See if there are any details."

I have my dad's old laptop, so it's slow, but it works. I dig it out from under the pile of books on my desk and hand it to Brandon.

He looks at me over the screen while it's loading. "Do you want to get your dad?"

Dad seems to be slowly crawling out of the fog that still holds me prisoner. I shake my head. "Not yet. Not until we know something for sure."

It doesn't take Brandon long to log on to the system. "Date?"

My mouth is suddenly dry. Could this be happening? Could we solve her murder right here? "May twenty-fifth."

He taps at the keys, then frowns at the screen. "I see a hit-and-run report, but the victim last names are Thorne and Rahman. Who's Rahman?"

"She was taking a taxi home from the airport. Rahman would have been the driver," I whisper.

Until today, I've never given a moment's thought to the driver. Does he have a daughter somewhere, carrying around the same sense of loss that I feel?

Rowan takes my hand.

"The accident took place on Hammonds Ferry Road? In Linthicum?"

"Yeah."

He frowns a little. "That's weird. Hammonds Ferry Road isn't on the way to the airport."

"What do you mean?"

"I mean, it's sort of *close* to the airport. Maybe he had more than one passenger and had another stop first. Or maybe he went a long way to get a bigger fare. Maybe there was an accident on the highway so he took side streets—I don't know, and we can't ask him. It's just not the most direct way between here and there."

Weird. But like he said, not a complete anomaly.

Brandon is still talking. "It was after dark, and that's a more remote part of town, so no witnesses, no cameras. When the paramedics arrived . . ." He hesitates, and his expression says he's reading details I don't want to hear read out loud.

He waves a hand. "Here. Let me see if I can find that loser's police report, and we'll see if anything matches up."

He's not a loser. I almost say the words, thinking about my conversation with Declan about how people misperceive him—but considering what we're researching, I don't say anything at all.

Brandon taps at a few keys, reads, then taps at a few more. We're all so quiet that I can hear three even breathing rhythms over the music.

After a minute, Rowan says, "You're killing us here, B."

"I know, I know. I just want to be sure. There's a report that might be Declan Murphy, but all the names have been obscured. That happens when the perp is a minor. This covers the whole state, so give me a second."

The perp. I almost smile. Brandon's life map is firmly intact, not lying in shreds like my own.

After another agonizing minute, Brandon looks up at me. His expression looks sorrowful. "I don't know if this is good news or bad news."

My fingers grip Rowan's hard. It's a match. It has to be. I'm breathing so hard I'm going to hyperventilate. "Tell me. Just tell me. It's him. It has to be him."

Brandon shakes his head. "It's not him."

What?

What?

He turns the computer around. "Look. The first call about your mother's accident came in at seven forty-six. According to Declan Murphy's police report, he didn't get behind the wheel until eight-oh-one, and he didn't crash into that building until eight sixteen."

It's not him.

I'm relieved. I'm devastated. I don't know what I am.

I feel like I'm going to throw up the nachos. I clutch my hands against my stomach.

"I'm so sorry," Brandon whispers.

Now I understand what he meant about not knowing whether this was good news or bad news. It's not Declan—but the crime is still unsolved.

"Just—turn it off. Okay? Turn it off."

He does, and I spend a minute talking myself off the ledge. I'm in the same place I was yesterday. I haven't lost anything.

And even if Declan were guilty, that wouldn't have brought my mother back.

"Is that your mother's gear?" Brandon says, nodding at the pile in the corner. My morbid little shrine.

I have to clear my throat. "Yeah. Her editor keeps trying to buy it back from my dad, but . . ." I let that thought trail off.

Brandon's expression shows no trace of recognizing the sentimentality. "Did the cops search her memory cards?"

The question is so unexpected that it shakes off some of my sorrow. "What? No. Why?"

He shrugs. "I don't know. But I remember reading about a murder case that was solved because they found photos a woman had taken on her cell phone. Apparently she started taking pictures as the guy was stabbing her, and they were able to find him based on that. Like . . . what if your mom was able to take pictures of the vehicle getting away?"

Rowan is making slashing motions against her neck, kind of like, *Stop talking about murders while my friend is suffering,* but my mind is revving up to normal speed.

"Do you think that's possible?" I say.

He glances at the equipment again. "Maybe?"

"No," says Rowan.

We both look at her, and her eyes are a little wide. "Do you realize how implausible that sounds? That someone would be alive enough to take pictures as someone is speeding away, but to be . . . to be . . ." Her voice trails off as she looks at me.

"To be dead by the time the ambulance gets there," I finish.

"They wouldn't necessarily be speeding away," says Brandon. "It says the car would have sustained some damage. It's possible someone stopped to check their own vehicle. Or it took them a minute to back up and keep driving. This wasn't a simple side-swipe." He pauses. His expression is pained.

"Say it," I tell him. My voice is hollow, but I've imagined her death hundreds of ways—he's not going to tell me anything surprising.

"She didn't die on impact," he says quietly. "It says internal bleeding. Probably from the seat belt. There's nothing in here about a head injury." He swallows. "So . . . there might have been time. Especially if she had her wits about her."

There might have been time. If she had her wits about her.

My mother, the woman who strolls through war zones in an effort to bring worldly reality to the American dinner table.

Has the clue to solving her murder been sitting in the corner of my bedroom for the last four months?

Holy crap.

I stride across the room, pick up the bag with her digital cameras, and practically bash them against the wall to get the memory cards free.

"Easy. Easy." Brandon stops me, prying the cameras from my shaking fingers. "Let me do it."

He works the latches with practiced ease, sliding the cards free, and we return to Dad's laptop.

We wait for his photo program to load, and it takes so long that I almost want to go down to the basement and fire up the high-powered Mac Mom uses—*used*—for photo editing. It hasn't been turned on since she died—mostly because I know the screen backdrop is a photo of me as a baby, snuggled into her neck.

My eyes fog, and I tell them to knock it off. We have a mission here.

The program finally loads, and the pictures on the memory card appear in thumbnails across the screen.

"Whoa," whispers Rowan.

The photos are horrific. Dead children in the streets. Bloodied doorways. Dust and dirt and sweat and tears everywhere. Wailing women. Men with injuries so terrible that these pictures should never be seen at anyone's dinner table.

Brandon scrolls through them steadily, but he looks a little green, too. "These are amazing. Your mom was a badass."

I know exactly how talented she was. "Those are all work shots. Check the other memory card."

He ejects and inserts, and again we wait.

Anticipation writhes in my chest. This will be it. There will be something there.

I don't know why I'm such a glutton for punishment. It's a blank memory card. There's nothing there.

Nothing.

Brandon looks up at me. "Did she have another camera?"

I shake my head. "Two more field cameras, but they were her cheap backups. They were in her suitcase."

"What's that?" He points to where light glints off a lens poking from a canvas bag.

"It's her film camera. We don't have a darkroom. And I have no idea what's on there. I can't drop off shots of carnage at CVS."

"Mr. Gerardi does. Does it have film in it?"

I grab the canvas bag, and it rattles. This was her carry-on bag, and when I pull back the flap, I catch the scent of her hand lotion. Loss hits me in a wave, and I need to close my eyes.

Work, Juliet. There's time for emotion later.

It still takes me a moment. Brandon and Rowan wait, like the good friends they are.

When I pull the film camera free, I see the rest of my mother's effects. Tubes of lip balm. A tiny pack of tissues. The edge of her boarding pass, tucked into a side pocket. An old *Us Weekly* magazine.

A sad smile finds my face. I would have given her hell for that if I'd seen it. If that Saturday night had turned out the way it was supposed to.

I need fluff sometimes, Jules, she would have said.

A tear snakes its way down my cheek.

"Do you want me to take it?" Brandon says softly. "I can develop it and tell you."

"No." I shake my head. She didn't use the film camera for work very often, and when she did, her shots were powerful. Anything on here would have been her own personal pursuits. Something she would have found personally meaningful. I can't imagine her grabbing this camera to take shots of a car as it sped away—if she did that at all—but if anyone is going to develop these photographs, it's going to be me. I hug the camera to my body. "They're her pictures. I want to do it."

"Okay." He sits back.

"Thank you," I say quietly. "I'm glad you guys came over."

Rowan wraps her arms around my neck from behind. "That's what friends are for."

CHAPTER THIRTY-SIX

From: Cemetery Girl <cemeterygirl@freemail.com>
To: The Dark <TheDark@freemail.com>
Date: Tuesday, October 8   10:31:57 PM
Subject: Friends

Yeah. I'm okay. False alarm.

 Did you talk to your mom?

False alarm? *False alarm?* What the hell does that mean?
The green dot sits beside her name.

TD: What's the false alarm?
CG: Declan Murphy didn't do what I thought he did.

It takes everything I have—and I mean *everything*—to keep

from writing back JULIET IT'S ME TELL ME EVERY-
THING PLEASE I'VE BEEN SO WORRIED I DID THIS
TO YOU.

My hands are practically shaking on the face of my phone.

TD: What did you think he did?

CG: He got drunk and wrecked his car on the same
night my mom died. I was worried he was involved
somehow.

TD: And he's not?

CG: No.

She is killing me.

TD: How do you know?

CG: My best friend's boyfriend did an internship in a
newsroom over the summer. He still has access
to their crime beat database. He looked up both
incidents. The times don't match. Mom died before he
even got in the car.

Oh.

I don't know what I'm feeling, but it's not relief. It's not even
a hollow victory. I didn't kill her mother, but she has no closure. I
still haven't told her who I am—and now it's too late.

I feel like I should apologize, but I'm not entirely sure how.
Or why.

Another message appears.

CG: It was a long shot anyway. A coincidence.

TD: I guess their paths didn't cross.

CG: No.

TD: Are you okay?

CG: I don't know what I am.

TD: What can I do?

CG: Talk to me. If you don't mind.

The words speak to me in her voice. I keep seeing her panicked eyes when she matched the dates in the cafeteria. I want to call her. I want to reassure her. She's the fiercest girl I've ever met, but I want to sit in the dark and hold her hand to show her she's not alone.

TD: Mind? I could talk to you forever.

She doesn't respond for the longest time, and I wonder if she fell asleep.

TD: Knock knock.

CG: You made me cry.

TD: Most people say, "Who's there?"

CG: Now you made me laugh. Who's there?

TD: I didn't really have a joke prepared. Why did I make you cry?

CG: I was so worried you were him, and I was going to have to stop talking to you.

I freeze. I read that sentence over and over again.

I was so worried you were him.

I can't breathe. I have no idea what to say. This is a thousand daggers striking me all at once.

CG: Sorry. I'm a mess right now. Brandon—my best
friend's boyfriend—thought maybe there was a
chance Mom took a picture of the car getting away,
so we looked at her memory cards. It's been an
emotional night.

Tell me about it. I'm sitting here, choking on my heart.

At least she's turned the conversation. I can force my suddenly numb fingers to type.

TD: Find anything?
CG: Nothing on the memory cards. But I'm going to
develop her film tomorrow at school.
TD: Do you think there's a chance?
CG: I'm scared to think there's a chance.

My brain can hardly process the words she's typing. I want to tell her that I can barely stay awake, that we can talk tomorrow, but I literally just told her I'd talk to her all night.

Maybe I *should* look up some knock-knock jokes.

CG: Did you talk to your mom?

Oh, good, something else I don't want to talk about.

TD: No.

CG: Why not?

TD: Because I got home from work late, and my stepfather was practically standing sentry outside her door.

CG: And you can't tell him you want to talk to her?

Her question is innocuous enough, but knowing that she doesn't want to talk to me—the *real* me—turns her words more critical than I'm used to. It's like talking to Alan. I hear accusations of failure between every word. It makes me angry, like I'm only good enough for her to see one half of my life, but the other half—the *real* half—is too screwed up for a girl like her.

My thoughts are a mess of exaggerations and hyperbole, and I know it.

I did this. *I* did.

I ruined it. This is my fault.

It's one more weight on top of so many. I want to brace my limbs and throw them all off—but they're too heavy. I can't.

My fingers stab at the screen.

TD: It's complicated.

CG: It's only as complicated as you make it.

TD: Well, I guess I'm good at making things as complicated as possible.

With that, I close the app.

And delete it.

Then I curl in on myself and do everything possible to keep from screaming.

I have to stop breathing. That does the trick. I sit there in complete, still silence until my muscles are crying for oxygen.

I need to get myself together. My room is stifling, and I want to get out of here, but there's only one place I can go that won't have Alan calling the cops.

I pull up my texts and send another one to Rev. He's ignored the last twelve, but those were all variations of me telling him to stop being such a pain in the ass.

DM: Please, Rev. I need you.

He responds immediately.

RF: I'm here.
DM: Can I come over?
RF: Always.

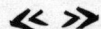

Rev is eating a bowl of Lucky Charms when I come in through the back door and find him in his kitchen. It's the kind of late-night snack usually reserved for potheads, but Rev has never smoked a joint in his life. When we were younger and our friendship was more evenly divided between our houses, Mom would keep a box on hand just for him.

He never eats sugared cereal for breakfast. He always treats them like a secret vice. Maybe it's a throwback to a childhood with a father who wouldn't let him eat Lucky Charms. Or maybe he likes the sugar. I've never asked him.

He pushes the box my way when I approach the table, but he doesn't look at me. He's still wearing the same hoodie he wore in school, which is unusual this late at night. I wonder if he hasn't taken it off, or if he put it back on when he knew I was coming over.

Either way, I have something to do with that. I don't like this feeling. I can't decide if I'm angry or ashamed.

"Hey," I say.

"Hey."

He still hasn't looked at me.

I don't sit down. "Still pissed?"

"Maybe. What's going on?"

"Juliet said she's glad I'm not me."

He takes a spoonful of cereal but still doesn't look up. "Maybe you could repeat that in English."

"She said she's glad I'm not Declan Murphy."

"I think I need more information." His eyes lift enough for him to nod at the cell phone in my hand. "Did she say this in an email? Read it."

"I can't. I deleted the app."

He gives a little laugh, but not like I'm being funny, then drinks the colored milk from his bowl. "Reinstall it. Let me see what she said."

"I just told you what she said."

"No, you gave me the Declan-ized version. I want to see what *she* said."

"What does that mean?"

Rev puts the bowl in the sink and finally looks at me fully. "Are you going to reinstall the app or not?"

His attitude is making me wish I hadn't come over here at all. "Not."

"Fine. Good night, then." He walks out, hitting the switch by the doorway. Leaving me in the dark.

I go after him, whispering furiously because I know Geoff and Kristin will freak if we wake the baby. "What the hell is your problem, Rev? If you have something to say to me, say it."

He doesn't stop walking. "I did."

"Would you stop and talk to me?"

He doesn't.

"Rev!"

In a second, he's going to be in his room, slamming the door in my face.

"Would you *stop*?" Without thinking, I go after him. I grab his arm.

Rev whirls and jerks free, shoving me away so forcefully that I hit the opposite wall. Picture frames rattle and swing.

His eyes are a little wild, but only for a moment. He blinks and the demons are gone. He's startled. Regretful. Ashamed.

"I'm sorry." My hands are up. I'll have a bruise tomorrow, but this is my fault. I know better. "I'm sorry."

The baby fusses, and we both freeze. After a second, she settles.

His parents' bedroom door opens, and Geoff leans out into the hall. "What are you boys doing?" he whispers fiercely.

"It's nothing," Rev says. "Go back to bed. We'll shut the door." He glances at me ruefully, and his voice is ironic. "Come on in, Dec."

In his room, Rev sits cross-legged on his bed, leaving me to take the desk chair. I straddle it and rest my arms on the back.

"Sorry," he says, his voice low. "I didn't mean to do that."

"My fault."

"No." He looks at me. "It wasn't."

"I shouldn't have grabbed you."

He shrugs, but tension radiates from his form. He's biting the edge of his thumbnail.

I frown and wheel the chair over to the end of the bed and rest my head on my arms. "What's the story, Rev?"

"I keep thinking about him."

His father. "Did something happen?"

"No."

"Do you want to talk about it?"

He finally looks away from his comforter. "Do you really think I'm a martyr?"

"No. Do you really think I am?"

"Sometimes."

Ouch. "I don't think I've ever heard you say 'damn' before."

He winces. "I shouldn't have lost my temper."

"I think you're allowed."

"No, I'm not. Would you reinstall the stupid app so we can talk about whatever you came over here for?"

"You're not allowed to lose your temper?"

His expression is pained. "Dec."

"Seriously, Rev, you're like the most laid-back person I know. If you don't go off on someone in the cafeteria once in a while, people are going to think you're inhuman. In fact, I was starting to worry."

He doesn't smile. He's quiet, locked inside his head.

I realize I'm probably in the running for the Most Selfish Friend award. And here I practically shoved my way into his room. For what? Because I don't have the balls to tell a girl who I am? *Boo-hoo, Declan.*

I edge the chair back a few inches. "Do you want me to go home?"

His eyes flick up. "No."

"Okay."

"But I do want you to reinstall the app."

"Rev—"

"Seriously. I need to . . . to . . ." His voice is tight, and he makes a circular motion with his hands. "Uncoil."

I hesitate, but he's watching me expectantly. "All right." I reinstall it.

There's an email waiting.

I can't make myself click on it. I can only imagine what it says. Her green dot is no longer lit. I toss the phone at him. "It's the most recent chat."

He tortures me by reading at the speed of someone who needs to look up every word in the dictionary.

After a few minutes, I want to grab it away from him. "You're killing me here, Rev."

"I was reading the earlier messages for context." He sighs and tosses my phone at me. "I agree with her. You *are* good at making things as complicated as possible."

"Do you think she hates me?"

"Which *you*?"

I wince. "Either one."

"No." He hesitates. "I think you need to tell her."

"You read what she said. She doesn't want to talk to me."

He shakes his head. "She said she's glad she doesn't have to *stop* talking to you."

"No, she said—"

"That's *exactly* what she said, Dec." His expression grows a bit angry. "Exactly. Verbatim."

"She said she's glad I'm not Declan Murphy."

"But you *are* Declan Murphy! *You are not two people.*" His fists are clenched, and his breathing has grown quick.

I shove my phone into my pocket and study him. "What is going on with you, Rev?"

He rubs his eyes. "I don't know. I'm just tired."

I think of how he sat in the hospital with me, saying nothing. His silence was more supportive than anything he could have said.

I don't know how to do that in return. Maybe I can offer something else, though. I pull out my phone and do a quick search, then turn it around and slide it across the bed.

He doesn't reach for it. "Did she send more?"

"No. It's a poem I had to read for English. Read it."

He looks up, and the expression on his face is exactly the one I'd wear if he suddenly said, *Hey bro, read this poem.* "What?"

"Just read it. I think you'll like it."

Because he's Rev, he doesn't give me a hard time. He picks up my phone and reads it.

His expression evens out. "You're right. I do like it." He slides it back to me, and for an instant, I think his face will crumple and he'll cry. His voice is a breath away from breaking. "But I don't feel like my head is bloody and unbowed. Not now."

The air feels weighted, like he's going to say more, so I wait.

"Lately," he says, more steadily, "I feel like everything is a test." He swallows. "And I feel like I'm getting closer and closer to failing."

"Like how?"

"I almost hit you in the hallway."

"I deserved it."

His eyes flare with anger. "No, you didn't!"

"Shh." I glance at the door. "Okay. I didn't. What's your point?"

"I almost hit you." He says this as if it's significant.

"And?"

"And what if I had?"

"People around school would probably want to shake your hand."

He glares at me. "Don't joke."

"You're worried that you almost hit me? I'm pretty sure I would have gotten over it."

"But what if I couldn't stop?"

I stare at him. This question is so incongruous of what I know of Rev that it's almost comical.

The expression on his face is anything but.

I wheel my chair back up against the bed. His voice has grown very quiet, so mine is, too. "You're worried that if you hit me, you'd keep hitting me?"

"Or anyone." He takes a breath. "When we went to Homecoming, everyone else made it look so easy. To have that kind of normal. But I'm so worried that one of these days I'm going to lose control. I don't . . . I don't know how it starts. And when it starts, I'm scared I won't know how to stop it."

Rev has never talked like this. When he does talk about his father or what he went through as a child, it's always in the vein of making sure no one ever does that to him again. Never a worry of him committing any kind of abuse toward someone else.

Rev is kind. Gentle. Geoff and Kristin open their home and their hearts to children from all walks of life—and Rev does, too. I see it every day. I envy it.

"You're not your father," I say to him.

"You're not yours, either."

And right there, in the middle of his own crisis, Rev knows exactly what I need to hear. This is why he's the perfect friend. And why I can't wrap my head around him thinking he could ever hurt anyone.

"Have you talked to Geoff and Kristin about this?"

"No." He rubs at his face again, and his eyes are damp. "I'm worried that they won't want me to stay here if something happens. I don't want to hurt any of the kids—"

"Rev. You will not hurt anyone. And they are your parents. They love you. Nothing is going to happen. I promise. Nothing."

He's quiet for a while, and I can see him rolling that around in his head. "But what if it does?"

Nothing is going to shake this loose right now. The thought has wormed its way into his brain and lodged there. I reach forward and hit his hand. "Then I'll keep you out of trouble. Like you do for me."

That seems to settle him. He looks across at me, then turns his hand to grasp mine, hard. "Deal."

CHAPTER THIRTY-SEVEN

From: Cemetery Girl <cemeterygirl@freemail.com>
To: The Dark <TheDark@freemail.com>
Date: Tuesday, October 8   11:19:27 PM
Subject: What happened?

If I upset you, I'm sorry. I didn't mean to.
    Please don't stop talking to me.

The morning air bites through my clothes when I cross Rev's yard into my own. The sun peeks between houses on the street, but frost glitters on the grass, the first hint of winter to come.

It's before six, so I ease my key into the lock, then put my shoulder against the doorjamb to keep it from creaking too loudly.

I might as well not have bothered. Alan stands in the kitchen, stirring a cup of coffee.

His eyebrows go way up. His eyes flick to the clock above the sink and back to my face. "Where have you been?"

"I crashed at Rev's."

"You've been gone all night?"

"Yeah." This conversation sounds like it's going south in a hurry, so I turn away, heading for the stairs.

Alan dogs me out of the kitchen. "You didn't tell anyone you were leaving?"

I keep right on walking.

He keeps right on following. "Declan." He grits out my name. "You stop right there. I want to talk to you."

I grab the bannister and swing myself onto the staircase— only to stop short when confronted with my mother coming down the stairs.

Now I'm trapped between them.

"Declan," she says.

For some reason, when I found out she was pregnant, I imagined she'd balloon overnight and start wearing massive, tentlike shirts with lace ties and long skirts. But this morning, she's in jeans and a pink T-shirt. Her hair is in a ponytail, and her skin is freshly washed.

My hand grips the staircase railing so hard that it's vibrating under the strain.

I don't know what to say to her. I swallow. My thoughts ricochet between the need to apologize for so, so much and the need to hear one from her.

My eyes flick over her form again. She's never been tiny, but she's not what you'd call fat, either. Mom-shaped, I guess. The shirt is loose, but not ridiculously so. If I hadn't been arguing with Alan in the ER two nights ago, I wouldn't believe she's pregnant.

But as I stand here staring, I notice she's a little more pale than usual. Instead of straining at the seams of her clothes, the jeans look a little looser than I'm used to.

"Are you okay?" I ask her.

She nods. Her mouth opens as if she's going to say more, but she must change her mind, because nothing comes out.

"What?" I demand, and she shrinks back a little.

Shame coils in my chest. I think of Juliet in the front seat of my car, pressing her back against the door. *You're pretty confrontational.*

"He was out all night," Alan says from behind me. "If you're not going to do something about this, Abby, then I will."

"Yeah?" I whirl on him. "And what are you going to do?"

"I can take your car until you learn a little responsibility."

He will have to knock me unconscious to get the keys. I struggle to keep my voice low and even so that doesn't become a real possibility. "You are not taking my car."

His arms are folded across his chest. "And maybe we can disconnect your phone, since you won't be going anywhere."

I hit the wall. The light fixture on the ceiling rattles. "I haven't done anything wrong!"

His eyebrows go up. "You don't think sneaking out all night is wrong?"

He says it like I was shooting heroin and gambling in South Baltimore. "I was at Rev's! Ask Geoff and Kristin!"

"You can't just walk out of here without telling anyone—"

I snort and move to shift past my mother. "Like you give a crap about me anyway."

She puts a hand on my arm. "Declan. Stop. He's not taking your car."

"Why do you always do that?" Alan says sharply. "You keep allowing this to happen, Abby. He needs to learn."

I ignore him. Her touch steals my strength. I stop on the staircase and look at her. My voice comes out rough and full of gravel. "Why didn't you tell me?"

Her eyes widen fractionally—but she doesn't answer.

"Why do you think?" Alan says, his voice tired. "After what you did at the wedding, you think we wanted to tell you about a baby?"

I jerk back, yanking my arm away from her. Anger constricts my chest, making it hard to breathe. Some small part of me had hoped that maybe this was as much a surprise to them as it was to me, but Alan's comment proves that the secrecy was very deliberate.

He moves closer to me, and I realize he's tracking my movement, like I'm a heartbeat away from shoving her down the stairs.

He thinks I'm a risk to my mother. To the baby. To their new attempt at a family.

Who am I kidding? I am.

"That night you were throwing up," I say to her. "You knew then."

She doesn't say anything, but that's answer enough.

"Replacing Kerry?" I say.

She flinches like I punched her in the gut. Her eyes glisten with sudden tears.

I hate myself right now.

"Maybe you should keep going," I say, continuing to move past her, finding no resistance now. "Maybe you'll get a boy next and you can replace me, too."

A sob breaks free from her chest.

Alan swears. "We should be so lucky."

His words are delivered with a viciousness that slices right into me. I move back down the steps as if walking underwater. I want to hit him so badly that my hands ache for the contact, but I keep my temper.

My mother says nothing. If we went at it, she'd cry and wring her hands and beg us to stop—but I have no idea whose side she'd be on.

That's not true. I know exactly whose side she'd be on. She proved that four years ago, when she let me get behind the wheel. She proved it last May, when she married this guy.

I think of my emails with Juliet, how she made me feel like my life was worthwhile, like I had something to offer. I think of my conversations with Frank and Mrs. Hillard, how, for a few minutes, they made me feel like more than just a loser with a record.

But the reality is here, *right here*, how two people who should have my back stand here driving me into the ground.

My chest is so tight I don't think I'll be able to breathe much longer.

"Give me your keys," Alan says.

"I didn't do anything wrong," I say again.

"You take every chance you get to do something wrong!" he roars. "You don't think about anyone but yourself, and when someone does something you don't like, you do everything you can to destroy it! Why the hell do you think we wouldn't tell you?"

Everything inside me turns to ice.

Mom pushes past me. She puts a hand on his arm. "Stop. Alan. Please. Stop."

But her voice isn't strong. It's weak, full of tears. She's not looking at me.

Maybe the tears do the trick, though. Alan swears and turns away, storming into the kitchen.

My body has gone numb. I'm frozen in place. I don't think I can move.

She turns around to look at me. I'm taller than she is, but now, standing two steps above her, she looks tiny. Microscopic.

I would give anything for her to close that distance. For her to talk to me. I want to fling my car keys and my phone at her feet. *Take everything*, I want to say. *I don't need any of it. I need* you.

But I don't get the chance. She turns around and follows Alan into the kitchen.

My legs don't want to hold me anymore. "I'm sorry," I yell, and my voice breaks. "I'm sorry, okay? I'm sorry I didn't drive him. I'm sorry I let Kerry go. I'm sorry."

She doesn't respond.

She doesn't come back.

They leave me there on the steps, alone.

CHAPTER THIRTY-EIGHT

From: The Dark <TheDark@freemail.com>
To: Cemetery Girl <cemeterygirl@freemail.com>
Date: Wednesday, October 9   07:22:04 AM
Subject: Talking

I don't know if I can keep doing this. You don't know anything about me. You don't know the real me. You only know what I've shared, but that's not the whole story. It's only a snapshot, just like your photographs. You've made a judgment of me based on the little you've seen, and I think it's all wrong.

I'm not a good person, Cemetery Girl. I'm not good at cultivating things, only destroying them.

You don't need me.

You deserve better.

I quickly close the email and go to the chat list. No green dot—his name has disappeared entirely.

WHAT.

I quickly type an email to him and send it.

The immediate response isn't what I'm expecting.

This user does not have a Freemail account. Please try again.

WHAT.

My chest is collapsing. He can't do this. *He can't do this.*

And I have no way to find him.

Like an idiot, I try to send him an email again.

Like an idiot, I expect a different response.

This user does not have a Freemail account. Please try again.

"Juliet? Are you okay?"

Mr. Gerardi peers down at me. Mom's canvas bag with her film camera is lying in a pile beside me, but I'm staring at my phone, trying to remember how to make my heart beat.

"Yeah." I cough. "Yes. I'm—" I choke and swallow and force my words to work. "I don't know what I am."

Keys jingle in his hand, and he reaches to unlock his door. "Do you want to come in? Are you here to work on the yearbook photos?"

"No . . . I . . . no." I need to get it together. I shove the phone into my pocket. "I wanted to see if I could use the darkroom."

He looks at the clock and grimaces. "I have a student coming to make up an exam in ten minutes."

"I know how to do it."

"I know." He sighs. "But I'm not allowed to leave students alone with the chemicals." He glances at the shoulder bag. "Do you want to leave it with me? I could run it through the developer, and you could come back later to make the prints."

I take a step back as if he were about to grab the bag from me. "No. I need to do it."

"Okay." He hesitates, and his expression softens. "Is that your mom's camera?"

"Yes."

"Do you want to leave her bag here? I could lock it up with my equipment."

I clutch it to my body. I've had it with me all morning, and it's like I can't get enough of the smell of the canvas and the hand lotion inside. It's like holding a piece of my mother.

I shake my head. "No." My voice is husky. "Thanks. At lunch, maybe?"

He winces. "Faculty meeting. I'm free after the final bell. Do you want to do it then?"

All day. I have to wait all day. I wasn't prepared for this.

My subconscious whispers that I've waited four months; another six hours shouldn't make a difference. My head bobs up and down.

"But come in for a minute." Mr. Gerardi flicks the lights. "I ran a few prints of that shot we want to use for the wrap. I wanted to show you."

The print is on glossy, legal-sized paper. He's cropped the original photograph for height so it would wrap around a yearbook well, but from what I can tell, he hasn't done any other editing.

"I know you might want to do some touch-ups, enhance the sky a bit," he says, "but honestly, I don't think it needs much.

I just needed a mock-up so we could get approval from the vice principal."

I stare down at the photograph. He's right—it doesn't need much. The sky is a vivid blue, with sparse clouds. Sunlight beams in from the left. Declan and Rev are visible with enough detail to see the expressions on their faces, though their clothes are turned dark by the light behind them. On the opposite side, the cheerleaders are a bright contrast in red and white, hair and skirts flaring dramatically. It's a great shot.

I want to feel pride, but compared with the horrifying shots Rowan, Brandon, and I were scanning through last night, this photograph is worthless.

Mr. Gerardi's eyes search my face. "What's wrong?"

"Nothing." I hand it back to him.

"You can keep that. I made a few."

"Oh. Okay." I don't know if I want to, but I roll it into a tube and put it in the side pocket of my backpack. I'm so off balance today, waiting to see what happens when the world stops spinning so wildly.

A hand knocks on the door frame, and a girl I don't know is standing there. She must be the other student he's expecting. I duck out of the room.

As soon as I'm down the hallway a bit, I fish the phone out of my pocket again. The Dark's name is still missing, and another email comes back unread. Why would he do this? What happened? What changed?

I go back and read through our stored chats.

I read them a second time.

I realize he never directly answered my question.

I need to find Declan Murphy.

We don't have any classes together, so I don't find him until lunch. He's sitting at the back of the cafeteria at the exact same table where I found him yesterday, and Rev has a near-identical spread of plastic containers.

After yesterday, brazen Juliet is gone, and I hover by their table like a nervous groupie.

Rev glances my way first. Today's sweatshirt is a very dark rust color, and the hood is larger, shadowing his face.

"Hey," he says.

Declan barely spares me a glance. He stabs his fork into a piece of cucumber. "Want to scream at me some more?"

I swallow. I didn't expect this kind of reaction. I don't know why not—he's right. I did go postal yesterday. For some reason I thought I'd walk up and he'd say, "Oh. Hey. You figured me out. Sorry I deleted my secret email account."

Instead, he bites the cucumber off the fork and glares at me. "So far we've covered drunk and murderer. Any other accusations you want to throw my way?"

Rev glances across at him but doesn't say anything. I can't tell if they're still fighting, or if the atmosphere is only tense because I've showed up.

The strap of my mother's bag is thick and damp under my sweating fingers. "I didn't call you a murderer."

"Close enough."

This isn't going anything like what I expected. "Could you please stop being such a jerk and talk to me?"

"Why?" He stands up from the table and approaches me. "What do you want to talk about, Juliet?"

He looks so predatory. The moments of vulnerability I've glimpsed in the past are locked down, nowhere to be found. This is the Declan Murphy everyone sees.

"What do you want?" he says.

I want to know if you're The Dark.

But I can't say it. I don't want to know, not right now. I can't bare myself in front of this Declan, especially if I'm wrong.

"I'm sorry," I say softly.

He leans in, his expression incredulous. "What?"

"I said I'm sorry." I study him. His eyes are dark, like he didn't sleep much last night, and his skin is rough with stubble. He never bothered to find a razor this morning. A small part of me wants to touch him, to put a hand against his cheek and feel his warmth—or share my own. I shift closer. "I'm sorry for what I said."

His walls don't crack. "What do you want from me?"

"What?"

"I said, what do you want from me? Your car runs. You don't need me. What are you even doing here? Slumming it with the rejects?"

"That's not what I'm doing."

"I think it's exactly what you're doing."

"Dec." Rev's quiet voice speaks from behind him. "Don't take it out on her."

Declan stares down at me, his breathing a little quick. I stare back at him. Despite all the anger, the aggression, electricity sparks between us. Once again, I wish so badly for him to be The Dark—but at the same time, the thought terrifies me. My hand almost aches to touch his, as if skin against skin will somehow solve the mystery.

"Here," I say quietly. "I brought you something."

He blinks. That throws him.

I pull the rolled photograph out of my backpack and hold it out.

He unrolls it, and blue sky on paper stretches between us. Declan is very still, his eyes on the photograph.

After a minute, he lets go, and it furls back into my hand. "If Rev wants it there, it's fine."

"Do *you* want it there?"

"I'm done with lunch." He grabs his backpack and walks away.

I follow him. "Please stop. Please talk to me. I need . . . I need—" My voice breaks. Tears fill my eyes, and I'm not ready for all this emotion.

I need you.

But I can't say that. I'm not even entirely sure it's him I need or if it's someone else.

He's not completely heartless. He stops. Turns. Looks at me. For the first time today, his eyes are heavy with feeling. I remember the same expression on his face when he held the weighted punching bag. *You're exactly as strong as I thought you were.*

I would give anything for him to touch me right now.

He doesn't. "I'm sorry, too," he whispers.

Then he turns around and walks out of the cafeteria, leaving me alone in the middle of a swarm of students.

CHAPTER THIRTY-NINE

INBOX: CEMETERY GIRL

No new messages

Every time I tell myself I'm not going to check my phone again, I do anyway. Not being able to email him is causing me physical pain. I grieved my mother's death, but this is a different kind of loss. A deliberate removal. I've reread his final email until I could recite it by heart.

You don't need me.

I *do* need him. I do.

I need him right now, while I'm sloshing chemicals in a light-safe tank, saturating my mother's film. It's been a long time since I've done this, and Mr. Gerardi is hovering. We had to start the process in complete darkness, winding the film onto a metal spool, but once it was in the tank, he flicked the lights back on and poured the developer in.

My heart beats so fast that my chest aches.

"Do you know what's on the film?" Mr. Gerardi says.

I shake my head quickly. I haven't told him about Brandon's theory about the hit-and-run, because I'm worried he'll stop the process and call my father.

I clear my throat and find it hard to speak around my galloping heartbeat. "They might be graphic."

Mr. Gerardi's eyebrows go way up, and his hand stops mixing the stop bath. "Graphic?"

I blush furiously and choke on nervous laughter. "Not like that. War zone shots."

"Oh." He nods and continues pouring chemicals.

"But they could be anything. Film was her hobby."

"I remember."

Of course he does. I used to spend more time in Mr. Gerardi's classroom than anywhere else in the school.

He keeps his eyes on the chemicals as he measures. "What exactly brought this on?"

"I don't know."

He's quiet, and he doesn't look at me. My words float there in the silence for a while, until guilt begins to prick at me. I *do* know, and he knows I know, and he's waiting for me to fess up.

"Brandon came over last night," I say quietly. "He had a theory that she might have gotten a picture of the car that hit her. We checked her memory cards, but . . ."

"Nothing there?"

344

I shake my head. "Just shots from her last assignment."

He straightens and looks at me. "I wish you'd told me this morning. I didn't realize—"

"No . . . it's okay." I shrug and fiddle with her empty camera, sitting on top of her canvas bag. The lens cap is worn in spots from the pressure of her fingers taking it on and off. "It's a long shot."

"True. But either way, it might be nice to see what her final photos were."

"Maybe." I swallow.

The timer goes off, and I pour out the developer, and he stands ready to pour the stop bath into the tank. I'm out of practice, but it's like riding a bicycle. I pour, he pours, and the lid goes on with a snap. He inverts the tank, and again we wait.

"Have you given any more thought to coming back to class?" he says quietly.

I shrug and start lining up the trays.

"How did it feel to shoot the Fall Festival?"

At the time, it felt like torture. But this morning, studying that photograph of Declan and Rev and the cheerleaders, I was reminded of how much I love photography. The chance to capture a moment of time, forever. Even if no one in that photograph ever saw anyone else after high school, that moment of friendship and separation was already immortalized.

"It felt . . . okay."

He waits, but I don't say anything else. He gives me teacher eyebrows. "And . . . ?"

"And . . . I don't know."

"Do you miss it?"

"Sometimes."

He nods, then studies me. "Does it make it painful, to know this is something you shared with her?"

"No. It's painful to know I'll never be able to do what she does. It makes it all feel so pointless." I freeze with my hand on a tray. That's more than I wanted to say. More than I think I've ever admitted to myself all at once.

He stops measuring chemicals for the trays and peers at me. "Pointless?"

I blush because it might sound like I'm insulting his career. I don't know how else to explain it. "She was making a difference with her photography. I can't do that. I can't go to Syria and walk through bombed-out buildings. I can barely drive through the city."

"Juliet, you're seventeen years old. That's nothing to be ashamed of. I think you'd have a hard time walking down the street and finding *anyone* who would have the physical and mental fortitude to do something like that. And just because you can't do it *now* doesn't mean you can't do it *ever*."

I stare at him, fiddling with my fingers. I don't know what to say.

He sets the bottles down and turns to face me fully. "My brother is a firefighter. I have no idea how he can walk into burning buildings—but he tells me he has no idea how I can stand in front of teenagers all day. Just because someone isn't risking their life doesn't mean their life's work is . . . *pointless*."

"I didn't mean it that way."

"I know you didn't mean it as an insult, but think about what you're implying here. Say you give up photography, which is your right. But . . . then what? What profession are you going to find that would live up to this vision you have of your mother's?"

I don't know. I've never thought about that. I've only thought about how I can't be *her*.

Mr. Gerardi keeps talking. "My wife is also a photographer. She takes pictures of babies. That's it—just babies. Do you think that's pointless?"

I swallow. "No." I hesitate. "But it's not life-changing for anyone."

"Are you kidding? Have you ever looked at a baby photo? As a parent, I'm telling you that having your children captured in a photograph is a true gift. The time goes so fast."

Mom's computer flashes in my mind, her desktop background featuring me as a baby, snuggled into her neck. My breathing hitches.

"I don't want to upset you," Mr. Gerardi says quietly.

"No. You're not." But he is. A little.

"Wait here," he says. He disappears for less than a minute. When he comes back, he's got a photo on his phone. In the picture, a woman is pressing her lips to the forehead of a newborn baby. Light comes from somewhere, and the baby's fuzzy hair gleams like a halo.

"My wife took this picture," he says.

"It's beautiful."

"The baby died," he says quietly. "Less than two hours later.

They hired my wife to document the birth, but he was born with a severe heart defect."

"Okay," I say, feeling my throat constrict. "Okay."

He shoves his phone in his pocket. "Have you ever heard of Humans of New York?"

I shake my head.

"A man named Brandon Stanton started a website where he'd take photographs of people in New York City and ask them a question, then publish their photo with what they said. Somehow people tell him their darkest secrets, their most painful memories—and they allow him to publish them online. His pictures have been seen by millions of people. *Millions*, Juliet. Millions of people have been affected by his photographs—and it was all because one guy started wandering around New York, taking pictures of strangers."

"But I'm not like that," I whisper.

"Maybe not yet. But you will find your own way to make an impact."

The timer rings, and he turns away to flick the light switch. The overhead lights go off, replaced by the red lights. He unloads the film and begins unwinding it. "Do you want to start at the end? Maybe do the last five shots?"

My heart is jumping around again, unable to settle after everything he's said. "Um. Sure."

He cuts the film and holds up the strip, but it's impossible to tell what might be on it now. We'll put the strip into the enlarger, shine it onto paper, then float the paper in chemicals to bring the images out.

"I could be wrong, but I don't think these shots involve a car," he says quietly. "It looks like a person."

My brain starts jumping up and down with *maybe*s. Maybe it's the person who hit her! Maybe she took their picture! But reality is heavy and stomps on those thoughts. I sigh.

He glances at me. "Do you want to stop?"

"No. We've come this far."

Once we've projected the images, we set the photo paper into the baths I've prepared. My heart trips along, and I remind myself to breathe.

"You know," Mr. Gerardi says, "there are some people who might not think your mother's job is all that brave at all."

I flash irritated eyes his way. "Like who?"

"Like the soldiers there to fight the wars."

Oh. I use tongs to make sure the paper is fully submerged. An image is beginning to appear. I know I can't rush it, but I want to.

"I'm not insulting your mother," he says. "Not at all. Her work is amazing, and important."

Yes. It is. There's no easy way to compare my mother to anyone. It's like the difference between my mother and my father. The difference between color photography and black-and-white. Vibrant rainbows versus shades of beige.

That's what makes this so difficult.

Lines begin to appear on the paper. I still can't make out much of anything.

My throat tightens. These were her last shots. Possibly some of her final moments. It's a chance to see through her eyes.

I look at Mr. Gerardi. "Can I . . . can I finish developing them alone?"

He hesitates, glancing at the baths again. He's not allowed to leave me with the chemicals, but I was once a special student with special privileges. I think of his precious Leica. Maybe I still am.

"Please?" I whisper.

He sighs. "Okay. I'll walk down to the teachers' lounge and get a cup of coffee." He hesitates. "Are you sure you want to be alone?"

I nod and swipe at my eyes. The image is becoming clearer. Wild hair, the slope of an arm.

Mr. Gerardi slips through the door, and the latch clicks. I'm alone. Silence presses around me.

My eyes blur, and I blink to clear them. The image has processed.

I have to blink again. My mother smiles up from the photograph, her eyes bright, her hair a wild mess of curls and tangles.

She's naked. She's in a bed. An arm covers one breast, but the other is unashamedly bare.

I stop breathing.

The next tray develops. Another of my mother, still naked. She's laughing in this one, reaching for the camera.

The next tray. A tangle of arms. A blurred neck, some dark hair. The edge of a jaw.

The tears go cold on my cheeks.

The next tray. Mom laughing and struggling, a muscled arm around her neck, trying to pull her into the photograph. An old-fashioned selfie, taken with a camera instead of a phone. The other face is mostly cut off, but my eyes lock on that muscled arm.

It's not my father's.

The next tray. This selfie caught them both. I seize the picture with my hands, ignoring the chemicals that drip down my forearms.

It's Ian. Mom's editor. He's shirtless, holding her against him. Her face is turned up, nuzzling into his neck.

I think of my father, moving through a fog for months.

She was cheating on him. *She was cheating.*

I pick up her camera and throw it at the door as hard as I can. Glass and plastic explode and tinkle across the floor.

How could she? Her bag is sitting open in front of me, and the smell of her lotion mixes with the chemicals. How could she do this to him?

I grab the lotion and throw it after the camera. I'm sobbing. I hate her. I hate her.

I seize her tissues. I press the pack to my eyes and then fling it. *I hate her.*

I grab the boarding pass, wanting to tear it into shreds, crumpling it. The folded corners press into my skin. I want to slice into all of my skin if it will take the edge off this pain.

She was cheating.

I feel like she was cheating on me, too. Her love was supposed to be for *us*. Not someone else.

"How could she?" I whisper.

I stand there and sob into my hands. Mr. Gerardi is going to find me like this, sobbing into her boarding pass.

The thought is enough to jerk me back to the present. Shards of glass and plastic litter the floor, glittering in the red lights. Chemicals have splashed everywhere. Mr. Gerardi is going to freak. I smooth out the thick paper, as if that will somehow put everything back the way it was. The boarding pass is a wet mess, but the date is in huge letters, right in the middle.

WEDS MAY 22

Wait.

There's no mistaking it, though. The characters are almost an inch high.

WEDS MAY 22

I blink a few times, as if my tears could have somehow turned "SAT" into "WEDS" or "25" into "22."

My breathing stops again.

I flatten the boarding pass again and press it against the edge of the table. There must be some mistake. This must be an old one. This must be for some kind of connecting flight.

It's not an old one. This was her flight home.

Three days earlier than we expected her. Three days before she died.

All of a sudden, Brandon Cho's voice echoes in my head.

Hammonds Ferry Road isn't on the way to the airport.

She came home early, exactly like I'd begged her to do. She came home three days early.

Just not to be with us.

CHAPTER FORTY

From: Elaine Hillard - HAMILTON ENGLISH
<EHillard@AACountyPublicSchools.org>
To: Murphy, Declan
<Declan.Murphy@AACountyStudentMail.org>
Date: Wednesday, October 9   03:11:53 PM
Subject: Invictus

Declan:

I've had a chance to read your in-class essay regarding "Invictus," and I'd like to discuss it. Would you have time to stop by my classroom tomorrow morning before homeroom? I'll be in my classroom by 6:30 a.m.

Sincerely,

Mrs. Hillard

I read the email while mowing, because Frank will go off at me if I stop. Then again, after yesterday, maybe not. But after weeks of emails from Cemetery Girl, this one is kind of a downer. Nothing says *awesome day* like meeting with an English teacher at six thirty in the morning.

I shove the phone back in my pocket and slide my hand into my glove.

For the twenty-fifth time today, I wish I could return to that moment in the cafeteria. I wish I could tell Juliet. I wish I could hold her and whisper the truth.

Instead, I'm stuck on a mower, unsure if she'll ever speak to me again.

Unsure if I'll ever sleep at home again.

Rev said that Geoff and Kristin will let me sleep there for a few nights, but they think we should all sit down with Mom and Alan and talk things out.

The thought makes me want to avoid Rev's house almost as much as my own.

I apologized. I apologized, and my mother said nothing.

That put a vise around my chest that refuses to loosen.

The sky is overcast, bringing a light drizzle to the cemetery, but I don't mind the rain trickling down into my shirt. The weather keeps people away, making my job easier. Music pours into my headphones, deafening me as effectively as the mower.

A flash of motion to my right draws my attention, and I look up from the monotony of grass and gray granite. A girl is running across the cemetery.

Juliet.

Panic flashes through me. She must have figured it out. She's coming to confront me.

But no. She skids in the wet grass and falls in front of her mother's grave. She's across the field, but even from here, I can see her face is a mask of anguish and pain.

She's screaming.

She's punching the gravestone.

I turn the key and kill the mower. And then I run.

By the time I get to Juliet, her fingers are bleeding and swollen. Tears streak her face, and her voice has gone hoarse. I can't understand what she's saying through her sobs, but she barely recognizes I'm there. She slams her hand into the gravestone again.

I grab her and wrestle her back, pulling her against me. "Juliet. Juliet, stop."

Her rage is so pure I expect her to struggle and fight to get back to her assault on the gravestone. Instead, she collapses against me, sobbing into my chest. Her hands clutch my shirt like it's a lifeline.

"It's okay," I say, even though it's so obviously not. I hold her tight, whispering against her hair. I pull my work gloves off with my teeth and stroke her back. "It's okay."

Cold rain has formed a mist through the cemetery, offering us the illusion of privacy. The scent of cut grass hangs thick in the air, mixed with the scent of Juliet, cinnamon and vanilla or something warm.

When the worst of her tears seems to subside, I lower my head to speak along her temple. "Do you want to sit down?"

She sniffs and shakes her head fiercely. "Not near her."

"Okay. Here, then." I pull her back a few yards, to an older gravestone that's never seen a visitor in the time I've been here. We sit and lean against the back of the stone.

She hasn't stopped clutching me. Even when we sit, she leans against me, a warm weight against my side. Light rain trickles through the clouds to chill my face and mix with her tears.

"Do you want to talk about it?" I say.

"No." She swipes at her face.

"Okay." I look down at her. Enough rain has collected in her hair to fill it with droplets of light. Mascara runs down her cheek in a long stripe. Her weight against me is both the best thing and the worst thing I've ever felt in my life.

I reach up and stroke a finger along that line of makeup.

She sighs and closes her eyes. "I wish I hadn't done it." Her voice breaks and she starts crying again.

"Shh." My lips brush her temple. I would hold her in this cemetery forever. "What do you wish you hadn't done?"

She straightens a little and pushes rain-damp hair away from her face. Her fingers are shaking. All of her is shaking. "My mother was a photographer. I developed her film. The pictures she took before she died. I wish I hadn't."

That's right. She was going to do that today.

My knee-jerk reaction is to play this the way I've played everything else, putting up a front like I don't know every detail of her sorrow from the other side of an email conversation.

But I can't do that. Not with her tears soaking into my shirt.

I brush a strand of hair away from her eyes. "What did you find?"

Her face crumples, and she presses her face into my shoulder. I expect a fresh round of tears, but she breathes through it and speaks into my shirt. Her voice is very small. "She was cheating."

"She was what?"

"She was cheating. On my father. She came home three days earlier than we thought."

Oh. Oh, wow.

"So the pictures . . ."

"I didn't know what to expect, you know? I thought maybe they'd be shots for work, or maybe some interesting people she met. She'd do that sometimes, take pictures of people who caught her eye, not because she thought they belonged in the *New York Times*, but because she thought they deserved to be captured on film."

"But they weren't."

"No." She snorts, and it's partly a sob. "They were shots of her in bed with her editor."

My eyebrows practically hit my hairline. "In bed? Like—"

"In bed. Naked. No mistake."

"Naked?"

"Yes. Naked."

"Wow."

"I hate her." The words fall out of her mouth like daggers. She's tense against me now. Rage is building, replacing the misery.

"You developed the pictures at school?"

She nods stiffly against me.

"Was a teacher there?"

"No. He went to get coffee so I could develop them alone."

"I bet he would have crapped his pants."

She giggles in surprise. It's a good sound, and I'd give anything to make her laugh again, especially now.

"Probably," she says. She straightens to look at me, and her expression sobers. We sit in the mist, breathing the scent of rain and cut grass.

I want to reach out and pull her against me again.

I can't. I have no idea how much she knows, and the *not* knowing is killing me.

Tell her. Tell her. Tell her.

Before I can, she shifts away, sitting up against the gravestone. It puts an inch between us, but it might as well be a mile. "God. I don't know what I'm going to tell my father."

"Do you have to tell him anything?"

"I don't know." She turns to look at me, and her mouth is a hand's width away from mine. "It seems unfair to tell him— but it seems unfair to watch him mourn a woman who doesn't deserve it."

"None of it's fair, Juliet." I shake my head and think of Alan. "None of it."

"I know." Her voice is soft, her eyes heavy with resignation.

"I know you know."

"If it were your father, would you tell him?"

She's still so close, and her words are so intimate, it's like our exchanges as Cemetery Girl and The Dark. I could close my eyes and forget our real lives and talk to her forever.

"Yes," I say.

She snorts and looks away. "Of course you would. You're not afraid to tell anyone anything."

I go still, unsure if that's an insult or a compliment.

Unsure if what she's said carries any truth at all.

Rev called me a martyr for not reaching out last May, when I sat in that police station, terrified when the officers said that no one was coming for me until the next day. But there's only so much rejection you can take before you finally give up and stop trying.

Or maybe me thinking that is exactly what he means.

Juliet looks back at me and swipes at her cheeks. "I'm sorry I lost it."

I look at her like she's crazy. "You don't have to apologize for that."

"I know . . ." She hesitates, then finds courage. "I know you don't want to talk to me anymore."

I stare into her eyes. Is she talking to *me*, or is she talking to The Dark? I have tangled this up so thoroughly that I have no way of knowing.

Tell her.

"Oh, Juliet," I say softly. I rake a hand through my hair. "That's not it at all."

She rotates until she's sitting on her knees, putting her eye to eye with me. "Then what is it?"

"We're traveling different paths," I say. "And yours will lead you out of this mess. Mine seems determined to run me into the ground."

She goes very still. A breeze runs through the cemetery and cuts between us. Her eyes narrow, just a little, and she looks at me carefully. "How did you know I was here?"

"I didn't. I saw you." Heat finds my cheeks, and I point at the mower. "I work here. Sort of."

"Community service." There's no judgment in her voice.

I find her eyes and wish this moment could stretch on forever. "Yeah."

"Juliet!" A middle-aged man is running across the cemetery, slipping on the grass a bit. "Juliet!"

She scrambles to her feet. "Dad!"

Even from fifty feet away, the relief on his face is visible. "Oh thank god," he calls. "Thank god."

"What's wrong?" she says. Tears are in her voice again.

Then he gets to us, and he sweeps her into his arms. "Your teacher said you left a mess and ran out of there. We've been so worried. I was going to call the police."

He's holding her so tight, and Juliet is crying. "I'm sorry, Dad. I'm sorry."

"It's okay," he says. "It's okay. I've got you now. We can go home."

I take a step back, away from them. I'm on the outside, looking in. A real family on display right here in front of me. I'm pretty sure her dad isn't going to get her home and crack open a case of beer—or start telling her that he's counting the minutes until she ends up behind bars.

I stoop and fetch my gloves from the ground. Frank is going to come around here any minute and start going on about how we're losing light.

"Wait!" Juliet pulls away from her father, and once again, she's breathless and looking up at me. "Declan."

I hold myself at a distance. The spell is broken. "Juliet."

She closes that distance, though, and then does one better. She grabs the front of my shirt and pulls me forward. For half a second, my brain explodes because I think we're going to have a movie moment and she's going to kiss me. And then it's going to be super awkward because of her father.

But no, she's only pulling me close to whisper. Her breath is warm on my cheek, sweet and perfect.

"We were wrong," she says. "You make your own path."

Then she spins, grabs her father's hand, and leaves me there in the middle of the cemetery.

Dusk cloaks the streets when I finally leave the cemetery, and the drizzle seems to be keeping people off the roads. My heart can't find a steady rhythm in my chest and instead seems content to alternate between lighthearted skipping and drunken stumbling. I'm heading for Rev's, but adrenaline races beneath my skin in short bursts. Everything feels undone, a scattered mess of emotions that keep drifting away when I try to gather them into some kind of order.

You make your own path, she said.

I've been thinking about that since she left with her father, winding it up with Rev's martyr comment, and letting it spin through my thoughts. *We were wrong.*

A car ahead sits on the shoulder, flashers blazing through the mist. Déjà vu hits me square in the chest—this is right where I helped Juliet.

Then I realize I recognize this car, too. It's a silver sedan that tries to be pretentious but fails miserably, like the guy wanted a BMW but could only afford a Buick.

I know this because it's Alan's car.

He's standing beside the car, on his cell phone, looking down at the hood.

For a tenth of a second, I think about running him over.

Okay, maybe a full second.

Steam is escaping from beneath the hood. Alan looks up as I approach. His face looks expectant. He must be waiting for a tow truck.

I see him recognize my car. I see him wait to see if I'll stop.

I see a big target in khaki pants and a button-down shirt.

His words from this morning pelt my skin as if he's shooting me with a pellet gun.

I think about how I stood on those stairs and apologized, and they said nothing. They did *nothing.*

I clench suddenly shaking fingers on the steering wheel and keep going.

And then, out of nowhere, a line from that stupid poem pops into my head.

I thank whatever gods may be for my unconquerable soul.

I brake and turn around at the next cross street. My heart keeps cranking along in a syncopated rhythm, and I'm not sure if I'm going to help Alan or if I'm going to punch him in his stupid face.

When I pull over and stop behind his car, his eyes register surprise, but he's good at tamping it down. His phone is still pressed to his ear, and when I step out of my car, he shoos me off with his hand.

"I'm fine," he calls. "Go ahead."

He is such a prick.

I head toward him anyway. Steam continues curling from beneath the hood. The idiot hasn't even turned the car off. "Do you want me to take a look at it?"

"I'm on the phone with the auto club right now."

"So, what? You're going to stand out in the rain for two hours? Pop the hood, Alan."

He puts a hand over the speaker. "Go on home, Declan. I don't need you."

"Trust me. I got the memo." I open the door to his car anyway and pull the lever to pop the hood. Then I turn the keys to kill the engine.

When I straighten, Alan is right there. The phone is gone from his ear.

"What are you doing?" he demands.

"I'm stealing your car," I tell him. "Call the cops."

He sets his jaw and glares at me, but I step around him and lift the hood. Steam pours from the engine and we both have to step back, waving it away.

Then we both stand there, staring at the engine.

In a flash, I remember standing like this with my father. He'd quiz me and clap me on the shoulder when I got everything right. Then he'd call to one of his buddies in the shop and tell him to come listen to "the kid" rattle off the engine components of a 1964 Thunderbird. I still remember what it felt like to be a part of something.

I can't remember the last time I felt that way.

Alan clears his throat. "See anything?"

"Yeah. I see a blown top radiator hose." I point to where the black rubber has obviously cracked open.

"So I need a tow truck anyway." He sounds a little smug.

"Sure," I say. "If you want to pay a mechanic three hundred bucks. All you really need is twenty dollars and an open Auto-Zone. I could fix it in ten minutes."

He studies me. His jaw twitches.

This is *killing* him.

I wish I could say I was loving this. I'm not. I'm exhausted.

"Come on, Alan. I spent the last three hours working at the cemetery. Do you want my help or not?"

He doesn't answer right away, but some of the apprehension has leaked out of his expression, and he's evaluating me.

Does he think I'm screwing him somehow? I don't need to stand here for this. I turn and head for my car. "Fine. Whatever. Wait for Triple-A." I slide behind the wheel of my Charger and turn the key. She fires right up.

"Wait!" Alan jogs through the path of my headlights, then stops at my passenger-side door. He pulls up on the handle, but it's locked.

I heave a sigh and lean over to flip the lock. A moment later he's in the seat beside me, and we're both so uncomfortable it's a miracle I can put the car in gear. In a weird way, it reminds me of the night Juliet sat beside me. Alan has pulled so far away from me that if I hit a turn hard enough, he'll go rolling out.

My eyes flick his way. "You think I'm going to shank you or something?"

His eyes narrow. "Are you making fun of me?"

"Yes."

He swears under his breath and shifts in his seat. It puts him about a tenth of an inch closer to me.

We drive in absolute silence for a few miles.

"Do you really think you can fix it that easily?" he says.

"Yes."

More silence.

A cough. An uncomfortable shifting in the seat again. "You know where there's an open auto shop?"

"No, I'm looking for a cliff. Buckle up."

His eyes flash with anger. "Watch the attitude."

"Thank you, Declan," I say under my breath. "I really appreciate you taking the time to—"

"You want to say something to me, kid? Say it."

"Fine." I jerk the wheel to the right and all but slam to a stop on the shoulder. The emergency brake cranks hard under my foot, and I unbuckle my seat belt.

Alan doesn't move, but I can feel the apprehension in the car, like maybe I drove him out here so I'd have a place to dispose of the body. I don't deserve that, and yesterday's Declan might have slunk out of the car and walked home.

You make your own path.

This one's going to take a bulldozer. I'm not sure what's going to come out of my mouth, but I inhale to speak.

"Wait," says Alan. His voice is quiet, almost hushed. He's put up a hand between us, but he's staring out the windshield. "Wait."

The word is thrown down like a gauntlet. I wait.

"You're right," he says. "Thank you."

Even my heart stops for a moment, to make sure I heard him correctly.

He doesn't stop there. "I owe you an apology for what I said to you this morning, too." His voice is rough, but steady. "I was way out of line."

It's a good thing I've got the car on the side of the road because I'd be veering into a ditch right about now. I keep my eyes on the steering wheel. I don't know if I want this apology—but hearing the words chips away at something inside me.

"I'm not my father," I say. I finally look over. "And I want you to stop treating me like I am."

"I know." He nods slowly. "I know you're not." He's quiet for a contemplative moment. "But . . . you sure don't miss a moment to remind me that I'm not, either."

I go still. "What are you talking about?"

He looks over at me. "I may not know about muscle cars or run an auto shop or drink hard liquor or smoke cigars or whatever hypermasculine things your dad did, Declan, but I'm not a bad man. Just because I know more about insurance regulations than carburetors doesn't mean I'm some pathetic loser. I love your mother, and I treat her well. I make a good living, and I do my best to provide for both of you. But never—not *once*—have you spoken to me without contempt."

I think of my savings, dried up in an instant for my legal defense fund. I think about their wedding night, when he left me in jail. I set my jaw and glare out the windshield. "That goes both ways."

"I know."

We both fall quiet, until the whisper of rain on the roof of the car fills the space between us with white noise. It's late, and I should drive, but this is the first time Alan and I have spoken directly to each other. It's infuriating, but it's also addictive. I don't want to stop. I want to see where it goes.

No, I want to see where I can take it.

I peer over at him. "Why?"

"Do you want the honest answer?"

I don't know. "Yes."

He rubs at his jaw. "I love your mother, but in a way, she's very passive. She has a good spirit, but she's too permissive. It's easy for her to get taken advantage of. When we first started dating and I learned about your father, then saw how much freedom she gave you, combined with your attitude . . . I built a picture in my head. I thought I had you all figured out. I thought you needed someone to set limits." He hesitates, and his voice turns rueful. "I didn't realize that your mother and father left you to figure out your own limits, way before I came around."

His voice is calm, reasonable. In a way, I don't want to trust it, but this *feels* like the truth. "I don't know what that means."

His voice is low and steady. "It means you refused to get in that car with your father."

My breath catches before I'm ready for it—but I will *not* cry in front of him. I speak through the gathering warmth in my chest, but my voice is barely more than a whisper. "I was selfish."

"Kid, there's a big difference between *selfish* and *self-preservation*." He pauses, then looks away. "Until this morning, I wasn't aware of your role in your father's drinking. I had no idea."

I have to clear my throat, but my voice is still rough. "You knew about Kerry."

"I knew your sister died, and your father was responsible. I had no idea they expected you to cover for him. Not like that." Alan pauses, and his voice has an edge. "I was so angry when she told me this morning."

I study him. I want that to be a lie. Every breath makes my throat feel raw.

He shakes his head, and he looks like life has thrown him up against a wall a few times, too, now that I'm staring at him. "I can't even stay mad at her. Abby has been so anxious about you and this baby," he said. His breath shudders, just a bit. "So anxious. I think that's what might have put her in the hospital. All this stress, plus everything she eats makes her sick."

Anger and shame make me want to curl in on myself. I feel like a monster again. "I would never hurt her." My voice shakes. "I'd never hurt the baby."

"Hurt your mom?" He looks stunned. "We weren't worried you'd hurt your mom. Or the baby."

"But you said—"

"We were worried about *you*, Declan." He's turned to face me fully now. "We were worried about you hurting *yourself*."

I press my arms against my stomach and clench my eyes shut.

"Don't you know that?" he says. "Every time you walk out of the house, she's terrified you're going to do it again."

No. I didn't know that. I had no idea. I think of her face on the night of the Homecoming dance, the way her eyes stared up into mine, the softness of her fingers as she pushed the hair back from my face.

"She never talks to me," I say, and my voice breaks. "This morning, she wouldn't talk to me."

"She feels so guilty," he says quietly. "She's so worried she's going to say the wrong thing and push you farther away. She's terrified of losing you, too."

"You don't know that." I sniff and wipe my eyes on my sleeve.

"Kid. That is literally all she talks about." Alan puts a hand on my shoulder. I stiffen and keep my eyes locked on the steering wheel, but he leaves it there.

"Then why doesn't she talk to *me*?" I demand.

He hesitates. "I don't know. She's not perfect. Neither of us is. I don't think she knows how to fix it. I sure don't. But fifteen minutes ago I didn't think you and I could have a civil conversation, so maybe things can change."

I nod. Maybe.

"If I ask you a question," he says quietly, "will you give me an honest answer?"

I nod. My head is still reverberating with his words from earlier. *We were worried about you, Declan.* Those words have swelled to fill every nook and cranny of my brain.

"Do you think about trying again?"

I'm so glad it's dark outside the car windows. I can't look at Alan now. I wish I hadn't promised him an honest answer.

"Sometimes," I say. "Never like . . . that night. But . . . sometimes."

He nods. "Do you ever think you want to talk to someone about it?"

"Like a therapist?"

"Sure. I told Abby we could all go. Or just her, or just you two, or even just you, or—"

"Okay." The word feels good to say. I feel drained. Wrung out. And while I'm not optimistic enough to think that this conversation is the beginning of a magically great relationship with Alan, I am crazy enough to acknowledge the spark of hope that's flared somewhere in my chest. I miss my mother. I miss feeling like I'm part of something.

I nod again. "I'll go."

"I'm glad." He gives my shoulder a squeeze before letting go. "Your mom will be really happy."

I glance at him. "I'd do anything to make her happy."

"I know," he says. "Me too."

CHAPTER FORTY-ONE

From: Declan Murphy
<Declan.Murphy@AACountyStudentMail.org>
To: Juliet Young <Juliet.Young@AACountyStudentMail.org>
Date: Wednesday, October 9   10:21:07 PM
Subject: Making new paths

I thought I'd be spending the night at Rev's tonight. I had a huge fight with Alan and my mother this morning, and I thought that was it. There was no coming back from what any of us said. Forget making a path—this morning's conversation was like the aftermath of a nuclear bomb.

But tonight Alan's car broke down. I helped him out. We talked. It's the first time we've ever done that. Like—ever. He wants to go to family therapy. I said okay.

This is a lot harder to write under my own name. You have no idea. I reactivated The Dark's account, but it's not the same now. That felt like hiding. And it was.

So here I am.

I should have told you that night on the side of Generals Highway. I should have told you a thousand times since.

I hope you don't think I was trying to trick you.

The opposite, really. I was trying to trick myself.

I wasn't ready to let go of what we had.

My dad is half asleep on the couch in front of some HBO special, and he startles when I come down the stairs and into the living room. He fumbles for the remote and turns off the television.

"I thought you were already in bed," he says.

"Not yet." I was lying in bed, reading the email on my phone, tracing my finger over Declan's name.

He's right. We were hiding.

Dad yawns and rubs at his eyes, then studies me. "Are you okay? Do you want some warm milk to help you fall asleep?"

I smile, but it feels wobbly around the edges. "I'm not six, Dad."

He smiles back at me, but his eyes are shadowed and tense. He's worried about me.

Mr. Gerardi didn't tell him about the pictures. When he called my father, he said I was developing Mom's photographs, saw something upsetting, and destroyed them.

I wonder if that makes him a coward.

I wonder if not saying anything makes me one.

"Do you want to come sit with me?" he says.

I'm about to refuse because I haven't sat with him in years—but then he holds open his arm and pats the cushion beside him. "Come on," he says, teasing gently. "Sit with your old man so you can tell your kids how I used to torture you."

When I drop onto the couch, his arm falls across my shoulder, giving me a tight squeeze. His body is warm beside me, and I feel secure and loved under the weight of his arm.

I've spent years idolizing my mother and her vibrancy, thinking of my father in boring shades of beige, when he's been right here beside me the whole time.

And she's been with someone else.

"Shh," he says, and I realize I'm crying.

I press my fingers into my eyes, and he holds me close, stroking my arm.

"Do you want to talk about it?" he says.

"I don't—" My voice breaks, and I have to try again. "I don't want to hurt you."

"Hurt me?" He kisses my forehead. "You won't hurt me. I don't want to see whatever it is hurt *you*."

I stare into his compassionate eyes. My own well with fresh tears. "Mom came home early." The tears fall, hot and heavy, and my breathing hitches.

My father goes still. "What? How do you know that?"

"Her boarding pass was in her bag." I can't look at him. I can barely breathe through these tears. This is going to destroy him, but I can't carry this weight on my own. "She came home early to be with Ian."

"Juliet . . . how—"

"I saw it, okay?" The words practically explode out of me. "I saw it. There were pictures of them on her camera. In bed. I'm sorry, Dad. I'm so sorry. Please don't hate me."

"Juliet—oh, sweetheart." Breath comes out of him in a long sigh, and he pulls me back against his shoulder. His hand strokes over my hair again. "Juliet, I could never hate you."

"I'm so mad at her," I say. "How could she? How could she do this to you?"

"Shh," he whispers. "It's okay."

"It's not okay!" I draw back and look at him. "I hate her. I wanted her to come back. So badly."

He grimaces, and his eyes fill, too. "Don't hate her, Juliet. Don't hate her."

"Did she love us at all?"

"You?" His voice breaks. "Oh yes. She loved you more than anything."

I snort. "Not more than three days with Ian."

He laughs, but it's a sound full of sadness. "Yes, more than even that." A pause. "She loved you so much that she stayed with me."

"What?"

He shakes his head a little. "Your mother was—a bit of a free spirit."

My voice won't raise above a whisper. "You knew."

"Not the details. I never wanted the details." He snorts, the first sound of anger I've heard from him. "Now I know why he wanted that damn camera so badly. If I'm mad about anything, it's that you found out this way."

"But . . . but . . ." I swallow, my head spinning. "But you were so sad."

His expression shifts. "I was sad. I am sad. Regardless of what she did, she was my wife. She was your mother. I was used to her being gone for long stretches of time, but this is a different kind of permanence. If that makes any sense."

It does. "How long did that go on?"

He shrugs, a motion full of resignation. "I don't know. Forever, probably. But I didn't know for sure until a few years ago."

I can't wrap my head around this. "But . . . why did you stay with her?"

He chucks my chin and gives me a sad smile. "Because I loved you, and you loved her. I couldn't take that away from you."

My brain begins realigning the moments I've seen them together over the last few years. My memories are crowded with special times with my mother, but moments shared between my mother and father are suddenly understandably absent. I always thought this was a failing of my father's, not being able to live up to her brilliance.

I never realized it was a failing of hers.

I swipe my hands across my face. "I wish I'd known."

He cocks his head. "Do you really?"

"Yes. I thought she could do no wrong. I thought she was the bravest woman alive."

"There's nothing wrong with that, Jules. Your mother was a brave woman. She did amazing things."

"She was selfish," I snap. "Coming home to play house when she felt like it, and leaving you to do everything else."

He winces. "Maybe a little. But we all have different capacities for failure. This doesn't take away from her work. This doesn't take away from her love for you."

"She came home three days early for someone else." I sniff and swipe tears off my cheeks again. She doesn't deserve any more tears. Not now. "That's going to take some time to get over."

"I know," he says softly. "I know." He pauses. "But I was here for those three days. And I'll be here for all the other days, as long as you need me."

I throw myself into his arms.

He holds me, and it's the best feeling in the world.

CHAPTER FORTY-TWO

From: Juliet Young
<Juliet.Young@AACountyStudentMail.com>
To: Declan Murphy
<Declan.Murphy@AACountyStudentMail.com>
Date: Thursday, October 10   5:51:47 AM
Subject: Letting go

I'm glad you never told me. I didn't want to let go, either. In fact, I'm a little sad that it's over. I keep thinking about our conversations in real life and replaying them with the knowledge of who you were on the other side of our letters. There's a part of me that still doesn't quite believe it's really you.

There's a lot you don't show the world, you know. I think you should. Give them a new snapshot. Show them what you showed me.

And on that note . . . what now?

There's an envelope on my dresser when I wake up. My name is written on the front, and it's in Alan's handwriting.

Inside, I find three hundred dollars.

My eyes almost fall out of my head.

I don't know what to make of this. I pull on a T-shirt, grab the envelope, and go down to the kitchen. Mom and Alan are at the table, drinking coffee, speaking in low voices.

I hover in the doorway, immediately off balance.

"Declan," says my mother.

"Hey." I fidget with the envelope. The money is making me uncomfortable. I don't like the feeling that they're trying to buy me off somehow. It seems to weaken everything that happened between me and Alan last night.

I walk over to the table and throw it down. "I can't take this."

"We want you to have it," my mother says softly.

I frown. "I don't want your money."

"It's your money," Alan says. "You earned it."

"I didn't do anything."

"You fixed my car. Didn't you say three hundred was the going rate?"

"I said I would go to counseling or whatever you want." I take a step back, my jaw set. "You don't need to buy me off."

"No one is buying you off," he says, his voice matching mine for intensity. "You said that's what a mechanic would charge, so I'm choosing to pay you." He hesitates. "And maybe we were a little too harsh when we took *all* of your money to pay for representation last May. You spent years saving that."

Yes. I had. It takes a lot of odd jobs and oil changes to make three thousand dollars—and this doesn't come close to replacing that.

Which is okay. Which is better somehow.

"Besides," says Alan, "you got a call from a guy named John King. He says he has a few friends who want you to take a look at their cars. I figured I should get your services while they're cheap."

Frank's neighbor. I feel light-headed. "John King called?"

"His number is by the phone. He said they're willing to pay you for a consultation."

Like I'm a doctor or something. I swallow. "Okay."

Mom slides out of her chair, walks over to me, and puts her hands on my face.

It's so unexpected that I freeze.

"I'm sorry," she says softly. "I'm sorry I haven't been there for you. I want to try to be better."

"You don't need to be better," I say softly.

"I do." Her face crumples a little, but then she catches it and takes a long breath. "These crazy hormones." She swipes at one eye. "I'm getting another chance. I want to do it right."

My words from yesterday morning echo in my head, and guilt tackles me. *Replacing Kerry?*

I can barely speak through the shame. "I'm sorry for what I said," I say. "I'm so sorry."

"Stop," she says. "It's okay. We're all getting another chance."

With that, she puts her arms around my neck and squeezes tight. I hug her back. I can't remember the last time my mother held me, and I hold on for a good, long time.

Then she jumps back. "Did you feel that?"

"Feel what?"

"He kicked! First time!"

I smile, thinking of the lady in the hospital. "I have that effect." Then I realize what she said. "He?"

"Yes. A boy."

"A brother," says Alan.

A brother. I've spent so much time thinking they were trying to rebuild our family that a baby brother didn't occur to me. My brain almost can't process this. I step back. "I need to get ready for school."

She nods. "Okay."

I stop in the doorway and pull a twenty out of the envelope, then walk back and slide it in front of Alan.

"What's this for?" he asks.

"Parts," I say. "You bought your own."

"Why are we at school this early again?" says Rev.

We're sitting on the darkened front steps of the school, waiting for the security guard to unlock the main doors. It's freezing, and I'm about to fight Rev for his hoodie. He's even got his hands pulled up into the sleeves. Fog has settled across the parking lot.

"I have to meet with my English teacher." I give him a sideways look. "You don't have to be here."

"You're my ride."

"Then shut up."

Shoes shift on pavement, and Mrs. Hillard appears out of the fog. "You're even here early," she says in surprise.

"Lucky for me," says Rev.

I punch him in the shoulder and shove to my feet. "You didn't say what you wanted to talk about. I thought maybe it was important."

She shifts her bag to her other shoulder. "You ready to go inside?"

"Sure."

Rev steps forward, and she looks alarmed for a moment. The dark and the hoodie make him look like a criminal. Then he says "Do you want help with your bags?" in his disarming voice, and she smiles.

She holds out her shoulder bag. "Such a nice offer."

The school is nearly silent at this hour, the hallways shadowed by intermittently lit security lights. Mrs. Hillard's classroom is a well of darkness until she flips the switch. Rev and I drop into chairs in the front row.

She glances at Rev, then back at me. "Do you mind if your friend stays?"

Rev smiles and leans back in the chair. "'One who has unreliable friends may come to ruin, but there is a friend who sticks closer than a brother.'"

Most people look at Rev like they can't figure him out and they're not sure if he's worth the effort. Mrs. Hillard just raises her eyebrows. "I might need more coffee if we're going to start reciting Proverbs."

I kick his chair. "Ignore him. But he can stay."

She unzips her bag and pulls out some notebook paper. I recognize my handwriting. She's put comments in red in all the margins.

She slides it in front of me. "Where did this come from?"

I bristle at the question. "I wrote it right in front of you. I didn't cheat."

"I'm not accusing you of cheating. I'm asking why you were able to put together five hundred words about a poem, when I can rarely get more than a compound sentence out of you."

I flush and look down. "It made me think."

"You're a good writer. You make solid points, and you express yourself very well."

I can't remember the last time a teacher offered praise. Who am I kidding—I can barely remember the last time a teacher made eye contact. My chest warms with a glow, and I fidget with my pencil. "Thanks."

"Do you plan to write like that from now on?"

This feels like a trap. "Maybe."

"Because I was going to ask if you wanted to try transferring into AP English."

Rev whips his head around. I'm choking on my breath myself.

"AP?" I say when I can finally put a thought together. "I don't have any AP classes."

"Are you looking at colleges? Might look good on a transcript."

I look away. Most of my teachers expect me to be getting a higher education courtesy of the Maryland State Penitentiary.

I've never considered taking an AP class, much less transferring into one a month into the semester.

"I don't know if I could catch up," I say.

"Do you want to try?"

You make your own path.

Yeah, but this is a path straight up a mountain. Pushing a wheelbarrow full of bricks. "I don't know."

"You don't think you're good enough? I promise you are."

I look away. "No . . . they're all the smart kids. They're going to think I'm some stupid thug."

"Prove them wrong."

I hesitate.

"Are you afraid of the work?" she says.

"No."

She turns away, pulls a book off her shelf, and hands it to me. "Are you sure?"

I look at the title. *A Farewell to Arms* by Ernest Hemingway.

"Have you read it?" she asks. "This is what we're reading right now."

I wouldn't know a Hemingway book if he stood in front of me and read it out loud. "No."

"Want to give it a try?"

"I'll think about it."

I wait for her expression to turn disappointed, but it doesn't. She nods. "Keep it. Try it. Let me know by the end of the week?"

"Sure." I feel a bit breathless.

Rev and I walk to our lockers, and the early buses must have started to arrive, because the hallways are slowly filling with students.

"Are you going to do it?" he says.

"I don't know. What do you think?"

"I think you should." He pauses. "Are you really worried they'd think you don't belong?"

Normally, I'd deny it, but this is Rev, and I tell him everything. "Yes. Wouldn't you be?"

He shrugs a little. "Maybe."

I tug at the sleeve of his hoodie gently. "Maybe?"

He stops in the middle of the hallway, and for a moment, I worry I've pushed him too far after our conversation the other night. But he pushes the hood of his sweatshirt back. Slides the zipper down.

And then he freezes.

I raise my eyebrows at him. "Jeez, Rev, at least wait till we're alone."

He hits me in the arm and starts walking again. The hoodie is still on, but the hood is down. The zipper stays unzipped.

"I'm wearing short sleeves," he says after a moment.

"Okay." I glance over. "You don't have anything to prove, Rev."

"I'm not ready," he says. "Not yet."

I shrug and try not to make this seem like a big deal. "There's always tomorrow."

"Yeah," he agrees. "There's always tomorrow."

CHAPTER FORTY-THREE

Anne Arundel County Student Mail Server
INBOX - Juliet Young

No new messages

By lunchtime, he hasn't written back.

I have no idea what that means.

In the cafeteria, I linger in the line, then casually walk past the table where he usually sits with Rev.

They're not there.

It shouldn't, but this feels deliberate. And not in a good way.

Rowan and Brandon welcome me to their table, but they've moved to the point of their courtship where everything is teasing flirtation and double entendre. Rowan is currently feeding him grapes by tossing them into his mouth, and giggling a little too hard when he misses.

I'm trying really hard to keep from sighing heavily.

A denim-clad leg swings over the bench, and weight drops beside me.

I'm somehow surprised, yet not at all, when I turn my head and find Declan straddling the bench.

He steals my breath. He looks as striking and lethal as ever, but I know his secrets. I know how much of that is a front.

"Feel like taking a walk?" he says.

"Ah . . . sure."

And then he surprises me by taking my hand.

We're at school, so our options are limited, but I'm under his spell and I'd walk into fire if he asked right now.

He doesn't. He leads me out the back doors of the cafeteria and onto the quad.

The noonday sun blazes down, robbing the air of any hint of a chill. Students are scattered everywhere, but it's more private with the open air around us.

"I've been wanting to talk to you all morning," he finally says.

"You didn't email."

He shakes his head. "I wanted to *talk* to you." He looks chagrined. "And now that I'm next to you, I wish I could go back to The Dark."

I understand exactly what he means. Butterflies ricochet around my abdomen. "Want me to pull out my phone?"

He smiles. "I'll save that for my last resort."

My own tongue is tied up in knots, so I smile, and we keep walking. The silence presses down.

He inhales to speak—but hesitates.

"It's okay," I say softly. "We don't have to talk."

He laughs under his breath. "I don't know what my problem is. You know everything."

"So do you."

He rubs his jaw—another morning without the razor, I see—and runs a hand through his hair.

"Wait," he says, pulling me to a stop. "I have an idea."

He turns to face me, and before I'm ready for it, he moves close. Very close. So close that his cheek is against my cheek, and one hand is against my neck. If I take a deep breath, I'll be pressed up against him. His breath tickles my ear, his stubble brushing my jaw.

"Is this okay?" he says softly.

"Okay? This is about three thousand times better than my idea with the phones."

He laughs, and our chests do touch. One of his hands finds my waist. We could be dancing instead of sharing secrets. I have the sudden urge to wrap my arms around him.

"I need to tell you something," he says.

I wet my lips. "You can tell me anything."

"I'm sorry for the times I was mean to you. I'm trying to work on that."

I feel light-headed, drunk on his closeness.

His thumb brushes against my neck in a soothing rhythm. "I like you."

"I like you, too."

"I've liked you since the morning you ran into me."

I giggle and try to shove him away, but he uses the motion to pull us closer. "You have not," I say.

"I have," he whispers, and now his lips brush against my cheek. "I remember thinking, 'Nice job, dickhead. Add another girl to the list of people who hate you.'"

"I don't hate you. I've never hated you."

"Now, that's reassuring," he says, but I can hear the smile in his voice. He inhales along my cheekbone, and sparks flare through my abdomen. "You should write for Hallmark."

"All my future love letters will start with 'To whom it may concern.'"

"Are you going to send me future love letters?"

I flush, and I'm sure he can see it. Feel it.

But then his voice loses the smile. "You were the first person to see all of me, Juliet. The first person who made me feel like I was worth more than a reputation and a record. That's the hardest part of losing Cemetery Girl. I don't know if anyone will look at me that same way again."

I draw back and put both hands against his chest, then slide them upward until I find his jaw.

He looks away.

"I see all of you," I say. "And I'm looking at you that way now."

He takes my hand, puts it over his heart, and holds it there. His eyes close. "You're killing me, Juliet."

"Look at me," I say.

He looks at me.

"You can't make your own path with your eyes closed," I tease.

"Watch me." Then he leans in and captures my mouth with his.

Acknowledgments

Full disclosure: I'm writing this while I'm sick, and my eyes are kind of blurry, and I'm at that emotional part of an illness where you think about people and their kindness and you start crying. So if I sound like a blubbering mess in print, blame Influenza A.

First and foremost, I have to thank my husband. He's my best friend, my confidant, my rock. (Okay, I'm crying already. Second paragraph. Go me.) He has been unfailingly supportive of my writing career since day one, and I couldn't do this without him.

Tremendous thanks go to my agent, Mandy Hubbard, who is quite possibly Wonder Woman. (I know you have the gold wristbands, Mandy. ADMIT IT.) One day we will meet in person and I will tackle her with hugs. I imagine this happening in a field of daisies, despite the fact that I wouldn't even know where to find such a field. Thank you, Mandy, for everything.

Additional tremendous thanks go to my editor, Mary Kate Castellani, whose guidance and vision in the crafting of this novel have been invaluable. You can join me and Mandy in the field of daisies and we can all tackle-hug. Or shake hands, if that's your thing. But seriously, I am so lucky for the opportunity to work with you. Thank you for everything.

Many thanks to everyone at Bloomsbury who has been working on my behalf. I wish I knew all of your names so I could thank you individually, but please know that I'm very aware that a book "takes a village," and you've all played a part in mine. You have my sincere appreciation. I hope to meet you all one day.

Huge appreciation and love go to my close friends and critique partners, Bobbie Goettler, Alison Kemper, and Sarah Fine. You all mean so much to me, and I'm so lucky to have you in my circle.

This book took a ton of research, from legal issues to photography to automobile repair. Charles "Chuck" Allen, I owe you a lunch (or a dinner, or a restaurant of your own) for all the emails you answered in regards to photography and photojournalism. Officer James Kalinosky of the Baltimore County Police Department has been a constant resource for all matters regarding law enforcement, and this time was no different. Most of my automobile information came from Joe Clipston, Ryan Albers, Stephanie Martin, and Scott Prusik. All of these people provided brilliant assistance. Any errors in print are mine alone.

Many people read early pieces or drafts of this manuscript and provided feedback that helped make this a better finished product.

Huge thanks to Jim Hilderbrandt, Nicole Choiniere-Kroeker, Tracy Houghton, Joy Hensley George, Shana Benedict, Nicole Mooney, Amy Clipston, and Michelle MacWhirter.

My heartfelt appreciation goes out to all of my readers, whether this is the first book of mine you've read, or if you've been along for the ride since you met Becca and Chris in *Storm*. Without you all, I wouldn't be able to do what I love. Thank you.

As always, I must thank my mother for her eternal wisdom, guidance, and support, even when I was in second grade, writing a book about a dog. (Which she still pulls out to show people, folks. Seriously.)

Finally, as always, tremendous thanks go to the four Kemmerer boys, Jonathan, Nick, Sam, and Baby Zach. Thank you for letting Mommy follow her dreams, while I thank my lucky stars each day for all of you.